To Charlotte, the love of my life,
my biggest fan and with whom
all things are possible.

The Legend of Erin Foster

The Legend of Erin Foster

Darlene Duncan

First Paperback Edition © 2022 Darlene Duncan
ISBN: 978-0-9723324-9-1

Published by Ocean Breeze Publishing

This novel and its characters are a product of the author's imagination. Some locales may be factual but are used fictitiously.

CHAPTER 1

Erin heard the engine of the patrol car and then saw the headlights sweep the intersection as it turned onto the next street. Lying on the driveway under the SUV, she breathed a sigh of relief.

Staying to the shadows she made it the rest of the way home without incident.

She entered the dark house through the back door. Standing in the kitchen leaning against the door, Erin took a deep breath.

Thank goodness, Alice must have gone to bed already.

Suddenly the kitchen lights came on and Alice demanded, "Why were you out after curfew and where the hell have you been?"

Erin raised a hand to shield her eyes from the bright lights. Blinking several times to adjust her vision to the abrupt change in light level, she pressed her back against the door.

The pressure of the .38 revolver tucked into the waistband of her jeans was reassuring.

Smiling Erin moved across the room, toward Alice and said, "I was visiting with Yvonne and Donald." She shrugged. "I lost track of time and before I knew it, it was past curfew."

Alice studied her lover's face for several seconds. She wasn't sure if Erin was lying or telling her the truth.

Most likely only part of the truth. She's a lousy liar but half-truths, I learned she's pretty good at.

Alice turned away and started for the bedroom. "Turn out the lights and come to bed."

"I'm a little wound up right now. I think I'll stay up and read a bit."

Alice looked over her shoulder at Erin and after a moment said, "Suit yourself."

CHAPTER 2

"Parks."

Norris Parks recognized Lt. Joe Hardtack's voice. He stopped and turned around. He didn't know the young man standing next to Joe. However, the black military style uniform he wore identified him as a Peacekeeper of The Order for Morality and Justice. Norris' smile disappeared.

"Officer Norris Parks, this is Peter Snead."

Peter puffed out his chest, looked from the lieutenant to Norris and said, "That's Peacekeeper Snead, Officer Parks."

The two police officers exchanged amused glances. Lt. Hardtack cleared his throat. "Yes, that's right Officer Parks. This is Peacekeeper Snead. He'll be riding with you today."

"Excuse me, lieutenant?"

"Peacekeeper Snead will be riding with you today."

"Lieutenant, can I see you privately for a moment?"

The two men held each other's gaze, and after the briefest hesitation, the lieutenant motioned for Norris to follow him into his office. The lieutenant moved behind his desk. Norris closed the door and faced his long-time friend.

"What the hell's the big idea?"

"What do you mean?"

"Damn it, Joe, don't play stupid with me. You know exactly what I mean."

3

Joe sighed and sank into his chair. "Look, Nor, I don't have any more choice in the matter than you do. Ever since Congress activated Amendment 28, The Order has become more and more powerful. Word from on high is that we're to provide police training for their Peacekeepers."

"It's not right, Joe. I'm a cop, not a babysitter. Despite his uniform that boy out there can't be more than sixteen."

Joe smiled. "You're getting old, Nor. Peter Snead is nineteen. Old enough to vote, old enough to be drafted, old enough to get married. The only thing he's not old enough to do is drink."

"Nineteen. Sixteen. He's still wet behind the ears."

Joe got to his feet, palms down on his desk; he leaned forward and said, "He's riding with you, Norris. Get used to it."

Norris opened his mouth to speak but Joe cut him off. "Officer Parks" Lt. Joseph Hardtack straightened up to stand his full six foot two "until further notice, Peacekeeper Snead will ride with you. You will teach him proper police techniques and procedures."

Norris ground his teeth and thought about his pension. Just two more years and he could retire with a full pension and benefits. He took a deep breath and resolved to survive the two years. He performed a sharp about face, opened the office door and headed for roll call.

Norris' listened to the usual drone of the sergeant with half an ear. His mind was occupied with fantasy scenarios that would allow him to tell Lt. Joe Hardtack what he could do with his badge. The sound of his name being called brought him back to reality.

"Officer Parks!"

"Huh? What?"

"I'm sorry if we're disturbing your daydreams, Parks."

Norris looked around the room at his grinning brothers in blue.

"If it wouldn't be too much trouble, could you come up here and get the arrest warrants you're serving today?"

Norris was halfway to the podium when Sergeant Gillette added, "While you're at it, how about introducing your new partner?"

Glaring at Gillette, Norris snatched the warrants from him, spun around and on his way back to his seat he said, "Peter Snead."

Snead bounced to his feet like a Jack-in-the box and stated, "Peacekeeper Snead."

A quick look around the room showed Norris the serious faces of his brothers in blue. It occurred to him, there was a time when Snead's pomposity would have earned him a serious razzing by the rank and file. Norris couldn't identify the expressions on the faces around him and he pushed the concern from his mind as he tried to pay attention to the rest of the briefing.

Sgt. Gillette continued. "Each of you has at least two warrants to serve this shift. This group is suspected of being enemies of the state. In most cases, they're little more than deviants. Regardless, be careful." He smiled. "I don't look good in black. Dismissed."

Deviants. Shit! I don't understand how screwing somebody of the same gender makes you an enemy of the state. There was a time when being a cop meant arresting criminals, not policing people's sex lives.

5

Norris noticed that the usual banter between the officers making their way to their patrol cars was missing. He looked around, and for the first time, noticed Snead's was not the only black uniform among the blue.

Putting his briefcase into his vehicle's trunk, it dawned on him what it was he'd seen on his comrades' faces in roll call – fear. Every one of them was afraid of the boys in those black uniforms.

Jack Collins wasn't afraid of Peacekeepers. Yeah, and look where it got him. Fired on grounds of moral turpitude. A ten-year career shot to hell because he didn't marry the mother of his children.

The image of Jack and Helen's empty house popped into Norris' mind. A week after Jack was canned; Norris went by to see how he and Helen were doing. The neighbors told him a moving truck came the same day Jack was fired and loaded up everything.

A shiver ran down Norris' spine as he remembered the fear that crept over him as he stood in the living room of Jack's empty house, wondering if Jack's disappearance had been his own idea or if someone else had made him vanish.

"Officer Parks?" Peacekeeper Snead derailed his thought train.

"Yeah?" Norris slammed the trunk lid.

"Is there a problem?"

Yeah, kid, there's a problem and it starts with the Reverend Master James Calton III. But you'll never hear me say it out loud.

"No, kid, no problem. Let's go to work."

6

As Norris pulled out of the police parking lot, Snead opened the first warrant and read the address.

"Hold that thought, Snead. I want to do at least one full patrol of our zone before I start serving paper."

"But…"

"But nothing, sonny boy. I'm senior officer and I say how and when we do things." He paused. "If you don't like riding with me, you can always request a transfer."

Snead made no comment as he refolded the warrant and returned it to its folder.

Two hours later, Norris couldn't think of another legitimate reason to delay serving the warrants.

CHAPTER 3

Erin dropped a shell into the last empty chamber of the .38 she'd just cleaned and snapped the cylinder into place. The cold metallic sound matched the chill that gripped her heart at the thought of what was happening to America since The Order for Morality and Justice came to power.

"Erin." Alice's voice came from the living room.

"Yeah babe." Erin looked around the room to see if there was any evidence of her gun cleaning activities. She'd stashed the cleaning kit in the closet. *Alice hardly ever comes in here so there's not much of a chance she'll come across it.*

"Can you come out here? We need to talk about something."

"Be right there." Erin tucked the weapon into the front waistband of her jeans and pulled her t-shirt down to cover it.

Seeing the worried look on her lover's face Erin wondered if she'd already found out about the gun. "What's the matter?" Her eyes fell on the papers on the table in front of Alice and she knew the answer. Print outs of their bank records.

Looking up from the papers in front of her, Alice studied Erin's face as if looking for the answer to some question. Her eyes moved to the wall beyond Erin. "One of us has to find a job."

Relieved that this discussion wasn't going to be about the gun, Erin moved next to her and kissed her on top of her head. Then she squatted down so they were eye to eye.

"Ow!" Erin straightened up.

Alice stood up. "What hurts? Are you alright?"

"Yeah. I'm fine." Erin's mind was racing trying to find an answer that would require the least amount of explanation.

"If you're all right, what was the 'ow' about?"

The gun had shifted and was still poking Erin in the stomach. She needed to reposition it. The problem was that to do so would draw attention to its existence.

Maybe she's changed her mind. Things were different seven years ago. I didn't feel the need to have a gun back then. But now... She's got to understand. Things have changed.

Erin took a deep breath and started. "I went to a meeting last night and..." She hesitated and moved around the table.

"A meeting?" Alice folded her arms across her chest and followed Erin's every move. "You told me you went to see Yvonne and Donald."

"Yeah, well they were at the meeting." Erin looked up and met Alice's gaze. "It was a meeting with some people who think that we need to do something about the things that are going on."

Erin watched Alice's eyes grow wider. "What kind of meeting? Please, tell me it wasn't one of those underground political groups." Alice stepped toward her and placed her hands on Erin's upper arms.

To Erin, Alice's facial expression seemed the same as a mother trying to explain something to a child, something beyond the child's ability to comprehend. "Don't you understand how dangerous it is to get involved with those

9

people?

Erin straightened her posture and raised her head. "What do you suggest we do? Wait for the country to come to its senses and realize we've given up our freedom for a false promise of security and safety."

Alice allowed her hands to drop from Erin's arms, to hang at her side. "There are peaceful ways to get things done. Compromise is always preferred over violent confrontation."

"I disagree." Erin reached under her t-shirt and adjusted the gun, so it was comfortable. She watched Alice's eyes as they moved from the gun back up to her face. "I'm tired of being persecuted because I love you."

Alice stiffened. "Don't blame me for the violence you are about to participate in. I want no part of it and will accept no responsibility for it."

Erin saw a shadow ripple across the curtains on the living room window and knew someone was about to knock on the front door. She raised her hand to silence Alice. Unfortunately, it had the opposite effect.

"How dare you treat me like... First you lie to me for years."

"Lie to you? What are you talking about?"

"You told me back when we first got together that you'd get rid of that gun. Now after seven years I learn you've still got the damn thing."

A pounding on the front door was accompanied by a male voice. "Police. Open up." He paused. "Ladies, we know you're in there. Open the door before I'm forced to break it down."

"Now look what you've done. The police are threatening to break down our door because of you and that damn gun."

"I never lied to you. I sold the gun I had seven years ago."

Another male voice, younger than the first demanded, "What are you waiting for? Didn't you hear them talking about a gun? We should call for backup and break down the door."

"Junior, I'm still the officer in charge here and we'll do this my way." The pounding on the door resumed. "Come on ladies. Don't make me ..."

"Stop that pounding." Alice spoke as she moved toward the door." I'll be there in a moment." As she reached for the door knob a shot rang out.

For a brief second, she stood perfectly still; then her head dropped, and she stared at the blood leaking out of the hole in her chest.

"Alice. Alice, are you alright?" Erin reached Alice in time to stop her from falling to the floor. Under the dead weight of Alice's body, Erin staggered backward and lowered herself and Alice to the floor. Her ears still rang with the sound of the gunshot as she cradled Alice.

When she looked up, she saw two uniformed men standing just inside the door. The young man in the black uniform was pointing his gun at Erin.

Officer Norris Parks put his hand on top of the gun and pushed it down. "Put your gun away." He nodded toward Erin and Alice on the floor. "You've done enough damage."

Smiling, Peacekeeper Peter Snead said, "What damage?" He holstered his gun. "It's just a couple of queers."

His words repeated inside Erin's head until it was the roar of a million people screaming the words, 'just a couple of queers', over and over again.

Alice's body shielded Erin's hand from view and by the time the two men saw the gun she held; it was too late.

Prior training and instinct took over as Erin aimed and fired. The look of surprise on the police officer's face and the fear emanating from the young Peacekeeper were etched in Erin's brain forever.

The wail of approaching sirens broke through Erin's mental fog. She blinked several times, took in the scene before her and decided she would never allow herself to be captured alive.

Two patrol cars pulled up in front of the house and the cars were barely stationary before the officers were out of them. As the uniformed men moved toward the house a neighbor stepped outside and hollered to them, "She's gone. I saw her go into the woods out back."

"Ma'am, get back inside."

Mrs. Bonelli obeyed the officer.

CHAPTER 4

Erin stumbled over a root, scrambled to her feet, and kept moving. Her lungs burned with the effort. She stopped, leaned against a pine tree, and listened. She heard nothing beyond the roar of her own blood and her gasps for oxygen.

Calm down, girl, she told herself. You've got to think, but first you've got to know how close they are.

She inhaled deeply, held her breath, and listened. Ten seconds slipped by before she took another breath, held it, and listened. Silence.

If they were following her, either they were far enough back she couldn't hear them, or they were very good.

Her breathing quieted and Erin looked around. There were no trails in sight. Sunlight dappled the ground in the few places it penetrated the tree canopy. She licked her dry lips and swallowed. She was thirsty. Her stomach grumbled, a reminder her last meal was over twelve hours old.

Something brushed against her ankle, and she jumped. Her movement disturbed the water around her, masking the departure of whatever had swum past. Recent rains covered usually dry sections of the woods with standing water. She sighed and wondered how long it would be before thirst would drive her to drink the muddy liquid in which she stood.

She threw her shoulders back and started walking. A short time later she paused for a moment and glanced upward. Live oaks, palms, and pine trees blocked most of the sky. Directly overhead, the sun forced its light through breaks in the green blanket of limbs and fronds.

A dog barked in the distance. Erin jerked her head toward the sound as fear tied another knot in her stomach. With only a vague idea of where she was and no idea where she was going, Erin placed one foot in front of the other and moved away from the barking dog. Sweat seeped from every pore as the heat of the day continued to build.

She stopped on a dry patch of ground, dropped her left ear to her shoulder and wiped her sweaty forehead on her shirtsleeve. A dark stain on the front of her t-shirt caught her eye.

Blood. Alice's blood. Alice is dead.

"No!" Her agonized scream echoed throughout the swamp as she dropped to her hands and knees. Birds flew from the trees and every creature within earshot fell silent. Tears blinded her as a red fog rolled over her brain. She collapsed and welcomed the escape of unconsciousness.

CHAPTER 5

Sgt. Michael Donovan stood on the manicured lawn in front of the house where his long-time friend Norris Parks died.

"Sgt. Donovan."

Recognizing the man's voice, Donovan rolled his eyes, took a deep breath, and painted a stony expression on his weather-beaten face before he turned to face the bane of his existence.

"Deacon Withersby, what may I do for you?"

Withersby's lips were pressed into a thin line magnifying his perpetual look of disapproval. He moved from the street to stand next to Donovan.

"You can tell me why one of our best young men is dead. Our Peacekeepers travel with your officers to receive training so they can be of service during emergencies. My understanding was that their participation was limited to routine assignments."

Donovan's jaw tightened. "First of all, Mr. Withersby, our preliminary investigation shows that your boy fired the first shot. His bullet ricocheted and killed a woman. As best we can determine, Erin Foster then shot and killed, not only your Peacekeeper but a police officer." He paused, narrowed his eyes and looking into Withersby's eyes, continued, "I grew up with Norris Parks. We went through the academy together."

"I am sorry for your loss; however, I would appreciate if you used my title, Sergeant, unless of course you would prefer I call you Michael."

Sgt. Donovan didn't reply so the Deacon continued. "Regardless of who fired the first shot, Sgt. Donovan, the question still remains, why was Peter Snead with your officer if he was serving warrants on dangerous criminals?"

"Deacon Withersby, all police work has an element of risk in it. If you want your boys kept safe, perhaps they should stick to desk duty. The worst that's likely to happen there is a paper cut. Now if you'll excuse me, I have to find a cop killer." Donovan turned toward the house and walked away.

Donovan stopped in the foyer of the house and watched the crime scene investigator examine the area surrounding the three bodies. "What have you got Brad?"

Brad DeMarco continued to study the relation of the bodies to one another. "The same as I had ten minutes ago when you asked me that question, nothing."

"Look DeMarco, I've got the good Deacon Withersby trying to blame us for his boy being in a dangerous situation. The detectives will be here any minute and I need to know what happened here." He paused. "Norris and I were more than just friends. I'm the godfather of his only child. What the hell am I supposed to tell his wife? How do I explain why his son will grow up without a father?"

"I already told you more than I should." Brad held his arms wide. "What do you want from me? Until I've had time to piece everything together, anything I tell you is nothing more than speculation."

"So, speculate."

Brad dropped his arms to his sides and sighed. "Okay. The

way I see it, Officer Parks and his Peacekeeper sidekick arrived and probably knocked on the door." He moved away from Alice's body and stood about halfway between the foyer and the hallway to the back of the house. "The two women probably stood about here."

"What makes you think both of them stood in the same area?" Donovan asked.

"Tsk. Tsk. Patience, sergeant. They stood here when Wyatt Earp, otherwise known as Peter Snead, shot out the deadbolt on the front door. The bullet shattered the wood around the bolt and ended up striking Alice Davis in the chest. She was probably dead before she hit the floor." Brad paused. "Anyway, whoever was with her kept her from falling where she was shot."

"The other woman's name is Erin Foster and you've already told me this much." Donovan looked out the front picture window in anticipation of homicides arrival. He knew once they were there, he'd be banned from the crime scene.

"And it's all I'm going to be able to tell you for a while, even that much is guesswork. Until I get my prints back, I can't say with any certainty that it was Erin Foster with the victim." He sighed. Brad empathized with Donovan.

"But we'll assume that it was, for the moment. So, Erin staggers back to here under the weight of Alice's body." Brad walked backward, between the bodies of Norris Parks and Peter Snead, to where Alice's body lay. "Then she lowered the body to the floor. Parks and Snead entered. She got the drop on them and fired, killing them both. I suppose one of the neighbors called in the shots fired. Our shooter hears the sirens and scrams before anyone else arrives."

"How does a civilian, with no criminal past get the drop on an officer with eighteen years' experience?" Donovan knew it was a question he would ask himself for some time to come.

"Who knows? Sometimes experience makes us think we know it all and then we learn we don't. In this case, the lesson came at a high price." He paused. "Leave it for the detectives. That's why they make the big bucks."

Donovan snorted. "The detectives didn't grow up with Norris Parks and go through the academy with him." He held DeMarco's gaze. "And none of them are godfather to his son."

"Sorry Donovan. I know this is personal for you, which is why you should leave it to the detectives."

Donovan lifted his eyes from Alice's body and scanned the living room. Set in the east wall was a large picture window, with the curtains drawn against the morning sun.

A series of bookcases lined the south wall. Each deep shelf was home to a row of books. The center bookcase held a display of wildlife stamps on its upper shelf. On its middle shelf, in front of a row of books, was an assortment of liquor and wine bottles.

Michael Donovan stepped past the four bodies on the floor and walked to the bookcase farthest from the window. He picked up a framed picture of two women. One was obviously the deceased. Comparing the other woman in the picture to the corpse on the floor he figured her companion to be about 5' 8" and around 140 pounds. She appeared to be in her late twenties or early thirties, with short brown hair, and gray eyes.

"Hello Erin Foster." He removed the 8 x 10 photograph and tossed the frame back onto the bookshelf. Its glass broke, scattering slivers of glass across the shelf. He ignored

DeMarco's shouts about contaminating the crime scene and moved outside.

Deacon Withersby was waiting next to Donovan's patrol car.

Why are the religious ones always such a pain in the ass? Donovan thought as he moved across the yard toward the older man.

Oh well, maybe I can put his zeal to work for me.

"Deacon Withersby."

"Sergeant Donovan."

"I wonder if I might ask a favor of you, sir."

Deacon Withersby squinted at him in the bright sunlight. "What is it you need, sergeant?"

"Will you to take this picture to the station?" He displayed the photograph, which he'd folded to reveal only Erin Foster.

"Have them crop it the way I've folded it and then run off enough copies to paper the city." He paused. "This is the woman who killed Peacekeeper Snead and Officer Parks."

He took the photo from Donovan and stared at the smiling face looking up at him. "Of course, Sergeant, I'll be happy to run your errand for you. Actually, I'll do better than what you ask. I'll take this picture to my office, crop it and run off full color copies." Deacon Withersby smiled. "The people in the black and white copies I've seen posted from your department wouldn't be recognized by their own mothers."

Donovan wanted to tell him, "If your congregation were as generous with our funding as they are with church tithes, we'd have more modern equipment to work with."

But he swallowed the words and instead said, "That's fine as long as you understand the department can't pay you for

19

your service."

Straightening his shoulders the older man replied, "Sergeant, we too lost a member of our family here today." He paused. "Quite literally. Peter Snead was the only son of Bishop Snead. We will do anything and everything we can to assist in bringing his murderer to justice."

CHAPTER 6

"Someone's at the door, Donald. It might be the package your sister said she was sending you." Yvonne covered the phone's mouthpiece and called out, "Be right there." She turned her attention back to her husband on the other end of the phone. "If you don't want to have to track down this package, I need to go. Besides it's time for you to be headed home. I'll see you soon, sweetie. Bye." Yvonne dropped the receiver onto its charging cradle.

Moments later with a smile on her face she opened the front door. "I'm certainly glad I was…" Her smile vanished.

Two men in suits with gold badges hanging from their jacket pockets stood on her front porch. Behind them were two uniformed police officers.

"Yvonne North?"

"Yes." She used her body to block the doorway. "What can I do for you?"

"We need to ask you some questions and search the premises, ma'am."

"Search the… What on earth for?"

"May we come in, ma'am?"

"Do you have a warrant?"

"No ma'am, but if you insist, I'm sure we can get one."

She wanted to scream, "Yes, get a warrant if you want to search my house. You can't come in without one. It isn't right.

Why are you here?"

She knew she could insist they get a search warrant, but she was also aware of the consequences of such action. Her name would be added to a list of suspected subversives. She could hear the media now, "If she had nothing to hide why did she make the police waste the time of a judge to get a search warrant?"

Yvonne stepped back and opened the door wide. "No need for that. I've got nothing to hide. Please, come in." Yvonne walked into the house, giving room for the four men to enter. The last man in closed the door behind him.

The tall one said, "I'm Detective Robison." He nodded toward the other detective. "My partner, Detective Cusack"

Cusack nodded in her direction.

Robison looked at Cusack and made a slight head motion toward the two uniformed officers with them.

"Right." Cusack said. He walked to the two uniformed men. Cusack spoke to them in a voice so low Yvonne couldn't make out what he was saying.

"Mrs. North, can I trouble you for a glass of water?"

Yvonne tore her eyes from the trio invading her home and looked at the man before her. "I'm sorry, what did you say?"

The detective smiled. "May I have a glass of water?"

Yvonne noticed his smile never reached his eyes.

"Certainly." His words were a polite request yet there was something about him that made her feel as if he had simply ordered her to get him a glass of water.

She strode to the kitchen and tried not to let her nervousness show as she pulled a glass from a cabinet, added ice, and filled it with water. All the while she felt

22

Robison's eyes following her every move. She handed him the glass. "What's this all about, detective?"

Yvonne waited as he drained the glass of water and then handed it back to her. "Thank you, ma'am."

She set the glass down on the kitchen counter with a bang, crossed her arms over her chest and faced the detective. "You're welcome. Now will you answer my question?"

"When was the last time you saw Erin Foster?" He pulled a pad and pen from his jacket.

"Erin?" Yvonne inhaled long and deep. "I don't know. A couple of months at least."

"She didn't come by earlier today?"

"No. I told you it's been at least a couple of months. Maybe longer." Yvonne snatched the glass from the counter, dumped the ice in the sink, spun on her heel and jerked open the dishwasher door.

I've got to get a grip on myself. I can't appear to be sympathetic to Erin.

She placed the glass on the top shelf and gently closed the door. She drew in a deep breath and turned back to the detective with a smile. "What's this all about, detective? I haven't seen Erin since I ran into her in the grocery store back in, let's see that was probably the end of December."

Before he could ask her another question, his partner came in. "Mort, I sent the rookie to the tool shed out back." He entered the kitchen and looked around the room as he spoke.

"According to Mrs. North she hasn't been here but check the computers and the phones, let's see if she's tried to make contact."

"Right you are." He left the kitchen, humming.

23

"Mort." Yvonne called the detective by his familiar name, and he brought his attention back to her. She was again standing against the kitchen counter. "Are you ever going to answer my question?"

"I would prefer you call me Detective Robison, and yes, I'll answer your question." He paused. "Your friend, Erin Foster, is wanted for the murder of a police officer and a peacekeeper. We're checking out everybody connected with her. Your name was in her address book."

Yvonne swallowed hard and felt the blood drain from her face. Her legs shook; she felt weak and placed a hand on the counter to steady herself. Her eyes met Detective Robison's and she saw the cold hatred that burned within him. She looked away, staggered to a chair at the table in the breakfast nook, and sat down.

"How? I mean, what about... Are you sure it was Erin? I just can't believe she would..."

Robison eased into a chair across from Yvonne and rested his hands in his lap. "Mrs. North, the only thing we are sure of is that the murderer was Erin Foster." He leaned toward her. "If she shows up here, remember she's armed and has already killed. She's got nothing to lose by killing again. Get in touch with us and we'll handle it. It will be safer for all concerned." He leaned back, scribbled in his pad, and asked, "Where is your husband?"

"Work. He's at work." Yvonne looked up at the clock on the kitchen wall. "Actually, he should be on his way home now." She didn't want to have to look at the detectives face again. The hatred and cold murderous intent she saw there was more than she could handle. She ran her hands up and down

24

her upper arms as if to warm herself and stepped to the kitchen window.

Yvonne stared with unseeing eyes. *Where is Alice? Is she also being hunted? Why hasn't he even mentioned her? Where is Alice?*

The unspoken questions bounced around in her head like an echo that grew louder instead of diminishing. Just as she was about to ask Detective Robison about Alice, the sound of the garage door going up caught her attention.

She turned to face her inquisitor who still sat at the table staring at her. Displaying a calmness, she didn't feel Yvonne held his gaze, and said, "My husband is home. Perhaps you'll believe him."

Robison stood and with that false smile on his lips replied, "I never said I didn't believe you, Mrs. North."

Yvonne refused to back down. She tossed her head. "No, but you certainly implied it, and I don't appreciate being treated like a criminal."

Donald North entered the house on the heels of the uniformed officer who had been searching his garage. "What's going on here, Yvonne?"

"Mr. North, I'm Detective Robison." He dismissed the other policeman with a nod of his head. "We're looking for Erin Foster. When was the last time you or your wife saw her?"

"Erin?" Donald frowned and looked at his wife. He rubbed his jaw and returned his eyes to Robison. "The last time I saw her was probably six months ago. I don't remember seeing her since then."

"What about your wife? When was the last time she saw Ms. Foster?"

Donald opened the refrigerator, removed a bottle of beer, and asked, "Can I get you something to drink, detective?" He twisted the top off the bottle.

"No, thank you. When was the last time your wife saw Erin Foster, Mr. North?"

Donald smiled. "I couldn't say, detective. I told her not to mention the woman's name in my presence. So, if she ran into her somewhere, I doubt she would tell me about it."

Robison scribbled something in his notepad. "What was your problem with Ms. Foster?"

"I didn't have a problem with her other than her lack of manners." Donald turned his back on the detective and threw the bottle top in the trashcan under the sink. He straightened up and turned back to Robison.

"Then why didn't you want your wife to mention her name in your presence?"

Donald took a long pull on his beer before answering. "Foster had a problem with me." His eyes darted toward his wife, and then he looked back to Robison. "I'm not exactly her favorite gender. I'm sure you know what I mean."

"Why don't you spell it out for me, Mr. North?"

"She hates men. I told Yvonne that until the bitch apologized for insulting me, she wasn't welcome here and I didn't even want to hear her name."

"Donald, you know full well that Erin…"

"Shut up, woman." Donald punctuated his command with a slap across his wife's face.

Yvonne caressed the right side of her face that now bore the red imprint of her husband's hand. Her eyes filled with tears.

26

"Sorry you had to see that, detective. She's usually much better behaved." He turned to Yvonne. "Go to the bathroom and put some cold water on your face."

Yvonne obeyed him immediately.

The two men watched her go.

"I understand, Mr. North. You know, The Order offers programs to help women adjust to the changes our society is experiencing."

"Actually, I'm meeting with Deacon Withersby tomorrow about being accepted as a Novice in The Order. I'll make a point of asking him about those programs. Thanks."

Detective Cusack walked in from the back of the house, and said, "Mort, we're finished. Nothing."

"Fine, Wally. Send the uniforms to the next address on the list. Make sure they understand that they're to wait till we get there before doing anything. I'll be out in a minute."

"Right."

"Mr. North, if Erin Foster gets in touch with your wife or you, contact me immediately." He handed Donald a business card. "Don't try to detain her or capture her yourself. She's already killed two men."

"Wow! I mean I knew Erin didn't particularly like men, but I never would've guessed... What happened? What about Alice?"

"Ms. Davis was killed resisting arrest." Detective Robison turned and without another word walked out the door into the garage. Donald watched him walk down the driveway, get into his car, and drive away.

A short time later, Yvonne returned to the kitchen and found Donald staring out the kitchen window. "They're gone?"

Donald hung his head. "Yes, they're gone, for now." He drew in a deep breath and turned to face her. "Forgive me?"

She reached up and gingerly touched the cheek where his blow had landed. "There's nothing to forgive, my love." She stepped up to him and took his hands in hers and placed a kiss in the palm of the hand that had slapped her. "If we're going to be successful, we have to play by their rules."

Yvonne moved up against him and wrapped her arms around him. "Did they say anything about Alice?"

Donald hugged her and then lifted her to sit on the kitchen counter in front of him. "Detective Robison said she was killed resisting arrest."

Tears rolled down Yvonne's face as she bit her lower lip in an effort to hold back sobs of grief.

"Poor Erin, with Alice dead she has no one. Being hunted like an animal." She sniffed, took a ragged breath, and hung her head. "All alone, how will she find shelter and food? How will…"

Donald put two fingers under her chin and gently lifter her head. Looking into her eyes he said, "Hey, aren't you the one who told me Erin has a military background?"

Yvonne nodded.

"And that her training included weapons, hand-to-hand combat and survival training?"

"Yes, but…"

"No buts." He smiled. "I must have heard Erin say this a thousand times. I can't believe I'm actually going to quote her."

Yvonne grabbed a paper towel from the roll under the cabinets and wiped her face as she asked, "So what is this wonderful quote?"

Donald took a deep breath and looking into his wife's eyes said, "Why worry about things you can't change? Instead, do something about the things you can change."

Yvonne leaned forward and slid off the counter into Donald's embrace. Enveloped safely in her husband's arms she silently renewed her vow to fight The Order.

After a few moments she straightened up, wiped her face again and blew her nose. "I should fix us some dinner. Then you can tell me about your day, and we can figure out what to do next."

Donald brushed a couple of stray hairs from her face. "You are an amazing woman, you know that?"

She smiled. "Oh yeah, well I think you're pretty amazing. The look of admiration on the detective's face was worth the price of the slap."

"If you thought I scored points with the slap you should have been there when I told him I had an appointment with Deacon Withersby."

"You got the appointment? They're going to accept your application for Novice?"

"It looks that way. But right now, I'm far more interested in your acceptance of my apology." He pulled her to him and pressed his lips to hers. The kiss started out soft and gentle but grew in its intensity.

Yvonne pushed him back, breathing heavily. "Look lover boy, we don't have time for this right now. We've got to make sure you know all the proper answers when Withersby interviews you."

Donald groaned. "Maybe The Order has the right idea, after

all."

"What did you just say?"

He grinned at her reaction. "If I were really a follower of the Reverend Master you would be more compliant and less of a Drill Sergeant."

Standing in front of him, arms across her chest, she said, "This is not a joking matter, Donald North."

He sighed. "I know but I remember a time when you actually used to laugh." He paused. "I miss the sound of your laughter."

She gave him a quick hug, pulled away and said, "Me too. Unfortunately, at the moment, I can't think of anything to laugh about."

He cupped her face in his hands and gently kissed her on the forehead. "Come on, I'll help you with dinner."

Donald moved to the refrigerator and began piling the makings for a salad on the counter as he asked, "Do you think Erin will get in touch with us?"

Yvonne considered his question before replying, "Only as a last resort. She knows they'll be watching us, as well as any of her other friends." She sighed. "I can't even imagine what she's going through right now."

"After dinner we'll see what we can find out."

*   *   *   *

In the patrol car Det. Robison asked, "Did all the bugs get placed as I instructed?"

"Yeah, Mort. No problem." Det. Walter Cusack started the car. "Did you get the one set for the kitchen?"

"It's on the underside of the kitchen table."

"Great. Who's next on the list?"

CHAPTER 7

Erin eyes popped open, and she jerked to an upright position. Running a shaking hand through her short hair she told herself it was just a bad dream. Still, she wasn't sure if the gunfire that woke her was part of the dream or not.

The only thing she knew for sure, was Alice was dead and so was the man that killed her. His face would be with her for the rest of her life, his look of disbelief as he looked down at the bullet hole in his chest oozing blood. Each time the scene replayed in her mind she was confused by the look of relief on the cop's face as she fired and gave him a third eye.

Tears filled her eyes as she gazed into the darkness around her. Something large splashed nearby and for a brief second the cicadas stopped. Erin held her breath. The silence was worse than the deafening song of the small insects, when the singing resumed so did her breathing.

A nearly full moon emerged from cloud cover and peeked through the tree branches.

Erin swiped at her face, brushing away unwanted tears as she got to her feet.

I don't have time for tears. Have to pull it together. Make them all pay for killing Alice.

What now, she wondered. Where do I go from here? She inhaled a deep, calming breath and scanned her surroundings, trying to get her bearings.

31

Uncertain of where she was or which direction was best, Erin threw back her shoulders and pressed forward. Logical thought evaded her as the instinct to survive pushed her on.

Three questions created an infinite loop inside her mind. *Why? What next? Where to from here? Why? What next? Where to from here? Why? What next? Where to...* But no answers came.

Inky blackness filled the gaps between the trees and bushes, forming a shadowy wall. The aroma of wet ground and decaying leaves filled her nostrils as a new mantra replaced the questions, she had no answers for.

Must keep moving. Can't stop. Must keep moving. Can't stop. Must keep...

Chanting the words in her head, Erin placed one heavy foot in front of the other.

The invisible tangle of underbrush, palmettos, vines, and roots sent her to the ground, repeatedly. Each time she forced her aching body back onto its feet and resumed her forward trek.

No breeze stirred inside the forest. She moved from wet ground to dry without noticing the difference. Brackish water soaked her tennis shoes and her jeans from the knees down. Sweat rolled into her eyes and each new breath required more effort than the last.

A cool breeze stopped her in her tracks. She closed her eyes as she lifted her head and spread her arms. She tilted her head back as the light wind dried her moist skin and lowered her body temperature.

A rustling noise broke her reverie. She opened her eyes and her arms fell to her sides as she dropped into a crouch.

Before her was a wide-open expanse and silhouetted against the night sky was a house.

The gentle sound came again, and she realized it was only the wind moving the fronds of the saw palmettos.

She glanced around. Behind her the woods formed a wall in both directions as far as she could see. She moved back into the protective cover of the trees and flora.

Erin examined what lay before her. She squinted to try and identify anything familiar, with the moon behind the clouds it was too dark to discern any distinctive features.

She sighed and moved deeper into the woods. Sitting with her back against a tree, vegetation shielded all but the roof of the house from sight.

Erin thought of all the comforts held under that roof: food, drink, a shower, a protected place to lay down her head and sleep.

Shit, for all I know I've come full circle and that's my house. No way of knowing until the sun comes up.

Her eyes closed and she started to drift off to sleep. The needle-like bite of a mosquito woke her. Instinctively she slapped her bare arm. The sound of the skin-on-skin impact silenced the cicadas for a moment. Erin held her breath and listened but heard no evidence that anything higher up the food chain than a barn owl was aware of her presence.

Still, I can't keep beating myself up to kill mosquitoes.

She remembered slogging through a large mud puddle a short distance back in the woods and hauled herself to her feet.

After coating every bare patch of skin with a layer of mud, Erin returned to the edge of civilization to wait for daybreak.

CHAPTER 8

Erin woke atop a pile of moldy leaves and damp moss in time to see a vibrant Florida sunrise. An old saying ran through her mind. Red sky at night, sailors delight, red sky at morning, sailors take warning.

She listened but heard no indications there were people nearby, so she stretched her sore muscles, causing her mud coat to crack in several places. Erin brushed off as much of the dried mud as she could.

Her mouth was dry, and her tongue felt twice its normal size. Ignoring her growling stomach, she crawled to the edge of the tree line.

Dew glistened on the grass. The sparkling drops of water increased her thirst. Again, Erin ran her swollen tongue over her dry cracked lips as she scurried back a few feet. She pulled her t-shirt over her head, chose the cleanest part of it, and tore away a small piece of cloth. She slipped the damaged garment back on and returned to the edge of the lawn.

Lying on her belly, she observed the house and its surroundings for several minutes before reaching beyond the palmettos and dragging the piece of t-shirt over the grass. Startled by a noise, she yanked her arm back and brought with it the dew-soaked cloth. She shoved the wet fabric into her mouth and savored every molecule of moisture. She couldn't remember a time when mere water had tasted so good.

Moments later, she heard the same sound again.

She dropped her head onto her forearm in relief, realizing the noise was a screen door slamming.

Somebody must have stepped out for the paper. Wonder if I made the front page.

Erin repeated her dew gathering procedure several more times until her tongue felt almost normal again. As she sucked water from the rag, she heard an engine start. Peering from the foliage she watched a county Sherriff's patrol car drive away from the house.

A deputy. Robbing his house will be a pleasure. He's as guilty as the one who pulled the trigger on Alice. I just hope he lives alone… To hell with it, it really doesn't matter. It's not like I've got a lot of options.

She stood up and tucked the still wet cloth into a pocket of her jeans, pulled the .38 from her waistband, and checked the load. Four shots left. Erin returned the weapon to her waistband and pulled what was left of her t-shirt over it before stepping out of the trees.

She crossed the backyard, flattened herself against the house, and listened.

The only sound she heard above the pounding of her heart was the chatter of mockingbirds. The concrete block wall felt cool against her back. Her grumbling stomach reminded her that food and water were priorities. She crouched and peeked around the corner of the house.

There wasn't much to see in any direction. Across the street was an empty wooded lot. A dirt road ran in front of the house.

She could still see little clouds of brown dust where the car had passed.

Erin drew a deep breath, let it out slowly and walked to the front of the house. She moved with an assurance she didn't feel. She glanced up and down the road as she tried not to look out of place.

She stepped onto the front porch and knocked on the door. "Hello, is anybody home? I need some help. I'm stranded. Is anybody home?"

Erin looked around for indications the house had an alarm system. There were no alarm company signs on the windows or in the yard. A full minute passed without any response to her knock.

Erin moved to the window nearest the front door, popped the screen out and pushed up on the glass pane. It opened easily. Dropping the screen behind a bush, she jumped to a sitting position on the windowsill and swung her legs into the house.

She paused for a moment to let her eyes adjust to the light change. Then she moved through the house searching from room to room. The split plan ranch house was typical of a Florida house and Erin was relieved to find no one was home.

The door to what she believed was the master bedroom was locked. She tried turning the doorknob with no success.

What's so important in that one room that he keeps it locked? I could break it down.

She licked her dry lips and decided that she had more important issues with which to deal.

In the kitchen Erin turned on the faucet and let the water run into her hands. She brought the cool liquid to her mouth, gulped it down and spit the remaining mouthful into the sink.

"Shit!" she said. "Damn well water." Her stomach roiled at the sulfur taste. She yanked open the refrigerator door and grabbed the first canned beverage she saw, popped the top and took a long swig. As she rinsed her mouth, the taste of old beer curled her tongue. Deciding it wasn't much better than the tap water; she spit the offending liquid into the sink and watched the fizzless amber fluid disappear down the drain.

Eying the label of the cheap beer she thought, how do people drink this stuff? Tastes like piss!

She set the beer can in the sink and squatted down to examine the contents of the refrigerator.

Half-empty take-out containers that held what looked like long forgotten science experiments were the only food present. More generic beer and no-name sodas took up the rest of the space. Shoved way in the back, Erin spotted a gallon bottle of water. She extracted it, flipped up the plastic top, sniffed the contents, and tilted the container up to her lips.

As she stood up, she realized there was one door she hadn't opened yet, the door to the garage. She took another big swallow of water; set the jug on the counter and with gun in hand opened the door.

A smile split her face from ear-to-ear when she saw the dark blue pickup truck in the garage.

Looks to be in good condition. No rust, a couple of door dings, and a scratch or two, nothing major. But does it run?

Erin stepped up on the running board and leaned into the cab. No keys.

She said aloud. "The damn key is probably on his key ring.

37

Where would he keep a spare?"

On her hands and knees, she examined all four-wheel wells. She moved on to the underside of the front bumper. Almost to the curve on the passenger side her fingers grazed a protrusion. She grasped it and pulled.

Her trembling hands opened the small metal box, and she removed a key. She closed her hand around it, scrambled to her feet and climbed into the cab, inserted the key and turned it. The big engine roared to life.

"Yes!" Tears of relief streamed down her face.

The gas gauge showed a full tank and the other gauges all showed normal operation. She turned off the engine, popped the hood, got out and checked the oil. It was fine. A quick inventory of the garage revealed a couple of quarts of engine oil and one of transmission fluid. Erin grabbed them all.

She opened the truck topper to store her supplies. She stood on the bumper and looked at all the camping equipment she could have ever hoped for and then some. At a quick glance she could see a tent, a large first aid kit, a camp stove, and a propane tank for it, and sleeping bags. There was so much stuff it looked as if someone had dumped the camping aisle of a sporting goods store into the truck bed. She added the oil and transmission fluid to the supplies.

Back in the house she again moved from room to room. This time she was looking for anything she might need. In the dresser of the open bedroom, she grabbed some shorts, jeans and a couple of shirts that looked like they might fit her.

In the bathroom she paused. A shower would be wonderful. *What if he comes home? I'd be trapped and defenseless.* She sighed and left the room.

As she passed through the kitchen with the pile of clothes in her arms, she grabbed her jug of water and hurried from the house. Erin tossed the clothes in with the camping supplies, closed the topper door and climbed into the cab of the truck. She pressed the garage door remote on the visor and started the engine. As soon as she cleared the garage, she put the door down.

Stopping at the end of the driveway Erin looked around. The dirt road in front of her ran north and south.

This looks like some of the neighborhoods west of home. Think I'll go north, until I find something that tells me where I am.

The silence in the cab of the truck was getting on her nerves, so she turned on the radio.

"...Described as a white, 28-year-old female, approximately 5'8", short brown hair, gray eyes, and 140 pounds, Erin Foster is wanted for killing Officer Norris Parks, an 18-year veteran officer and Peacekeeper Peter Snead, son of Bishop Snead of The Order. Peacekeeper Snead and Officer Parks were serving warrants when Erin Foster resisted arrest. Do not attempt to detain or capture her. She is considered armed and dangerous. Her picture is being displayed on billboards around the state. If you see her, contact authorities immediately. For those who may have just tuned in, Erin Foster is described as..."

Erin snapped the radio off and yelled at it. "You bastards don't bother to mention that you killed Alice. Alice never hurt a soul but that didn't stop you holier-than-thou sons of bitches from shooting her. Resisting arrest! Hah! I'll show you what resisting really means before it's all over with."

39

Having let off some steam, she got herself under control and concentrated on not being pulled over for some minor traffic violation.

Two miles later Erin found a street with a familiar name, Barlow Road. She turned east. Her next turn took her south for a short distance to connect to another east bound road. She became aware of her destination about half a mile before she reached it.

Of course, the quarry is perfect. I don't know if today's high school kids still go there on the weekends, but I doubt they spend time there during the week.

Turning off the paved road onto the soft sand track that wound back to a clearing in the woods, memories of years gone by and the good times she experienced in this teenager's haven flooded her mind.

Back then it had been the perfect place to get away from authority figures. Today it would serve that purpose again. Only this time if she was found it wouldn't be a case of being grounded for a week.

A mockingbird flew across her line of sight and brought her back to reality.

She maneuvered the large truck so that it was facing out, careful not to get stuck in the soft white sand. Satisfied that she could leave quickly if the need arose, Erin turned off the engine.

CHAPTER 9

Deputy Henry "Hank" Bartholomew pulled into the driveway of his home, with a little over four hours of his twelve-hour shift remaining.

His last encounter with his shift supervisor convinced him he couldn't risk waiting any longer. The man knew something or at least thought he knew something, either case spelled disaster for Hank.

He'd managed to keep his homosexuality a secret from almost everyone in his life. He wondered who had turned him in, maybe one of his former lovers looking for a little leniency. Or someone he'd pissed off. It really didn't matter. What mattered was his cover was blown and he needed to seek sanctuary.

The screen door slammed closed behind him as he entered the house. Halfway across the living room he paused to let his eyes adjust to the light. Something didn't feel right. He reached for his sidearm and released the holster strap.

Standing in the middle of the room Hank listened but all he heard was the whirring of the refrigerator's motor.

Gun drawn he glanced into the kitchen. No one there and there was no place in that room to hide. He moved through the rest of the house checking each room.

The door to the master bedroom was still locked.

Satisfied he was alone Hank holstered his gun and logged

onto his personal computer, went to the site he'd been told about, and entered the code phrase. He didn't have to wait long before he received a phone number to contact for sanctuary.

Hank made a backup of everything on the desktop computer and put the external drive in the case with his laptop, zipped the case closed and slung the shoulder strap over his head. With the laptop secured he stood in the doorway of the room and took one last look around.

For over a year this single room had been his refuge. Three of the clean white walls were hung with pictures of half-nude and nude men. The fourth wall was covered from floor to ceiling with shelves, filled with books, magazines, and videos.

On those rare occasions when he brought someone home with him this was the only part of the house they saw. All the necessities of life were here from the small refrigerator to the port-a-potty.

He smiled, remembering how nervous Clark had been when Hank insisted, he wear a blindfold from the time they left the bar's parking lot until they were safe in Hank's room.

Hank headed for the garage. When he passed the kitchen sink, he spotted the beer can Erin had left in the sink.

Well, someone's been here. Shit!

Hank hurried the last few steps to the garage and flung open the door. His mouth dropped open and he rubbed his eyes, unwilling to believe what he saw or rather didn't see. His truck was gone.

"Damn it!" He looked at his watch. *I've still got three and a half hours before I'll be missed unless I get a call, then all bets are off.*

He weighed his options. If it weren't for the fact it would be suicidal, driving his patrol car to the sanctuary rendezvous would be amusing. Driving into town and trying to rent a car would take too much time. Besides if he was spotted outside his patrol area someone might get suspicious.

He grabbed the phone's receiver off the garage wall and punched in the numbers he dredged up from his memory.

"Star Tracking, this is Amanda. How may I help you?"

Hank hoped it was the same Amanda he'd worked with when he was on the car theft task force. "Mandy, this is Hank Bartholomew. How've you been?"

"Well, as I live and breathe. Haven't heard from you for a long time, deputy."

"You know how it is. They keep me pretty busy. As a matter of fact, as much as I'd love to chitchat with you, I should be giving you the information on a missing vehicle."

"Yeah, I know what you mean. I'm getting the evil eye from my supervisor too."

Hank gave her the information she needed and fifteen seconds later she gave him the coordinates of his truck's current location.

"You want me to dispatch a unit for you, Hank?"

"No, that won't be necessary. Actually, I'd appreciate it if you kind of forgot to log this activity at all. You see, well, it's a little embarrassing, but the vehicle is my personal truck and I'm not sure if it was actually stolen or if a friend of mine borrowed it."

"Woman troubles?"

He could hear the smile in her voice. "Well..."

"Don't worry about it deputy. It won't show up on my activity

43

log. I just replaced it with a search for my own vehicle. Seems my teenage daughter is at the mall again. Take care of yourself, gotta go."

"Thanks a million, Mandy."

The coordinates she gave him were outside his patrol zone, but he had no choice. He needed that truck; besides this was personal.

He pulled a map from his patrol cars glove box. The coordinates were to a location with which he was very familiar. When he was in high school it had been a favorite place to go after school and party.

Shaking his head in disbelief that a bunch of teenagers were probably responsible for the theft of this truck, Hank started up the patrol car.

Boy, are they in for a surprise.

CHAPTER 10

Erin bathed in the cold green water of the quarry pit and then dressed in a pair of cargo shorts and a t-shirt she'd taken from the deputy's house. She sprayed herself with a mist of insect repellant and then took inventory.

The truck contained two first-aid kits, a camp stove, propane tanks, and water purification tablets. There were two tents; one, still in the box looked like it would be big enough to live in and the other was more of an emergency shelter meant for short-term use. Several MREs that were supplemented by freeze dried foods, energy bars, and books on trapping and edible vegetation. While she finished looking through the contents of the truck bed she ate two of the energy bars.

"Damn! This guy has enough stuff here to live pretty high off the hog for quite some time." Startled by the sound of her own voice, she cleared her throat and in a much quieter voice said, "This is way more than anybody needs for a camping trip. Wonder what he was planning? It's almost as if he planned on disappearing into the wilderness."

Now that she was clean, and fed, exhaustion was catching up with her. She pushed aside a sleeping bag and noticed a hammock.

A short time later she was stretched out in the hammock, gently swaying between two trees. Her mind raced with a million questions. She did her best to not think about Alice or the fact that every law enforcement agency in the state was looking for her.

Instead, she closed her eyes and concentrated on the warmth of the sun, the salty aroma of the sea carried to her on a gentle breeze and the sounds of the birds flitting from branch to branch. The lizards scurrying across dry leaves accented the chattering squirrels.

On the verge of sleep, Erin was yanked back to full consciousness by the snap of a twig, followed by complete silence from the wildlife around her.

She lifted her eyelids just enough to get an eyelash filtered view of an individual in a forest green uniform approaching her. Erin closed her eyes and waited.

Something blocked the sun from her face and then a man's voice said, "Wake up."

Erin opened her eyes and squinted at a Deputy Sheriff looming over her but made no effort to rise from her hammock.

"You got a lot of nerve, lady." She made no response. "Get up from there." He reached for the edge of the hammock with the obvious intent of flipping Erin out of it.

"Stop." Erin pulled back the hammer on her .38. "I don't think you want to do that." She used her eyes to direct his gaze. He looked down at Erin's midsection and saw the gun in her hand, pointed at his crotch and the hammer pulled back.

"Now, you're going to back away from me and raise your hands, very slowly. Any sudden movement might cause me to shoot you."

He did as she ordered.

"Very good." Erin's eyes darted around but never left her

captive for more than a second as she placed her feet on the ground and stood up. "Did you come here alone?"

He smiled.

"It doesn't matter; I wouldn't believe anything you said anyway. However, I am left with a dilemma. What to do with you?" She shrugged. "I suppose I could shoot you and bury you here. It might be years before your body's found, by then..."

"You won't shoot me."

Erin cocked her head to the right slightly. "I'm curious. What makes you think I won't shoot you?"

"Why would you shoot me over a truck? Right now, all I want is my truck and its contents. Hardly worth killing for. Kill me and you add cop killing to grand theft auto."

He doesn't know who I am. Erin continued to hold his gaze as she moved so her back was against the truck. "How do I know there aren't more of you?"

He sighed. "You really are paranoid, aren't you? If there are other deputies hiding in the shadows waiting to pounce on you, it's not because I called them." He started to lower his hands.

"Don't even think about it."

"My arms are getting tired."

"Tough." She judged the length of his legs and was careful to stay out of kicking range. "Take off that gun belt and drop it."

He hesitated, studying her.

"Look, I've already killed two men; one more won't make a lot of difference to me."

Erin watched his face as it dawned on him who she was.

47

He dropped the gun belt in the sand. "Actually, the last I heard Officer Parks was in surgery and expected to survive."

"The radio said they were both dead. Besides, one, two, what's the difference?" Using her gun to indicate the direction she wanted him to go she said, "Move over behind the truck."

Erin moved in unison with him always keeping her distance, yet never losing sight of the bull's eye she imagined on his chest. She stopped him at the rear of the truck, with his back to the vehicle.

"Now lie face down, and scoot under the truck, feet first." He hesitated and studied her, as if gauging his chances, before complying with her demand.

When everything except his head was under the vehicle, she stopped him. Keeping a close eye on him she retrieved his handcuffs and tossed them into the sand in front of him. "Cuff your right wrist to the trailer hitch."

The ratchet of the handcuff closing was a comforting sound. "You can slide out from under there now."

Maneuvering out from under the vehicle he sat up, reached down toward his ankle and started to pull his pants leg up.

"Freeze!"

He sighed. "My leg itches. Think I could scratch it?"

"How stupid do you think I am?"

He smiled. "Do you really want me to answer that?"

"Smart guy, huh." Erin had him take off his boots and pull his pants legs up. She confiscated the .25 automatic strapped to his right leg and then had him tighten the handcuff one more notch.

"It's cutting off the circulation already."

"Yeah, well I wouldn't want you to think you could slip out of

48

that bracelet. Despite what I'm sure the media is saying about me, I really wouldn't want to have to shoot you." It was her turn to smile. "Someone might hear it."

Erin retrieved the gun belt and placed it in the cab of the truck.

"What makes you think the media is saying anything about you?"

"Don't even try to play me, green shirt. I'm not in the mood."

"Erin, would you listen to me for a minute?"

"No! I don't want to hear your crap. I'm not surrendering. If they want me, they're going to have to kill me."

"From what I've heard that's exactly how Sgt. Donovan wants it."

Erin held his gaze. "You can take your reverse psychology and shove it."

Hank squirmed in the sand trying to find a more comfortable position. "The only thing I want to reverse is the tightness of this cuff. Much longer and my hand is going to fall off."

Erin studied his hand. Its lack of color gave testimony to the truth of his words. She tossed him the handcuff key. "Loosen it one notch and toss the key back." She kept her gun trained on him throughout the process.

"Thanks."

She caught the key he tossed to her. "Yeah." Erin paced between the beginning of the road out and the footpath to the quarry. She refused to look at her prisoner, but she could feel his eyes on her.

"Did you know there's a quarry pit down that path? Some friends and I used to come here and go swimming when I was a teenager." He smiled. "It was a great place, if you know

49

what I mean."

"Big deal! You may have been some hotshot jock in school with all the girls just dying to jump into the back seat of your car but in case you haven't noticed, this isn't high school. And I'm not interested in whatever you have to offer."

"That puts us on equal footing because…"

"Do I have to shoot you to get you to shut up? I am trying to think here. So shut your face before I shut it for you, permanently." She enunciated each word carefully. "No, you do not need to reply. Just nod your head."

Hank nodded his head.

"Good boy." Erin wandered away muttering, "Maybe if he can't see me, he won't be inclined to talk to me. Damn fool. God, I'd kill for a cigarette right now."

Hank wrapped his right hand around the ball of the trailer hitch for support, stretched himself out so he could see Erin's feet at the other end of the vehicle. With his free hand he removed the spare handcuff key from an inside pocket in the waistband of his pants.

Maybe it's a good thing I didn't change out of uniform. My jeans don't come with an extra handcuff key.

Hank freed himself and silently lowered the chain to hang from the trailer hitch. Rubbing his wrist, he moved to the passenger side of the truck and stood up.

He examined the ground between himself and the front of the truck. *I know that twig I stepped on earlier is what gave me away. I won't make that mistake again.*

Silent as the clouds above, he walked to the front of the truck. He stopped behind Erin but before he could grab her, she dove to the ground, away from him.

50

He saw her reach into the fanny pack and knew she was going for her gun. He flung his body on top of hers. Her violent flailing made it impossible to get a firm grip on her. Finally, he grabbed her right wrist and tried to pull her hand out of the fanny pack.

Bam! The gun went off.

Erin stopped struggling. She released the gun and her hand fell from the leather bag. Hank pulled on the fanny pack so hard the clasp broke. Standing over her holding the pouch, he saw why she had stopped fighting him.

Her left short's leg had a hole in it and the fabric was growing dark with blood. He threw the bag aside and dropped down on his knees next to her. "Damn it, woman! Why did you have to fight me? I only wanted to talk to you. We're on the same side."

Lying flat on her back Erin looked up at him. "Do you always go around shooting people on your side?"

Hank exhaled in an exasperated manner and shook his head in disbelief. "You getting shot is as much your fault as it is mine." He paused. "Let me get the first aid kit."

When he returned Erin had propped herself up on her elbows, she glared at him. "If you had to shoot me, you could have at least been decent enough to make it fatal."

He knelt between Erin's legs and opened the first aid kit. Making sure it was within easy reach he ordered, "Stop whining and lay back down. I need to lift your leg." Without waiting for her compliance Hank grabbed her left leg and placed the ankle on his shoulder.

Erin fell onto her back with a thud and bit her lower lip to keep from screaming in pain.

51

"Looks like a through and through. That's good. At least I won't have to try and dig the bullet out." He studied the wound for a moment and then said, "The bleeding is minimal, considering. Anyway, the bullet missed the femoral artery, or you'd be dead by now." He glanced down at Erin.

"I'm sorry you got shot. We really are on the same side." As he talked, he cut the leg of the shorts open to allow greater access to the wound. He gently lowered her leg to the ground. "I'll be right back." Moments later he came back and set up a folding camp chair. Then he lifted her leg and placed the ankle on the edge of the chair's seat.

He grabbed the gallon jug of water Erin had nearly emptied and started to pour it over the wound area. "This may sting. I don't know how badly, but I do know I've got to get the sand from around that hole."

Erin didn't say a word, just nodded her consent. Hank poured the water over the area, gently washing the sand away. Using sterile gauze pads, he applied direct pressure to stop the bleeding.

Neither of them spoke for several minutes, then Hank released the pressure and said, "Look Erin, I'm no doctor and my first aid training is virtually nonexistent. However, I think we both know that infection is the biggest risk right now." He looked at the first aid kit and then back at Erin.

"What are you trying to tell me, green shirt?"

He ignored the common street slang used for sheriff's deputies. Shifting his weight from foot to foot, he stuck his hands in his pockets and said, "The only thing I have to sterilize that wound with is rubbing alcohol."

"Rubbing...you mean, you plan on pouring alcohol into the

hole in my leg?"

"Yes, and it's going to hurt like hell."

"No shit." Erin paused and studied the man before her. He looked like a young boy who has just busted the cookie jar he was caught snitching cookies from. "How about this instead, just take your gun and put me out of my misery?"

Hank shook his head. "I don't think so, Erin." He pulled his right hand out of his pocket. In it was a thin leather wallet. "Bite down on this."

Erin took the wallet from him and said, "You're certain this is the only way." She thought that he looked like he was about to cry.

"I'm sorry. It's the only way I know. Maybe if I had more first aid training… But I don't, and maybes really aren't going to help us." He removed the top from the small bottle of Isopropyl Alcohol. "Are you ready?" Hank repositioned her leg on the camp stool and straddled her leg at the knee. He put enough of his weight on her that she couldn't move the leg.

"No, but since that's not going to stop you…" Erin placed the wallet between her teeth and nodded her head.

The cold liquid touched her skin and instantly her leg felt as if it were on fire. Her teeth sank into the soft leather of the tri-fold wallet, her leg jerked, and she passed out.

Hank finished cleaning and bandaging Erin's wound. "Well, Ms. Erin Foster, it looks like you'll live. Though when you come to you may wish you could die."

He retrieved the .38 from the fanny pack, tucked it in his waistband and tossed the fanny pack into the truck. Then he set to work rigging a hammock behind the seats in the truck's extended cab. He heard a groan and looked toward his

53

patient. She licked her lips and her eyelids fluttered but didn't open.

Damn, I'm not ready for you to wake up. He watched her for several seconds before returning to his work.

With the hammock secured he got out of the truck and stretched his back. He tilted his head back and rolled his head from shoulder to shoulder. A sound brought his attention back to his surroundings. Hank opened his eyes in time to see a wobbly Erin trying to attack him. He caught her as she fell into his arms and passed out, again.

He scooped Erin up and started the difficult process of placing her in the hammock cocoon he'd strung in the truck's crew cab.

Now if she'll just stay there and not cause me any more problems, I can get a couple of necessities dealt with.

He popped the hood on the truck and reached under the battery shelf. After a couple of attempts he managed to get a good grip on the tracking device and remove it. Looking at it in the palm of his hand he hit the off button.

Hank looked in on Erin. She seemed to be asleep. So, he returned to where he'd parked his patrol car. He removed his personal laptop, riot gear, including weapons and ammo and tossed the tracker he'd taken from his truck into the trunk.

He stashed the items he'd removed in some bushes. Then he drove the car a short distance, aimed it at a canal, put it in neutral, placed a rock on the gas pedal and reaching in through the driver's open window with his night stick he knocked the gear shift into drive. He watched until the car sank below the surface.

The whole operation took about half an hour. When he

arrived back at the truck Erin was still in her cocoon.

He smiled, thinking to himself; even if she came to, I doubt she could get out of that cradle with her leg in that condition.

CHAPTER 11

The time Hank spent waiting for sunset he debated with himself the pros and cons of changing into civilian clothes before meeting with the Sanctuary people. In the end he decided he would be better off staying in his uniform. He figured by being up front about his former occupation he stood a better chance of earning their trust.

He parked the truck at the edge of the convenience store parking lot, shut off the engine, and pocketed the keys. He checked on Erin. She felt warm to him.

He tucked the blanket around her, pulled up the collar of his denim jacket, and stepped out into the cool evening air. A late afternoon rainstorm had dropped the temperature to a comfortable seventy-two degrees with a light sea breeze. Playing with the change in his hand he walked to the pay phone, slid the appropriate number of coins into the ancient device, and punched in a phone number.

The line stopped ringing. Hank thought he heard someone breathing but they didn't speak. He said, "Hello?"

"Yes."

"I, we, need sanctuary." Holding the receiver in his left-hand Hank rested his right hand on the Plexiglas frame around the instrument, shielding his face from any passersby.

"How many?"

"Two."

"Where are you?"

"The corner of James Street and Barbara Boulevard."

Silence. Hank could tell the line was still open. He was about to ask if anyone was on the other end when he was told, "Drive to Carson and turn left. Go two miles and take the dirt road to the right. Drive three miles, turn off the engine and wait. Repeat the instructions I just gave you."

Hank recited the instructions verbatim and then said, "Look the woman with me..." click. The people on the other end had disconnected. "...needs medical attention." He slammed the receiver down. "Damn!"

Hank looked around to see if anyone had noticed his outburst. He was alone. A glance into the nearby convenience store showed the clerk leaning on the counter, his nose buried in a magazine.

Back at the truck he noted the beads of sweat on Erin's face. He considered returning to the pay phone and recalling the sanctuary number when a patrol car drove by.

His chest felt as if an elephant just sat down on it. A faint smile tugged at the corners of his mouth as the irony of the situation sank in.

I don't think I like being on this end of the cops and robbers' equation.

He watched the cruiser round the corner down the block before he started the truck. "Well, Erin it looks like we'll just have to do what the fellow on the phone said and wait. Hopefully, it won't be long."

Ten minutes later Hank stopped alongside the dirt road, killed the engine, and waited.

The crickets chirped and the frogs croaked. Other than that,

57

it was quiet. Even with the windows up the sweet aroma of orange blossoms seeped into the cab. Hank inhaled the fragrance, leaned his head back on the headrest, closed his eyes, and thought of happier times.

His trip down memory lane was short lived. Erin moaned and weakly flailed the air, as if she were fighting someone.

"Shh. Quiet." He twisted around and wrung out the washcloth in the shallow pan he'd made from the gallon water jug Erin had taken from his refrigerator. He wiped down her face. "They'll be here soon and then we'll get you to a doctor."

A tap on the passenger side window made him jump. The grotesque Halloween mask that looked back at him gave him another start.

"Open the door." It was impossible to tell if the mask-muffled voice was male or female.

"Do as you're told." Another voice, this time from the driver's side ordered.

The guns displayed by both of his visitors left him little choice. Hank unlocked the trucks doors with the push of a button.

The one on the driver's side said, "Keep your hands on the steering wheel." He paused. "We were told there were two of you. Where's the other one?"

Hank nodded to the rear. "She's back there."

"Tell her to move forward."

"She can't."

"Why not?"

"If you hadn't hung up on me when I called, you'd know why not, damn it. She needs medical attention. She's been shot." Hank glared at the fright mask next to him and watched his captor give a couple of quick hand signals to his companion. Out of the corner of his eye he saw his initial visitor disappear.

"Keep your hands in sight and slide out the passenger side."

Hank slid across the seat. As his feet touched the ground a hood was slipped over his head, hands roughly grabbed him, and handcuffed his hands behind his back. They led him several feet then shoved him into the backseat of a car. The vehicle rocked with the slamming of the door.

Sensing someone nearby Hank asked, "Who's there?"

"No one you know, deputy." The voice was male with a slight southern drawl. "Who's the wounded woman with you?"

"Erin Foster."

Hank could hear whispering voices but couldn't make out the words. "Look, it really is her. We struggled over a gun, and it went off." He paused. "How is she?"

"I don't know, green shirt. I didn't bring the doc with me. But for your sake, you better hope she pulls through."

Hank sighed. "Yeah, I suppose so."

The man with the southern drawl ordered others Hank couldn't see. "Slide her in here. She can rest across us. Give me the blanket from the trunk. I'll use it as a pillow for her." He paused. "Careful of her leg."

Seconds later Hank felt a body sliding across his lap.

"You know what to do with the truck. Come home as soon as you're finished."

The car carrying Erin and Hank began to pull away when there was a ferocious pounding on the roof.

Someone lowered a window letting in the cool night breeze.

The man with the southern drawl demanded, "What the hell

is the problem?"

"You're not gonna believe it." The words tripped over one another in their rush to be spoken. "The truck, it's full of camping equipment, MREs, tents. You name it, it's probably in there. He's even got police riot gear in there."

Southern drawl didn't respond immediately. Then he said, "Scan the stuff for tracking devices, then stash it and get rid of the truck. Don't dawdle. You need to be home by sunrise." He paused. "If you find anything you think might be useful bring it back with you."

CHAPTER 12

The flat-bottom boat bumped against the dock closest to Camp Liberty's hospital. The once abandoned fish camp served as home for the Swamp Rats.

Dr. Upton waited in the building that served as the camp's hospital. His bedside manner was seriously lacking in any form of empathy. He was efficient and good at his job, beyond that no one had much to say about the man.

Colonel Linda Mason, the leader of Camp Liberty followed the two men carrying Erin.

"Put her on the table." Dr. Upton moved to Erin's side. He glanced at Nurse Barton and ordered, "Temperature and blood pressure."

"Yes, doctor."

"Can anyone tell me exactly what's under this bandage?"

Colonel Linda Mason said, "Paul, go fetch the deputy." Though no one spoke Colonel Mason noted the raised eyebrows among her people at the mention of the 'deputy'.

The toe of Hank's boot caught on the threshold as he blindly stumbled into the room; his head still covered with the black hood. His voice came through the cloth, "If you're going to kill me, I would prefer a quicker method than suffocation."

A voice from the group said, "Just tell me how and I'll accommodate you, green shirt."

Colonel Mason snapped her head toward the gathered

61

crowd. She thought she had recognized the voice and when she saw Andrea among those present, she knew she'd been right. "Andrea, this man has asked for our protection, and you threaten him with murder?"

"Remind me again, Colonel, why we're offering sanctuary to any who call? I say it'll be our undoing." Andrea looked around her for support. Some others in the crowd murmured their agreement. She turned back to Colonel Mason. "I say we feed them both to the gators."

"I'll pass your recommendation on to General Wayne. However, for now since we're under his command and not yours..."

Colonel Mason signaled the man closest to Hank to remove the hood. "Better, deputy?"

"Yes, ma'am. Thank you." He squinted and blinked as his eyes adjusted to the light. He aimed his comments at Linda, "My name's Henry Bartholomew, but most everybody calls me Hank." He looked around the room at many suspicious faces. Across the room he saw Erin lying on a table. "Is she going to be all right?" The concern in his voice was plain.

"That depends on a great many things." Dr. Upton said, cutting away the old bandage. Without looking up from examining his patient, he asked, "What happened, when did it happen, and what kind of treatment has she received?"

Hank swallowed hard, looked around the room, and then brought his focus back to the doctor. "We were struggling over a gun when it went off. I cleaned the wound by pouring rubbing alcohol into it. I soaked a clean t-shirt with alcohol and then bandaged her with the t-shirt."

Dr. Upton locked his gaze on Hank for a moment before

turning back to Erin. "How long ago?"

"What time is it now?"

Nurse Barton replied, "It's zero two thirty."

"In that case, about ten hours ago."

"Her temperature is 100 and the blood pressure is 90 over 50, doctor. Breathing is rapid."

"Very well." He handed Chris the bloody bandage. "Bring me the suture kit, sterile gauze and whatever antiseptic we have."

Chris pushed her way through the crowd, to dispose of the bloody bandage and fill Dr. Upton's order.

"Colonel, why are all these people standing around my hospital?" Upton's normally abrasive tone was sharper than usual.

Over the past few weeks Colonel Mason had learned not to take the doctor's lousy bedside manner personally. "All right, everybody out. Let's give the doctor room to work." She looked at the man holding the hood he'd taken from Hank's head and said, "Paul, take our guest to my office and wait with him. I'll be there shortly."

As soon as the others were gone Linda asked, "What's the prognosis, Dr. Upton?"

"From all appearances she'll live. The bullet missed the femoral artery, or she'd already be dead." He paused. "The fact that she's unconscious concerns me. I'll know more when she comes to." He dismissed the existence of anyone other than his patient and Nurse Barton. "While I get this wound sewn up, start an IV of glucose and saline. I'm certain dehydration is at least part of her issue."

63

CHAPTER 13

Sgt. Paul Skinner stood just inside the doorway of Linda's office, arms crossed over his massive chest, his eyes fixed on Hank.

When Linda entered the room Hank got to his feet. Paul started toward him.

"It's all right, Paul." She glanced at Hank. "He's just being a gentleman. Isn't that right, dep…Hank?" Paul resumed his position at the door as Linda moved behind her antique gray government-issue desk and plopped into a leather, high back, executive office chair that swiveled and tilted. It was her one luxury among the hardships of living in the swamp.

"Yes, ma'am."

"Sit down Hank."

"If you insist, colonel, but it's more comfortable standing." He indicated his hands cuffed behind his back.

Linda tossed Paul the key. "Cuff his left arm to the chair."

Paul did as he was told, though from the look on his face it was obvious he didn't agree with her decision. He offered the key to Linda.

"Keep it for now." Paul slipped it into his pocket and returned to his post near the door. Linda focused her attention on the man before her.

"Let's start with your full name."

"I told you most people call me Hank. My legal name is

Henry David Bartholomew."

"Okay, Hank. I want to hear again, this time in detail, how you came to shoot Erin Foster."

Sitting behind her desk Linda studied Deputy Bartholomew closely as he recited the events leading up to Erin being shot.

Colonel Mason prided herself on being able to read people and know right away whether she could trust them. She had a good feeling about Hank.

"Of all the trucks to steal, why mine?"

The colonel looked from Hank to Paul and back to Hank. "That has got to be the most unbelievable story I've heard in a long time." She glanced at Paul and asked, "Have you ever heard of anything so outlandish in your life?"

"No ma'am."

Hank worked his shoulders to relieve the tension. "You know, maybe you're right about it being unbelievable, the truth often is."

A light knock accompanied the appearance of Dr. Upton. He stood in the doorway. "Colonel Mason, my prognosis is for a full recovery. I've given her a mild pain killer that will help her sleep."

"Was that wise?" The words were no sooner spoken than she wished she could take them back. The look on Upton's face told her she was about to be handed her head. She continued talking, quickly. "I mean, you said she was already unconscious and…"

"Colonel," Dr. Upton cut her off. "Don't tell me how to treat my patients and I won't tell you how to fight The Order." He paused. "Besides, she regained consciousness and seemed to be in a great deal of pain."

"When can I talk to her?"

"Eight hours, maybe more."

"Thank you, doctor. Would you please ask Chris to let me know when Ms. Foster wakes up?"

A nod of his head was all the reply she received to her request. "Good day, Colonel."

She covered a yawn with her hand, as she tried to remember the last time her head made the acquaintance of her pillow. Soon the heat and humidity of a 90 plus degree day in the swamps of Florida would make sleep impossible.

"Paul, take Hank to the mess for some food and then find him a hammock." Linda stood and stretched. "You can remove the handcuffs. I don't think he'll try to run". She looked at Hank and added, "Without a guide you'd never find your way out of here and Paul wouldn't appreciate you trying."

"No worries on that score, ma'am. I'm too tired to think much less run."

CHAPTER 14

Peeking at the world through partially opened eyes, Erin could tell she was in some kind of clinic or dormitory. Curiosity won and she lifted her eye lids all the way. Gradually, the room came into focus, starting with the palm frond roof supported by pine poles. Looking to her right a line of cots confirmed her initial assessment, that this was some kind of clinic or dormitory.

"Good morning, Ms. Foster. Let me be the first to welcome you to Camp Liberty."

Turning toward the voice Erin was careful to keep her face expressionless. She stared at the petite blonde with pale blue eyes wearing camouflage shorts and a t-shirt.

The woman smiled and said, "Don't worry, Colonel Mason will explain everything. But right now, I need to have someone get Dr. Upton." She moved a few feet to the open doorway and called, "Billy. Find Dr. Upton please. Tell him she's awake. Then give Colonel Mason the same message."

Erin tried to speak but her voice wouldn't cooperate.

"My name is Chris Barton. I'm the nurse for Camp Liberty." She talked as she moved next to Erin's cot. "How are you feeling? Thirsty? Hungry?"

Working her mouth to create some moisture Erin tried to speak. The noises she created were unintelligible.

Chris took a clean cloth, soaked it in some cool water and

dabbed Erin's lips with it. Erin grabbed the cloth with her mouth and sucked the moisture from it.

Chris smiled. "If you let me rewet that, I promise to give it back."

Reluctantly, she opened her mouth and allowed Chris to take the cloth.

True to her word she rewet it and returned it to Erin. "The doctor will be here in short order."

Erin removed the rag from her mouth, swallowed the room-temperature water and asked, "Why didn't you let me die?"

"Excuse me?"

"It's a simple question. Why didn't you let me die?"

A male voice answered, "Because I took an oath to do no harm." A narrow-faced man entered the room. "To have done nothing for you would have been to harm you, therefore I did what was necessary to save your life." He maneuvered Chris out of his way and stepped up to Erin's cot. "What are her vitals?"

"I was just preparing to take them when you arrived."

He sat on the cot's edge and placed a stethoscope to Erin's chest. He listened for a few seconds. "How long has she been conscious?" Without pause he told Erin, "Take a deep breath."

"Approximately ninety seconds."

He moved the stethoscope and said, "Again." He removed the listening device from Erin's chest and looking at Nurse Barton said. "Harrumph. And you haven't taken her vitals yet?" He paused again. "Well, what are you waiting for?" Erin didn't see where the scissors came from; all she knew was that suddenly the man was cutting through the bandage around her thigh.

Chris walked to the other side of Erin's cot, wrapped the blood pressure cuff around her arm and stuck a thermometer in Erin's mouth.

Dr. Upton examined the sutures and then scribbled notations on the clipboard from the foot of the cot. "In any case, my prognosis is for a full and complete recovery. As for your lack of gratitude…"

"Her blood pressure is 131 over 82. Her pulse rate is 77. Temperature is 98.9"

"Very well. Replace her bandage. Dietary restrictions are on her chart." He paused. "Has Colonel Mason been notified that Ms. Foster is awake?"

"Yes, I have been." A smiling woman with the most beautiful green eyes, Erin had ever seen walked up behind the doctor. "Billy came and found me right after he spoke to you."

Upton replaced the clipboard and said, "Five minutes, Colonel. No more. She needs rest." He turned on his heel and brushed past the camp's commanding officer.

A ray of early morning sun danced across Colonel Mason's hair creating the illusion it was sprinkled with ruby dust. Erin watched her sit down in a chair Chris placed next to the cot.

"Thank you, Chris." She turned back to Erin. "I suppose I have an unfair advantage; I know who you are even though we haven't been properly introduced." She smiled. "My name is Linda Mason. I'm in charge of Camp Liberty."

She leaned forward in the chair, resting her forearms on her legs. "Ms. Foster, I heard the doctor say he expects you to make a full recovery."

Erin didn't speak. She just continued to stare into those mesmerizing green eyes.

Linda cleared her throat. "I need to ask you some questions, about your shooting." She paused as if expecting Erin to speak. "I've heard Deputy Bartholomew's version of what happened. I need to hear what you have to say about it."

Erin pulled on her lower lip with her teeth and then after a couple of false starts, told the story.

"...Somehow the deputy got free from his handcuffs. I saw his shadow on the ground and dove away from him and went for my gun. We struggled. The gun went off and I was hit." She paused. "I asked him to just put me out of my misery, but he refused. He doctored the wound as best he could and the next thing I know, I'm here."

Erin looked around and then brought her attention back to Linda. "I know that you people call this place Camp Liberty but that really doesn't tell me much."

"For the time being, all you really need to know is that you're safe here."

"I suppose."

Linda started to say something else but was interrupted.

"Colonel Mason?" asked a young woman standing in the doorway.

"Yes, I'm Colonel Mason." Linda stood up. "And you are?"

"A messenger from The Outside."

Linda bent down and touched Erin on the shoulder. "Excuse me, Erin. I'm sure my five minutes are up. Get some rest and I'll come back to see you later."

The woman standing in the doorway stared at Erin as if memorizing her features for future reference. She gave Erin an uneasy feeling.

As the colonel and the messenger walked past the window

70

above Erin's head the colonel asked, "So, what news do you bring from the outside world?"

"I would prefer we discuss my news in your office."

CHAPTER 15

Boredom and the residual effects of the painkiller the doctor gave her eventually lulled Erin to sleep. When she woke, Colonel Mason was across the room talking with Nurse Barton. A few moments passed and the colonel came over and sat down next to Erin's cot.

"How are you feeling, Ms. Foster?"

Last time she was here I was Erin, now I'm Ms. Foster. This is not a good sign.

"I have a hole in my leg. How do you think I feel?"

"Point taken." She sighed. "Regardless, there are some questions I have to ask you."

"So ask."

Linda took a deep breath. "All right. I don't suppose there's any polite or gentle way to ask this…"

What questions could this woman want to ask me that she really doesn't want to ask me?

Erin's automatic defense of exhibiting anger went into effect. She looked at the other woman and said, "Just ask your damn question."

"As you wish. Did you shoot Alice to keep her from leaving you for a man?"

"What?" Erin sat up straighter on the cot.

"Did you shoot…"

"I heard you the first time. I just can't believe you're asking

72

me such a ridiculous question." Erin closed her eyes for a second. She opened her eyes and holding Linda's gaze said, "No, I did not shoot Alice, period."

She sighed. "Though I suppose I might as well have."

"Now, that's a statement that needs clarification."

"Yeah, I guess it does." Erin took a sip of water from the glass on the table next to her cot. "Long story short, Alice hated guns. She was against violence of any kind. Just before they came for us, she found out I had a gun. We were" she paused "discussing the issue when the bastards started pounding on the door."

She shrugged. "They probably heard the word gun and panicked." Erin bit off each word. "One of them shot out the front door lock and the bullet ricocheted and hit Alice. So, if you want to get technical about it, yes, it's my fault she's dead."

Linda's attitude softened. "You don't know that. They might have shot out the lock even if you didn't have a gun."

"Now I have a question, what made you think Alice was going to leave me for a man?"

"Roger Slinder. The media are interviewing him and he's claiming…"

Erin cut her off. "Yeah, I've got a good idea what he's claiming."

"So, you know this man?"

Erin fidgeted. She needed to move. Sitting still was never her style. "I don't know him. I know of him."

Linda waited for more information, when she didn't get it, she said, "I'm going to need more than that, Erin."

"Look I don't really see why I need to air personal

73

information about Alice and my relationship."

Linda leaned in close and in a gentle voice said, "Because you've got to defend yourself. If you can't come up with a plausible story to counter the propaganda the media is spreading…" She sat back in her chair. "Let me put it this way, if you're a murderer, the general may be forced to turn you over to the authorities. In any case, we will no longer be able to offer you sanctuary."

Erin studied the wall across the room as she ran through the possible outcomes of refusing to defend herself. Worst case scenario was being turned over to The Order.

Better to be dead than turned over to that bunch of bigoted zealots. If I thought they'd just take me out and shoot me. I'd tell them it was none of their business. But I've got a feeling…

She sighed and let her head drop back to rest against the wall behind her. "Alice went to school with Roger Slinder." Erin lifted her head and looking directly into Linda's eyes continued. "When The Order came to power, Alice could see the writing on the wall. She was always a very non-violent person, and she was terrified of what she could see coming." She paused.

"Alice had a brief affair with this clown. She wanted to see if she could pass as a heterosexual, until, as she put it, the craziness was over." Erin smiled at the memory of Alice's confession. "When she ended it with him, she told me about it and said, it wasn't in her nature to live a lie."

Erin closed her eyes and swallowed hard. "So, what happens now? I'm sure they can produce witnesses and all kinds of manufactured evidence, while I have nothing but my word."

74

Linda stood up. "To be truthful, I don't know what happens next." She started to go, then turned back and said, "I don't know if it matters or not, but I believe you. Try to get some rest."

CHAPTER 16

The next day, Colonel Mason entered the hospital and went straight to Erin's cot. "Good morning, Erin. How are you doing today?"

Things must be looking up. She's back to calling me Erin.

Erin scooted back on the cot and leaned against the wall with her arms across her chest. "You tell me."

Colonel Mason smiled. "I imagine you're concerned about the campaign being waged by The Order to discredit you."

Erin snorted. "Is that what you're calling it? How about calling it what it is – a pack of lies told by a group of bigoted cowards."

The colonel sat down on the canvas stool next to the cot. "Headquarters isn't using those words, but the sentiment is the same." She paused and looked around the room. Erin followed her gaze.

They were alone.

Their eyes met and Erin said, "Nurse Barton went off to breakfast a short time ago."

"Yes, well," Her tongue darted out to moisten her lips and she twisted her wristwatch around. She stood up and moved a few steps back. "Headquarters has passed the word that the media propaganda regarding you is to be ignored. According to General Wayne, only idiots and the faithful believe the news."

Erin gave the colonel a brief smile and then looked beyond her, as if looking at something miles in the distance. "Yes, well, we all know the official line doesn't necessarily help when you're on the front lines."

"I'm not sure what you mean by that."

"I mean," Erin brought her eyes back to meet Linda's "that those in charge can pass all the proclamations they want. It doesn't mean that the rank and file will abide by those proclamations."

Before the colonel could form a reply, Erin said, "Look, I'm kind of tired." She slid down and rolled over on her side facing away from Colonel Mason.

"Yes, you rest. I'll come by and see you again tomorrow."

CHAPTER 17

The doorbell and the phone rang at the same time. Yvonne was closer to the door than to her phone. She looked out the peephole.

The sight of a uniformed police officer and a peacekeeper on her doorstep sent a surge of panic through her. She took a deep breath and fought off the desire to run.

A forced smile on her face she opened the door. "Good afternoon, gentlemen. What can I do for you?"

The stoic young man in the black peacekeeper uniform asked, "Are you Yvonne North?"

"Yes."

"You'll have to come with us, ma'am."

"What for? What's going on? Is it my husband? Has he been in an accident?"

The police officer started to speak but his Peacekeeper partner cut him off. "Ma'am, all I know is that I was told to bring you to headquarters." He took a firm hold of Yvonne's right arm just above the elbow. "Will you come peacefully or are you going to force me to handcuff you, ma'am?"

Yvonne looked to the police officer for help and found a closed face. Despite his expression she appealed to him. "At least let me get my phone, in case he tries to call me."

A hint of a smile pulled at the blonde giant's mouth as he said, "Your husband is being notified as we speak, Mrs. North.

Shall we go?"

A hundred different thoughts ran through her mind as she looked into the eyes of the Reverend Master's errand boy and knew their resistance activities had been uncovered.

What was the mistake that gave us away? Did someone turn us in? If so, who? Is Donald already in custody? Maybe he managed to avoid the men sent to arrest him.

The two men marched Yvonne to an unmarked black sedan sitting next to the patrol car in her driveway. The front door of the house remained open, giving the house the appearance of a huge face with its mouth open wide in a silent scream.

Yvonne slid into the back seat of the car next to a woman with a humorless expression. She promptly slipped a hood over Yvonne's head, while saying, "Don't fight it Mrs. North. We're not going to hurt you. The hood is simply procedure for all individuals suspected of terrorist activities."

Before the hood stifled her ability to smell anything other than the aroma of its freshly laundered cotton, it crossed Yvonne's mind that the new car smell of the sedan was out of place. A vehicle used to steal people away from their lives shouldn't smell like a showroom floor vehicle. It should smell like sweat and fear.

"Terrorist activities? You've definitely got the wrong person. There must be a mistake. My husband and I..."

"You and your husband have been under surveillance for some time now. Even before your friend, Erin Foster committed murder. Her actions combined with her connection to you simply intensified our scrutiny of your activities." The tone of voice was that of a mother who has caught a child with its hand in the cookie jar.

Yvonne closed her eyes and took a deep breath. Thoughts of torturous interrogation and prison came to mind. She pushed them aside, not willing to believe the stories that she'd heard were true.

Despite The Order this is still the United States of America and I have rights.

She tried to concentrate on the number of turns, the length of time between them and the direction of travel. Her efforts were short lived when she realized they had done at least two figure eights since leaving her house.

Obviously, they don't want me to figure out where they're taking me. This is not a good sign.

"Why are you putting so much effort into making sure I don't know where you're taking me?" *Maybe if I can get her to talk to me, she'll let something slip.*

"I don't know what you're talking about Mrs. North. What efforts are you referring to?"

"The hood. The driving around in figure eights."

Yvonne could hear the smile in the other woman's voice. "As I told you the hood is procedure."

"And the figure eights?"

The car stopped, since the engine kept running Yvonne figured they were at a traffic signal. Unable to see she strained to hear any sound that might identify their location. The only sounds she heard were the gentle purr of the vehicle's engine and the air conditioner's fan. Her hands felt the inside of the door. No armrest. No handle, not even a way for lowering and raising the window.

"Why are you so concerned about where you're going?"

They were moving again.

"Wouldn't you be concerned if you were being taken somewhere with a hood over your head by people you don't know?"

The woman sighed. "You must learn to have faith, Mrs. North. And by the way, you can stop searching the door for a way out. There is none."

A couple of more turns, a speed bump and they stopped. The door closest to Yvonne opened.

She recognized the voice of the peacekeeper at her house. "Please, step out of the car, Mrs. North."

She maneuvered herself out the door and searched for the ground with a foot. She got to her feet with little effort.

"Please, turn around and put your hands behind your back, Mrs. North." Yvonne did as she was told.

When the cold steel handcuffs touched the skin of her wrists, panic consumed her, and she began to struggle.

"Get this thing off my head. I can't breathe." Her entire body thrashed around until the peacekeeper grabbed her arm, twisted her around and shook her violently.

"Calm down, Mrs. North."

Panic was replaced by anger. "Go to hell you sick bastard."

"My parents were married long before my conception and I'm afraid that hell is reserved for the likes of you, Mrs. North." He paused.

"You have a choice; you can walk under your own power, or I can sling you over my shoulder and carry you."

The calm matter-of-fact tone of his words made it clear to Yvonne he really didn't care which she chose.

She jerked away from the hand placed on her arm. "Keep your filthy hands to yourself." At the moment she was thankful for the hood. It hid the expression of terror that covered her face.

The ground she stood on was paved. The heat of the day radiated through the soles of her sandals. She stepped forward, ran her foot into a concrete curb, lost her balance and ended in a heap on the ground.

This time she made no attempt to shake off the hands that brought her to her feet. "Mrs. North, I will guide your steps and keep you from losing your footing. I have no desire for my superiors or the members of the press to say I mistreated you."

She heard a door open. A blast of cold recycled air hit her legs. A few steps later they were inside. The flooring was hard and cold.

Too hard to be linoleum. No grout lines, so it can't be ceramic tile. That leaves terrazzo or concrete. The faint odor of fresh paint. The paint job can't be more than a few days old.

Another door opened to their right and they entered another corridor.

Yvonne tried to remember her instructions for dealing with situations such as this. She smiled at the irony of the situation as she recalled her cynical words to the teacher.

"Do you honestly think any of us will ever be in a situation where we have to figure out our surroundings without being able to see where we are? I mean, it'll be great advance training if I ever lose my eyesight but beyond that..."

She cocked her head, straining to pick up any sound that might give her a clue about her location.

She coughed. The sound told her the corridor was bare

concrete walls. Another turn this time to the left, through a doorway and into a quiet room. It felt small.

If they hadn't driven around in circles to confuse me, it would have probably only taken about fifteen minutes to get here. If that's true, I'm within fifteen to twenty minutes of my house. The building is either very new or newly remodeled. It's been a long time since terrazzo was used for flooring.

They stopped. A chair was gently pressed against the back of her legs and at the same time the handcuff on her left wrist was released. "Please, sit down Mrs. North."

Still unable to see, Yvonne reached for the chair as she lowered herself into it. The metal of the chair was cold on the back of her legs. The chair was pushed forward, her right arm was lifted, and a handcuff attached to it. She tugged and realized she was now attached to the chair. Someone took her left arm, and she heard the ratchet of another handcuff closing. Tugging on her left arm she found it too was now attached to the chair.

Then her hood was removed.

Yvonne tried to raise her hands to protect her eyes from the bright light shining in her face. But the handcuffs she shared with the chair arms made that impossible.

Blinking and squinting against the brightness, she turned her face from one side to the other to escape the light.

"What do you people want from me? Where is my husband?" No response. "I want a lawyer. I have rights, you know. This is still America." She could hear the panic in her voice.

A soft chuckle came from behind the light. It was followed by a voice that reminded Yvonne of the southern gentlemen of the old Hollywood movies she liked to watch.

"Mrs. North, this is indeed America. However, you have no rights because you are a terrorist and a traitor to your country and to God." He paused. "As to whether or not you know anything, well, that's what we're here to find out."

Pictures slid across the slick metal table and stopped in front of her. "Who are these people?"

Without even glancing down Yvonne replied, "I have no idea. I've never seen them before."

Unseen hands came from behind her, and a leather harness was placed across her torso. It was pulled tight. Yvonne found herself firmly attached to the chair back.

"It's for your own protection, Mrs. North. We wouldn't want you to fall off your chair during our – discussion."

Yvonne fought off the fear and panic that threatened to rob her of the ability to reason as she realized the horror stories she'd heard were true.

Where's Donald? Did he escape? Does he know what's happened to me? Must remain calm. Cannot let them know how terrified I am.

A slight tingling sensation ran through her body.

"I'm sure you're wondering what that little tingle was." She could tell he was pacing back and forth behind the light by the sound of his voice. "Your chair is wired to a device called The Persuader. It's capable of delivering a tiny charge of electricity up to a fatal charge and everything in between."

"Go to hell." Her words were brave but inside she was trembling. She had heard rumors about The Persuader.

He chuckled again. "I think not, Mrs. North." All traces of humor left his voice. "I think it's you who shall be experiencing hell, at least for the next hour. I've set The Persuader to deliver charges at random intervals with varying levels of intensity. When its cycle is complete, we'll talk again." She heard a door open and close.

She was alone.

Yvonne struggled against her restraints until every part of her body was sore and her wrists bled. Before she could catch her breath the first jolt of electricity hit her. She felt as if her blood were on fire. The unexpected shock released the contents of her bladder. Her cotton shorts absorbed most of the urine. The remainder trickled down her legs.

In lock step with the jolt of electricity the boisterous voice of the Reverend Master James Calton III, leader of The Order for Morality and Justice filled the room.

"Woman was made to serve man. God created her as a help mate. Not as an equal. Woman was made to bear man's children, to raise them and help him improve the world. She was not created to be a shrew and order man about as if he were a child. Women, like children, are meant to be seen, not heard. If in church you don't understand a sermon, ask your husband to explain it in the privacy of your home. If you have no husband, then you must speak to your father. Woman is a weak vessel. Her sole purpose for existing…"

Yvonne shouted, "The Bill of Rights. Number one, Congress shall make no law respecting an establishment of religion or prohibiting the free exercise thereof; or abridging the freedom of speech or of the press, or the right of the people peaceably to assemble, and to petition the Government for a redress of grievances."

Another jolt of electricity coursed through her body.

85

"...Wives submit yourselves to your husbands, in all things. The man of the house, the husband is the head. He is the first and last word on all things. Just as Christ is the head of the church, so the man is the head of the family. This is God's plan. Our society has wandered so far off the planned path of righteousness. It's time...no, it is past time for us, as a society, to return God to the head of all our lives. Just as woman must give control back to the man in her life, so man must listen to and obey the word of God. Men must take back control of their women. Women should dress modestly. Righteous women are known by their modest dress. Their long hair is a glory to God. It was given to help cover them. A woman is not allowed to shear her head. Such things are an affront to God."

As the Reverend Master's rambling sermon continued, so did Yvonne's recitation of the Bill of Rights. "Number six. In all prosecutions, the accused shall enjoy the right to a speedy and public trial, by an impartial jury of the State and district wherein the crime shall have been committed..."

A scream of agony was ripped from her throat as another jolt of electricity sent her body into spasms.

Though her voice was barely audible Yvonne continued to recite the Bill of Rights. She lost track of time and the number of shocks. Sagging against the harness that held her upright, Yvonne wondered if anyone knew what was happening to her.

Am I one of those women people hear about on the news? The ones who disappear and are never heard from again. Must keep my wits about me. What number was I on? Doesn't matter. I'll just start over at one again.

Another spasm of pain shook her body and took away her

breath.

In the observation room Deacon Withersby asked, "Has her husband been apprehended yet?"

The interrogator with the southern drawl said, "No, Deacon. It appears the police have once again proven their incompetence by losing track of him." He smiled. "However, I do have some of our own people on the hunt. We'll get him."

Deacon Withersby glanced at Yvonne just in time to see her experience another taste of The Persuader. He turned away and holding the gaze of the interrogator he said, "You do understand this" he pointed toward Yvonne "method is useless unless her husband is here to watch it."

"We're softening her up in anticipation of his arrival. One look at her and he'll tell us anything we want to know if we agree to stop interrogating her."

Deacon Withersby turned to leave, at the doorway he looked back. "Just make sure she's still alive when he gets here."

*　　*　　*　　*

Donald climbed into his car after a boring day spent listening to one speaker after another explain the new distribution of electricity.

Not one of those men had the balls to call it what it really is – rationing. I suppose I should go back to the office before I go home.

His frustration with the apathy of those around him was exhausting. He started the engine, aimed the air conditioning vents at his chest and face, and then turned the fan up full blast. The roar of the air almost drowned out the sound of his cell phone.

Dreading another crisis call from the office he sighed and said, "Donald North, how may I help you?"

A voice he didn't recognize whispered, "Seek Sanctuary. Don't go back to your office. Seek Sanctuary."

Click. The person with the warning hung up.

Seek Sanctuary. Fear gripped him. *If they're after me, then they're after Yvonne as well. Did someone call and warn her to seek sanctuary?*

Without hesitation Donald speed-dialed his home number. He considered the possible consequences of the call as he listened to the ring.

Yvonne could answer the phone and tell me everything's all right. Meaning some asshole at my office is yanking my chain. Or maybe someone in The Order is testing me to see if I'll run. Of course, if we've really been outed Yvonne may already be in custody and no one will answer the phone.

He waited. In his mind he pictured Yvonne cussing the interruption as she tried to figure out where she'd left the phone this time.

The third ring was interrupted by a male voice. "Mr. North, please do not hang up. We have your wife in custody. Why don't you make it easier on everyone concerned and turn yourself in? You're in need of counseling. I'm certain that Deacon Withersby will be glad to assist with your reintegration."

"Go to hell you bastard and take Deacon Withersby with you." Donald mentally kicked himself as he terminated the call. His exhaustion was swept away by his survival instinct he lowered the car window and hummed the cell phone into the canal at the edge of the parking lot.

88

Ten minutes later he parked at the mall and went in through the main entrance. Despite the air conditioning in the building a layer of sweat covered his entire body.

He paused just inside the bookstore, studying the layout as if trying to determine where to find a particular book. Fearing the rapid flub dub of his heart would give him away, Donald didn't approach the man at the counter.

The clerk noticed him and asked, "May I help you, sir?"

Donald didn't respond immediately. He held the other man's gaze, trying to decide if this was his contact.

"Are you all right, sir?" the clerk asked, moving from behind the counter and toward Donald.

"Uh. Yes, of course." Donald cleared his throat and then quietly said, "I'm looking for a copy of Red Badge of Courage."

The clerk glanced around the store as he stepped back behind the counter and locked the register. Then he motioned for Donald to follow him toward the back of the store.

"That would be in the history section, sir."

"It should be in the current events section."

"That is a matter of opinion."

"Opinions are like assholes; everyone has one and everyone else's stinks."

Donald followed the clerks gaze to a security mirror. They were alone in the store.

"Follow me." The clerk walked to the back of the store and unlocked the door to the employee's only area.

As soon as the door clicked shut behind them Donald said, "I need Sanctuary. My wife's been arrested and they're looking for me."

CHAPTER 18

Donald North came to and rubbed the sleep from his eyes, then stretched his stiff muscles. He sat up, yawned, and examined the room. Whatever they had used to knock him out had virtually no residual effects. In a matter of minutes his mind was clear.

Light seeped in from the window high above his cot. The room was unremarkable. Its furnishings were Spartan, a small table with two chairs and the cot on which he sat. Unpainted cinderblock walls and a bare concrete floor.

Donald felt the cool breeze from the air conditioning vent in the ceiling. He watched the bare bulb hanging in the middle of the room sway in the rush of recycled air. The air smelled of rusting metal and oil.

On the far side of the room the door opened.

"Good morning, Mr. North."

"If you say so." Donald blinked against the bright light from the hallway. He stood up and took a step toward the shorter man in the doorway. "Where am I? Have you found out anything about my wife? When…"

Though the other man was shorter than he, Donald felt intimidated and stepped back as the man moved into the room.

"Mr. North, we have no information about where your wife was taken. All we know for sure is that she was arrested around the same time you received the phone call advising you to seek sanctuary."

One of the armed guards at the doorway reached in and flipped on the light switch.

Donald blinked until his eyes adjusted to the new light level. "How do you know when I got the phone call?" He paused. "Who are you?"

"My name is Jack Collins. I'm the leader of ATO."

"ATO?"

The stocky bulldog of a man smiled. "Yeah, it stands for Against The Order." He indicated one of the chairs at the table. "Mind if I sit down?"

"Help yourself." Donald paced the room and ran his hand through his hair. "How long do you think it will be before you know what they've done with Yvonne?"

Jack sighed. "Mr. North…if we're going to be working together I think we should drop the formalities. I'll call you Don and…"

Donald spun around, slammed the palms of both hands down on the table and leaned toward the other man. "You can call me asshole if you'll help me find my wife! But if you're not going to help me find her – I won't be around for you to call anything."

Jack maintained eye contact with Donald and kept his voice even and neutral. "Mr. North, we'll do everything we can to locate your wife. Not because of any threats or incentives you level but simply because that's part of what we do." He paused, never breaking eye contact. "Why don't you have a seat, Don?"

Something about his demeanor told Donald to be careful.

91

This man was dangerous. Donald sank into the chair across from Jack, rested his elbows on the table and held his head with both hands.

"Don, I understand your concern over your wife, and I promise to do everything in my power to help you find her. In the meantime, we have a common enemy, The Order." He paused. "From what I understand your wife was as much a part of the resistance as you." Donald looked up at him as Jack continued. "Your knowledge and skill could be of great help to us, especially on issues regarding the city's power grid."

"What the hell do I care about the city's power..." He stopped. It dawned on him that his knowledge of the region's power distribution system would come in very handy when planning raids and such.

Maybe I can use it as leverage to make them find Yvonne.

Donald straightened up and held Jack's gaze. "I suppose you want to know how to shut off the power."

Jack smiled. "Something like that. We'll discuss the details in my office, whenever you're ready."

No more hiding in the shadows and pretending I'm helping the resistance fight these bastards. I'm in it for real now. Damn it, Yvonne! You should be here instead of me. You were the one who wanted to fight. That's all right; you'll join us soon. I know you will. They'll find you and then we'll rescue you.

Getting to his feet Donald said, "There's no time like the present."

CHAPTER 19

Yvonne had no idea how long she'd been in the interrogation room. As far as she knew it could have been days or weeks. She had a vague memory of someone giving her water and then showing her a bunch of pictures and asking if she knew any of the people in the pictures.

She ran her tongue over her lips and tried to remember what she had said. Allowing her head to drop back, she stared at the ceiling as she combed her memory.

Were the pictures of people in the resistance? Did I give them up? Damn it! I can't remember the pictures or what I said. Please, dear God, tell me I didn't implicate anyone. I don't want to be responsible for anyone sitting in this chair. Except the bastard that put me in it.

On the other side of the one-way glass Deacon Withersby spoke with her interrogator. "Her husband has disappeared. She has told us nothing of value." He paused. "I'm transferring her to a reorientation facility."

"But Deacon Withersby…"

Withersby held up a hand. "No. This is not an issue that is debatable." He turned to leave. At the door he stopped, looked back, and said, "Clean her up and find her suitable attire. Deacon Miller's men will be here within the hour to collect her."

CHAPTER 20

Sgt. Michael Donovan knocked on Lt. Hardtack's office door and then entered without waiting for permission.

The door hadn't closed behind him when he spoke. "What the hell gives Joe? Why aren't Robison and Cusack working exclusively on catching the bitch that killed Norris?"

Lieutenant Joseph Hardtack rose from the chair behind his desk never breaking eye contact with the burly Donovan. His tone was even, and his words measured. "Sgt. Donovan, I don't like it any better than you, however unlike you, I don't have the luxury of barging into my superior's office and acting like a spoiled child who's not getting his way."

Donovan started to speak but Hardtack cut him off.

"The fact is that we don't have enough manpower to assign officers to any one case exclusively. Especially a case that's gone cold. It's been four weeks and not a single lead on Foster. Last night a National Guard convoy transporting a shipment of weapons and ammunition was hijacked on Highway 1 between Smather and Orangeville."

He moved from behind the desk his eyes never wavering and stood nose-to-nose with Donovan. "Do you grasp the implications of such an event, or do I need to draw you a picture? Now I suggest you get back out on the street and help find that hijacked shipment before the body count gets totally out of control."

Donovan stepped back and raised both hands. "Sorry, Joe. It's just Norris Parks was a friend."

"He was my friend too, Mike. Just because I'm a lieutenant now doesn't mean I've forgotten old friends." He sighed, motioned for Donovan to take a seat, and folded his own lanky frame back into his chair. "Look, for all we know Erin Foster is working with the group that hijacked those weapons. She's got to be getting help from somewhere. Either that or she's dead. Maybe a snake or a gator got her in the swamp." He rubbed the back of his neck. "We sure as hell can't find her."

"No, she's not dead."

"How can you be so sure?"

Donovan smiled. "Because I haven't killed the bitch yet."

Someone knocked on the door and then opened it.

Hardtack snapped. "Don't any of you people know you're supposed to wait after you knock until someone tells you to enter?"

"Sorry lieutenant. Deacon Withersby is here to see you."

"All right." Hardtack sighed. "Tell the Deacon I'll be with him in a moment." The officer nodded and closed the door.

"Better you than me, Joe. That guy and the rest of his holier-than-thou bunch give me the creeps."

Hardtack stood up, straightened his tie, and studied his old friend. "Mike, let me give you some advice. The Order is the way of things now and it's only going to become more powerful and influential as time goes on." Joseph pulled his uniform jacket off the back of his chair. "Have you considered joining?"

"Join that bunch of…" Donovan squinted at his childhood

companion as if he wasn't sure who he was. "You're serious, aren't you?"

"Dead serious."

"Have you…"

"Yes, sergeant. I am a member of The Order." He slipped his jacket on and straightened his tie.

Donovan noticed the black armband bearing the symbol of The Order for Morality and Justice on the right sleeve. He snapped to attention. "My apologies, Lt. Hardtack. If there's nothing else, I'll get back to work, sir."

"Dismissed."

Outside Joe's office Donovan turned left. Hardtack watched him disappear around a corner before turning in the opposite direction. He tried not to think about the inevitable result of his old friend's attitude toward The Order.

As Lt. Joseph Hardtack entered the lobby Deacon Withersby stood up and walked toward him.

"Deacon Withersby it is good to see you." The two men shook hands. "Shall we go to my office?"

The Deacon smiled and nodded.

The short walk was conducted in silence. Joe closed his office door. He didn't want anyone to overhear this conversation.

"Have a seat, sir. The chairs aren't the most comfortable, but they are functional. Can I get you anything? A cup of coffee? A glass of water?" He stood behind his desk silently praying an emergency would require his presence elsewhere. Hardtack was the one who had set up this meeting, but it wasn't a conversation he was looking forward to.

"No Joseph. I'm fine." He paused. "Sit down and relax. Tell

me why you needed to see me, son."

He rolled his chair up close to the desk, rested his arms on the work surface and stared at his clasped hands. He lifted his eyes to meet those of the older man who patiently waited. "It's my wife, Deacon."

"What about your wife?"

"Well, she's having a hard time adjusting to the ways of The Order."

Deacon Withersby chuckled. "That's not at all unusual, Joseph." He sighed. "Unfortunately, our society has corrupted the natural order of things and now we have to realign those things that have been allowed to wander off the proper path. The biggest one is the relationship between men and women. It's not your wife's fault that she was raised the way she was. It will take great patience and considerable time for you to recondition her way of thinking."

"I'm not sure I can do it, Deacon Withersby." He pushed his chair back, got to his feet and began roaming the room, rubbing the back of his neck. "I mean, look, we got into an argument last night. She was being so stubborn that I, well, I slapped her."

His words came out in a rush tumbling over one another in their haste to be heard. "I wanted to apologize afterward but I remembered my mentor's words. About being firm and making sure the woman knows her place and I wasn't sure if I should apologize or not. I was afraid it might make me look weak." He continued to pace behind his desk like a caged cat all the while rubbing the back of his neck. "But Deacon I felt weak, weak for striking her because she was being stubborn. I don't know, I just don't…"

97

Deacon Withersby rose and stepped into Hardtack's path. "You were not weak and were perfectly correct to strike her, Joseph. It's a pity but it's true that sometimes one must first get a person's attention by doing something like what you did. No, we do not condone wife beating however there are times when the shock value of a slap or similar action can be beneficial, to both parties. Please, sit back down Joseph I'm an old man and I find standing tiring."

Hardtack sat down and Deacon Withersby returned to his chair.

"You were right not to apologize. It would have sent the wrong message. Your wife must understand that you are the man of the house and as such she is your helpmate. Her assistance and obedience are mandatory for you to have a successful marriage." He leaned back with his hands folded in his lap, a concerned look on his face. "Let me ask you something. Is your wife still working outside the home?"

"That's what we were arguing about. I told her to quit her job. That she needed to stay home, and we needed to start a family. She refused to quit and said she doesn't want to have children yet."

"I don't mean to be too personal Joseph but are either of you using any form of birth control?"

"I'm not. I don't know if she's still taking the pill or using the patch or whatever it is women do to keep from getting pregnant." He rubbed the back of his neck. "I tried to ask her about that too and she told me it was her body and to mind my own business."

"Oh my, you do have a bit of a rebel on your hands, don't you? A child would be the best thing for your wife but since it

98

doesn't look like she's going to cooperate on that issue"
Deacon Withersby stood up "let me do some checking and
see if there's an opening in the Women's Reorientation
Program. If there's a space available, I'll let you know."

"Thank you, sir. I do love my wife and I don't want to lose
her."

"I understand perfectly, Joseph. I'll be in touch."

CHAPTER 21

As he was preparing to leave the office for home, Lt.
Joseph Hardtack's phone rang. "This is Hardtack."

"Good evening, Joseph."

"Good evening, Deacon Withersby. What can I do for you,
sir?"

"I'm calling to let you know there is a space being held for
your wife at the local Reorientation Facility." He paused
waiting for his young protégé's response. "I understand your
hesitance, my son."

"I appreciate your efforts on my behalf sir. I'm just not sure
that such drastic measures are necessary."

"Go home, Joseph. Talk to your wife and then call me with
your decision. If you want, I can send a team out to collect her
or you can tell me that you've worked things out. I look
forward to hearing from you tonight."

Joe sat in his car on the driveway for several minutes,
steeling himself for the battle he was about to enter. Hesitantly
he pressed the button to open the garage door. As it rumbled
up, revealing his wife's car already inside, he took a deep
breath, drove in and parked next to her car.

Moments later he stood in the kitchen. The air felt charged
with electricity and the house was strangely quiet. He chalked
it up to his imagination. Emily had no knowledge of his
conversation with Deacon Withersby and the availability of a

spot in the Women's Reorientation Program.

"Sweetheart? Emily, are you here?" He hung his gun belt on the hook near the garage door; placed his jacket over it and his hat on top of the whole package.

Odd. I usually get some kind of reply.

He stepped into the living room as he called her name. "Emily?"

In a voice empty of emotion, the slight woman on the couch said, "I heard you, Joseph."

Crap. It's Joseph, is it? What did I do this time? Screw it! I'm tired of worrying about what I may or may not have done to irritate her. Still, I would prefer this be an amicable discussion.

"How about if we order Chinese delivered? We have some serious issues we need to discuss. We can talk while we wait for the food."

He moved to stand in front of Emily who sat on the living room couch hugging an oversized pillow with her feet tucked up under her. The curtains were pulled tight and the only light in the room came from a small table lamp behind the couch.

"Why are you sitting in the dark, sweetie?"

"What difference does it make?"

"It makes a lot of difference. I like to look at the beautiful woman I married."

Her words snapped like icicles broken from their moorings by a harsh north wind. "Is that all I am to you? Something beautiful to look at? A trophy?"

"No, of course not." He paused. "Look I don't want to argue tonight." He sat down in the chair across from her. "There are some issues we need to deal with, and I'd like to have an adult conversation and reach an understanding."

"Adult conversation? That translates to, you've already decided the way things are going to be and I'm expected to go along regardless of my opinion."

He ignored her words and bulled forward with his agenda, just the way Deacon Withersby had suggested. "Sweetheart, I want you to quit your job so we can concentrate on starting a family."

Emily pushed the pillow aside and purposefully got to her feet.

He watched her walk to him. He tilted his head back a little to look into her eyes. The rage he saw there didn't register with him in time to avoid the stinging blow as her right arm came down with all the power her petite 110-pounds could muster. His head snapped to the right as her hand connected with his face.

Emily Hardtack leaned down, face-to-face with her husband. "I wouldn't have your children if the survival of the human race depended on it."

He jumped to his feet; hands clenched in fists. "What the hell is your problem?" His abrupt movement forced her back a few steps, but she refused to give any more ground than absolutely necessary.

"As if you didn't know. You come home spouting about wanting me to quit, as if I had a choice in the matter." Her emotions began to get the better of her as spittle flew from her mouth with each word. "First you get me fired and then you come home acting all innocent…"

"Fired? What are you talking about? They fired you?"

Emily applauded. "Bravo! What a magnificent performance. You should have gone into acting instead of law enforcement.

You're a natural."

Hardtack started to deny her charges but changed his mind. "It really doesn't matter whether I had anything to do with you being fired or not, Emily. The reality is that you have been fired and since you're not working and not likely to be able to find a job you might as well give in to the inevitable."

"The inevitable?"

He relaxed his hands and let them hang at his sides. "Yes. You will be the mother of my children. You're my wife and as such you have certain, biblical, obligations."

Emily laughed derisively and moved away from him. "Is that what your friends in The Order tell you? That a wife has certain biblical" she flung the last word out as if it were something dirty "obligations to her husband. Here I thought they were a bunch of puritanical prudes, but it turns out they just want to make sure the men keep the women barefoot and pregnant by exercising their biblical rights." She slouched on the couch, legs spread with her skirt halfway up her thighs. "Sex is what you mean by 'biblical obligations' isn't it, Joseph?"

He licked his lips and swallowed hard as his eyes traveled up Emily's body. From her dainty perfectly formed feet, past muscular calves, the hips he rode to ecstasy, the small firm breasts. The flawless face was marred by the wrath that twisted its delicate features.

"The only way you're ever getting any sex from me is if you rape me, you bastard."

"Emily, why can't you be reasonable about this?"

My God, she's so angry. I just want to take her in my arms and tell her it'll be alright. But I have to be strong, for both our sakes.

"Reasonable?" She sat up with her elbows on her knees. "You think it's reasonable to get someone fired and then insist they give you children?"

Pacing the room and rubbing the back of his neck he muttered, "Deacon Withersby warned me it might come to this."

"What are you mumbling about?"

He stopped in front of her, staring into her eyes as if looking for something he desperately wanted to find. After a few moments he said, "I'm sorry Emily but I have to go out for a while." Without another word he went to the kitchen and grabbed his hat, jacket, and gun belt.

As he closed the door to the garage behind him, he heard the shattering impact of a heavy glass object against it.

"And don't come back you cowardly bastard!"

Emily's words rang in his ears as he backed down the driveway. He parked a block away, pulled his personal cell phone and punched in the numbers.

"Good evening, Joseph."

"Deacon Withersby, you were right." Joe paused. "Yes. She's home alone."

CHAPTER 22

Dr. Upton stopped in and examined Erin's wound. "It's time you started physical therapy. Nurse Barton will provide you with a set of exercises; in addition to that you can start using a cane, instead of the crutches." He hung the clipboard back on the foot of Erin's cot. He took one of several canes hanging from his forearm and handed it to Erin. "Here, this will give you the mobility to get to and from meals on your own. Nurse Barton will no longer deliver your meals."

Erin took the cane and got to her feet. Cautiously, she put some weight on the injured leg and took a small step.

"Wait," Upton said. He moved forward and exchanged canes with Erin. "Try that one." She took a step. "Yes, that's a better fit." He moved off a few steps and said, "Walk to me."

Her steps were clumsy, but she achieved her goal. The doctor took her elbow and helped her into a chair. "Good. Just don't overdo. I'll notify Col. Mason that I'm releasing you. She'll probably assign you a hammock near one of the troop quarters."

He removed a small planner from his pocket. "Today is April 15th. I'll see you here at 9 a.m. sharp on the 24th for an exam."

That afternoon Nurse Barton provided Erin with instructions on how to find the mess hall.

"There are six buildings connected by the wooden boardwalks."

Leaning on her cane, Erin stood next to the petite blonde and listened. The nurse pointed west. "The first crosswalk you come to, turn right, at the second intersection, turn left." She pointed at a ramshackle building. "That's the mess hall."

Wooden boardwalks connected all the buildings, with walkways around each building so that you didn't have to go through any building to get to the one beyond it.

Nurse Barton continued, "If you turn right instead of left at that intersection, you'll end up at the supply building."

Erin pointed down the walkway to the building immediately west of the hospital and asked, "What's that building used for?"

"That's Colonel Mason's office."

"And the one beyond it?"

Barton sighed. "Quarters and before you ask, the one beyond that building is also quarters."

"Why do I need to go to the second intersection before turning left? The first intersection connects to a walkway that hooks up with the mess."

Barton faced Erin and said, "Yes, that will get you there. However, it puts you in much closer proximity to the quarters."

"So?"

"Look, you have to know that some of the Swamp Rats don't exactly look upon you has a hero. They think you killed your lover to keep her from leaving you."

Erin smiled. "Yeah, I told the Colonel you can't order people to believe what you want them to." She paused. "Thanks for being honest with me."

There were a million questions Erin wanted to ask Chris, about Colonel Linda Mason. Instead, she questioned her on a safer topic. Sweeping her cane across the walkways and buildings before her, Erin asked, "How did all this get here?"

"General Wayne is a man with great foresight. He saw the direction things were headed and got a group of people together. Every time he or any of his group went camping or fishing, they came here. This used to be a fishing camp. When the owner died his heirs couldn't find a buyer for it and they just abandoned it." Chris looked around as she spoke. "General Wayne and his friends began repairs some time ago. They mostly used what nature provided with a few extra items that are manmade."

"So, nobody knows about this place other than its inhabitants?"

"Pretty much."

At dinner time, Erin slipped into the mess hall as the kitchen staff was setting up the food line. She filled her plate and took it to the dock on the east side of the hospital. Her meal finished, Erin leaned back against the rough cedar wall and watched the clouds change colors as the sun began to sink in the western sky.

The sound of voices woke her.

"Chris, have you seen Erin?"

"Not since I gave her the lay of the land earlier today." She laughed. "Maybe she lost her footing and ended up as a gator's snack."

"Nurse Barton! I don't find that possibility the least bit amusing."

The tone of Barton's voice changed. "My apologies, Colonel. It was just a joke. If you would like, I'll ask around and…"

"No, that won't be necessary." She paused. "I've already asked at the mess hall. One of the kitchen workers saw her come in early and leave with a full plate. But no one has seen her since."

Erin pressed her ear to the wall to make sure she didn't miss a word.

"Linda, are you worried because her disappearance might make you look bad or" she paused "or is this more personal?"

Colonel Mason's tone became defensive. "What are you trying to imply, Chris? I'd be upset over the disappearance of any one of my people. Are you insinuating that there's an improper relationship between Erin Foster and me?"

"Calm down, Linda. I know there's no relationship, improper or otherwise. I've watched you try to befriend her. She's about as friendly as Peacekeeper to a drag queen." She paused. "However, I think you have feelings…"

"Nurse Barton!" The pounding of running feet on the boardwalk accompanied the urgent cries. "Nurse Barton!" The footsteps stopped and between gasps for air a woman said, "Dr. Upton needs you in the mess, there's been an accident."

Erin listened until she couldn't hear footsteps before she struggled to her feet and entered the hospital.

Obviously, I have to let the colonel know that I'm all right or she'll have a search party looking for me.

Erin hobbled down the walkway to Colonel Mason's office. At the open door she knocked on the frame and called out, "Colonel Mason? Anybody home?" Her leg throbbed, so she went inside and took a seat to wait for the colonel.

It didn't take long before sitting up was an uncomfortable position. She needed to lie down.

I suppose I could wait in the hammock I noticed outside. But that would leave me in plain sight of anyone walking nearby. Not a good plan.

With the help of her cane, she pushed herself up from the chair. It was almost full dark now, but in the waning light she saw a full-size bed in the corner.

I guess rank does have its privileges, she thought as she pushed on the soft mattress. I'll just lie down for a few minutes. I'll hear her coming and have plenty of time to get up.

CHAPTER 23

Part of her mind knew it was a dream, but it didn't matter. Fear filled her, clouded her ability to reason and she began to flail her arms. She felt as if her feet were encased in cement.

"Erin! Erin, wake up." Hands grabbed her shoulders and shook her. "It's just a bad dream, Erin. Wake up."

Her eyes popped open. At first, she wasn't sure where she was. Then everything came flooding back; Alice's death, running through the swamp, getting shot, and being accused of murdering Alice.

Colonel Mason sat on the edge of the bed, still holding Erin's shoulders. "It's okay, Erin. You're safe here."

That simple phrase of reassurance was the final straw. Erin collapsed, sobbing into Linda Mason's arms.

"It's all right, Erin. Everything will be all right." She petted Erin's hair and rubbed her back trying to calm her. "You go ahead and cry. It's long overdue."

Erin quickly got control of herself. She stopped sobbing and pulled back. "I'm sorry, Colonel. I was waiting for you and my leg started to hurt. I just meant to…"

Erin pushed away from the colonel, who reluctantly released her from her embrace.

"It's all right, Erin." Colonel Mason gently brushed Erin's hair out of her eyes.

Guilt flooded through Erin like a raging river. In Linda's arms

110

she'd felt things she didn't think she had a right to feel. Her nipples hardened, her pulse quickened, and a tingling sensation spread throughout her body.

She thought, "I don't have time for feelings. I have to kill The Reverend Master. It's his fault Alice is dead."

"No!" She moved deeper into the corner. "No, it's not all right."

The colonel stood up and walked to the desk. She struck a match and lit a kerosene lantern. Her back still to Erin, she cleared her throat and as she turned around said, "I'll ask Nurse Barton to come and make certain you didn't reopen your wound."

Erin slid forward and with the aid of her cane got to her feet. "That won't be necessary, colonel. I assure you, I'm fine." She hurried toward the door and stumbled. Linda raced forward, caught her, and gently lowered her to the floor.

She lingered a moment longer than was necessary to ensure Erin's safety. Looking into Linda's eyes, Erin knew what Chris Barton said earlier was right, Linda had feelings for her. What Chris Barton didn't know, what Linda must never know, was that the attraction was mutual.

Erin closed her eyes. She felt Linda move away from her. *I want her. I want to feel her hands, her lips exploring me, and I want to explore her. But I don't dare go there, for so many reasons. If I do people will really believe that crap The Order is spreading about me.*

"No arguments this time. Nurse Barton is going to come and look at that leg." Erin started to get up off the floor. "Oh no you don't, you just stay right where you are until Chris is here. Then we'll both help you get to your feet."

111

Erin didn't offer any argument or attempt to rise. She decided that it would be better to have a third-party present. She no longer trusted herself to be alone with Colonel Linda Mason.

Linda moved to the doorway and whistled. It was a sound reminiscent of a whippoorwill's call. Seconds later someone repeated the whistle.

"She'll be here in a minute."

Erin didn't respond. She stayed on the floor with her eyes closed, thinking about the way being in Linda's arms made her feel.

Chris arrived and was given a synopsis of the circumstances leading to Erin being on the floor of Colonel Mason's office. When she opened her eyes, Erin caught a glimpse of Chris' face and saw a smile, a smile that was a half of a step away from becoming laughter.

She thinks the situation is funny. Erin considered it from Chris' point of view. *She's right; it is funny, in a sad sort of way.*

"There doesn't appear to be any damage to your stitches." Chris got up and motioned for Linda to move to the opposite side of Erin. Each woman grabbed one of Erin's upper arms and helped her get to her feet.

"Don't put any weight on that leg yet. Linda, keep supporting her while I get her cane."

Chris released Erin, leaving Linda as her sole support. It was barely two seconds that Linda and Erin had alone while Chris bent down and picked up the cane. It was more than enough to get Erin's blood racing again.

I can't do this. I have to get myself under control.

112

Erin snatched the cane from Chris. "Thank you, Nurse Barton. I assure you I'm fine." She cleared her throat and moved away from both women, toward the door.

"I merely stopped by the Colonel's office to let her know I've strung a hammock on the far side of the hospital. Thank you for your help, Nurse Barton. Colonel Mason. Good night."

"Good night" came in stereo from Chris and Linda.

CHAPTER 24

The Fourth Shift catered to off-duty police officers. Pictures of officers killed in the line of duty hung on the wall of honor, alongside those of retired officers. Norris Parks' photo filled one of the spots left empty, when all the female officers' photos were removed.

Donovan stared at Norris' reflected image in the mirror behind the bar and said, "I'll have another." The bartender hesitated. "I said, I'll have another. What's the matter with you, are you deaf?"

"No, he heard you just fine." The voice behind Donovan replied.

Donovan turned and glared at Det. Robison.

Robison, you worthless piece of shit. If you were any good at your job, Erin Foster would have been caught already.

Looking sideways at Robison, he said, "You know Norris Parks was a real cop. A pity he was killed instead of a jerk like you and I'm off duty. So, fuck off."

Robison ignored the insult. "Off duty or on is irrelevant. You're a police officer and as such there are certain things expected of you."

Donovan stood up, kicked his stool out of the way, and using his body weight to add power to the blow, swung a roundhouse punch at Robison. The slender man stepped out of the way and allowed Donovan's momentum to land him on the barroom floor.

Across the room a couple of other off duty uniforms took note of the commotion. One of them started to get up but his buddy stopped him, nodded toward Robison, said something, and his friend sat back down.

Robison knew the reputation he had around the station. He couldn't have been any more distrusted by his fellow officers if he were with Internal Affairs. He ignored the others, reached down, and tried to help Donovan to his feet.

Donovan pulled his arm away and grabbed a table to pull himself from the floor. "Get away from me you freak. Christ, I'd rather have some faggot touch me than one of your kind. At least I know their perversion won't rub off on me."

Robison's expression never changed. "Let me call you a cab, sergeant. You've had enough to drink for one night."

Donovan stood with his back to the bar, one hand rested on its rolled wood edge for support as he gestured with the other one. "What the hell's wrong with the rest of you?" His booming voice filled the building. "Don't you know what he is? Can't you see what him and his kind are doing?" His bleary gaze pierced the darkness. Men who risked their lives every day lacked the courage to meet Donovan's stare. "Cowards. The whole fuckin' lot of you. A bunch of little…"

He turned toward the bar, muttering under his breath, and slouched against the newly resurfaced, highly polished wood.

"What exactly is it that you think my kind are doing to you, Sergeant Donovan?"

"What?"

Det. Robison stepped over and stood next to Donovan and repeated the question.

115

Donovan smiled, leaned toward the man, and opened his mouth as if to speak, instead the greasy sandwich he'd eaten earlier mixed with beer and whiskey spewed all over the front of Robison.

Robison looked at the disgusting mixture running down him and then lifted his eyes to look into Donovan's. He never raised his voice as he said, "Sergeant, you need to learn to control yourself and to respect your superiors. I intend to see you get both lessons."

The bartender offered Robison a damp towel. Robison ignored it and ordered, "Call Sgt. Donovan a cab. He's going home."

Then he looked around the room. His eyes stopped on the patrolman that had started to aid Donovan earlier. He pointed at the man and said, "You, come here."

The young man obeyed immediately.

"What's your name, officer?"

"Sweet, sir. Matthew Sweet."

"Officer Sweet, will you see to it that Sgt. Donovan takes a cab home?"

"Yes sir. I'll take care of him."

"Thank you." Det. Mort Robison turned and left without a backward glance.

CHAPTER 25

Donovan opened one eye and immediately closed it. He hadn't drawn the shades last night and the room was flooded with bright Florida sunshine. The brilliant light stabbed his eyes like needles in a pin cushion.

The sound that woke him came again. It reverberated through his head like a sledgehammer against an empty oil drum.

"I'm comin'." He shouted and grabbed his head in pain.

This wasn't Mike Donovan's first hangover, but it was certainly his worst. He staggered from bed and managed to get to the front door before his visitor resumed knocking.

Donovan squinted at Lt. Joseph Hardtack standing on his threshold wearing a reproving expression.

Lt. Hardtack nudged Mike aside and stepped into the tiny apartment slamming the door behind him.

"Oooh. What'd ya go and do that for?" Mike whispered holding his head with both hands. He wobbled to the window and managed to close the blinds.

Once the room was properly darkened, he could open his eyes without too much pain. He took a deep breath, fought the urge to vomit, and faced his friend.

He watched the lieutenant look him over from head to toe and could see he didn't measure up to his friend's expectations.

Well, ain't that just too damn bad. Cause he isn't exactly meeting my expectations either.

"You look like death warmed over, Mike."

"It's my day off so you can take your self-righteous ass the hell out of my home, lieutenant."

Hardtack rubbed the back of his neck, dropped his hand to his side, and extended his lanky frame to his full six feet two inches. "No, I'm afraid it's not your day off. All days off and leaves have been cancelled until further notice."

Donovan worked his mouth, clamped his lips tight, and swallowed the bile that threatened to erupt from him like a shaken beer. He filled his lungs through his nose and willed his stomach to calm down. Through clenched teeth he said, "I'll get a shower and report right away."

"No, you won't. You're on suspension."

The volcano in his belly seemed to go dormant and Mike asked, "What the hell for?"

Hardtack closed his eyes and shook his head in dismay. He opened his eyes and looked into the bloodshot orbs of his childhood friend. "Do you remember what you did last night?"

Donovan moved to the sofa and sank into the soft cushions. Elbows on his knees he rubbed his forehead and then ran his hands through his tousled hair before looking up to meet Hardtack's critical gaze.

"I went to the Fourth and had a sandwich and a few Boiler Makers. Must have been something wrong with that sandwich I ate. I didn't drink near enough to be this sick, Joe."

"You drank enough to puke all over Det. Robison, right after you tried to cold cock him."

Donovan hung his head and stared at the floor. The

118

previous night began to come back to him in disjointed puzzle pieces.

The image of him puking on Robison popped into his mind. With it came a smile. He continued to stare at the floor until the smile covering his face was gone.

I really hate that holier-than-thou bastard.

Hardtack sat in a chair opposite Donovan. In a softer tone he said, "Mike, you've got to straighten up and fly right or you're going to be in some serious trouble."

Donovan lifted his head. "You better watch out yourself old buddy. They'll be having second thoughts about allowing you into the fold if you keep hanging around me."

"Yes, I know." Hardtack locked his gaze with Mike's. "That's why I'm suspending you for a week without pay."

Donovan grunted. "I'll bet that bastard couldn't wait for you to get to the office this morning."

"Robison never said a word to me."

"Then how…"

"There was a Proctor in the bar last night."

"A Proctor? What the hell is that?"

"Proctors are a special branch of the force, sort of like Internal Affairs only with more authority. As police officers we're expected to set a positive example for the community. Proctors are out there to watch and make sure any officer not up to standard is disciplined and if necessary, removed from the force."

The pain in his head and stomach were nothing compared to the rage that swelled throughout his entire body as Joe's words sank in.

"As long as I don't break any laws when I'm off duty, I'm

free to do as I please. This is America for crying out loud. I'll sue for violation of my civil rights."

Hardtack stood up. The look on his face told Donovan this was his old friend's last effort to help him. "Mike, straighten up and join The Order. If you don't, you'll be out on your ass in no time. It's that simple. I know it and you know it. The days of suing the government for violating your civil rights are gone. Grow up."

After Hardtack left him, Donovan showered, dressed, and walked to the corner bar. In his book the hair of the dog that bit you was the best cure for a hangover.

He downed his first beer of the day quickly. It didn't make him feel any better, so he nursed the second one, wondering if he was coming down with the flu or something.

"Hey Donovan."

Donovan looked at the new arrival sitting next to him, Sgt. Bobby O'Brien.

O'Brien indicated Donovan's beer and said, "It's a little early in the day for that isn't it?"

"Shove it, O'Brien."

Bobby smiled, looked at the bartender and ordered, "Club soda with a twist of lime, please."

Donovan snorted. "What the hell happened to you, O'Brien? You used to be able to drink me under the table."

"Times change, Donovan. You either change with them or they roll over you."

"Why are you here? Hardtack send you?"

"No." O'Brien glanced around the room. He got off the stool. "Let's go sit at a table and talk."

"I got nothin' to say."

O'Brien's jaw tightened. "Then listen." He paused. "Look, what have you got to lose? If you don't like what you hear I'll buy you another beer and go away."

O'Brien picked the table in the farthest corner of the small room. Sitting with his back to a wall he studied Donovan.

"What the hell are you staring' at?"

O'Brien leaned forward and spoke softly, "That's what I'm trying to figure out."

Donovan's eyes narrowed as he pondered whether or not he'd just been insulted.

"Look Mike, I know you're never going to join The Order, not as a convert and not as a pretender. You're too honest for that." O'Brien's eyes scanned the room. It was virtually empty.

There were two men sitting at another table in the opposite corner and the bartender, who was busy slicing limes. "You and I both know your suspension is just a holding action until they can decide how to deal with you on a more permanent basis."

"So, tell me somethin' I don't already know."

"Do you remember Sgt. Jack Collins?

Donovan set his beer bottle down and held O'Brien's gaze. "Yeah, I remember Collins. He was a good cop."

"How would you like to join him?"

"Rumor has it that he's rotting in some reorientation facility somewhere. Do I look like I want to join him?"

Never blinking O'Brien continued to look Donovan square in the face. "Rumors have been known to be wrong." He swallowed half of his club soda. "Collins knew better than to go home that day. He's now part of a resistance group fighting The Order."

"What are you trying to pull O'Brien? You trying' to get me arrested for treason?"

"Hardly, but I can understand your concerns." He paused. "I have my own reservations about bringing you into the organization." He indicated the beer. "You drink too much, and drunks can't keep a secret."

This time there was no doubt, he'd just been insulted. Donovan stood up forcing his chair to slide across the floor behind him. "Who the hell do you think you are, calling me a drunk?"

O'Brien remained in his chair and signaled the bartender not to worry. They weren't going to be breaking up his place. "Sit down, Donovan."

Donovan's abrupt movement created a nauseous feeling combined with a light headedness he hadn't felt since his last bout with the flu. He reached behind him and pulled the chair back and slowly sank into it. With his elbows on the table, he held his head and moaned. "Damn, I hate being sick."

"Stop drinking."

"No man, this ain't a hangover. I think I'm coming' down with something."

"Trust me, you're healthy as can be expected for a man your age."

Something in O'Brien's voice caused Donovan to look up. "What are you talking about?"

"I've seen the proof myself. All alcoholic beverages are being treated, if you overindulge in alcohol, you get sick." He paused. "How many drinks did you have last night before you got sick on Robison?" A little boy smile spread across O'Brien's face. "By the way, you're a hero to a lot of guys for puking on that prick."

"I was nursing my third boiler maker."

"Shit, Donovan, I've seen you drink six of those things and then walk a straight line. Think about it." He watched Donovan's face. "Anything more than the equivalent of two shots of booze in any forty-eight-hour period will make you sick. The more you've had to drink, the sicker you feel."

Donovan studied him, looked at his beer bottle, and then pushed it aside. He scooted his chair forward, and said, "There's just something so totally wrong about that. I don't even know what else to say."

"I can tell you what Jack wants you to say."

Donovan narrowed his eyes. "Yeah, and what's that?"

"He sent me here to get you to join us before you end up in a reorientation facility."

CHAPTER 26

Donovan held no affection for the great outdoors. Wandering around the ruins of an ancient sugar mill plantation wasn't his idea of fun but this was where O'Brien said to meet.

The meeting with Jack Collins was scheduled for sunset. Donovan decided to get the lay of the land. It was just past noon when he arrived and quite warm for April. Dressed in jeans, tennis shoes, and a t-shirt, sweat trickled down his back and his legs.

Sunlight draped itself over the crumbling moss covered rock walls of the disintegrating structure. Ancient oaks at the edge of the woods, twenty feet away, provided pockets of shade. Within seconds of entering the woods a person could be rendered invisible in the dense shadows.

Staring into the mass of scrub pine, palmettos, oaks, and potato vines Donovan searched for signs of someone watching him.

The hair on the nape of his neck stood straight up. Donovan spun around.

Other than the family on the far side of the ruins he was alone. He worked his shoulders and hooked his thumbs in his back pockets. Reassured that the flask of whiskey was safe in his left back pocket, he performed a full circle scan of his surroundings.

The truth is that there could be a platoon of men hiding just feet from here and I'd never know it.

He took a deep breath and exhaled slowly.

It's time for a drink.

Satisfied with his reconnaissance in preparation for his sunset meeting, he walked to the parking lot, got in his truck, and drove to the small seafood bar and grill he'd spotted about a mile from the park entrance. The parking lot held one car when he arrived.

Great! Getting served shouldn't be a problem.

As he stepped down from the cab of the truck, Donovan reached back and pushed the flask in his hip pocket down. He licked his lips in anticipation as he headed toward the building.

He paused just inside the doorway while his eyes adjusted to the poor lighting. A quick scan of the interior revealed one person, the bartender.

Fishing and cargo nets draped the walls. Lobster pots and crab traps hung in decorative displays from the rafters. Wooden tables with bench seating were lined up in the middle of the open floor. Round tables and wooden chairs were strategically placed at intervals around the edges of the room. Everything except the bar seemed to be covered in an almost invisible layer of dust.

"What can I get for you?"

Donovan spotted his favorite beer on the menu board behind the bartender and silently cursed The Order. Letting the door close behind him, he walked to the bar.

"A cola. Whatever brand you've got. It doesn't matter, as long as it's cold."

The bartender filled a glass with ice and pulled a glass bottle of cola from an under the counter cooler. He expertly popped the top off the bottle and started to pour it into the glass.

Donovan stopped him. "I'll take it just the way it is."

"Suit yourself." The bartender shrugged and set the bottle and glass on the bar.

Donovan dropped a five-dollar bill on the smooth wood surface. "Keep the change." Cola bottle in one hand, glass in the other he turned toward the dining area.

"Hello, Donovan."

Standing in front of him was Jack Collins. *Where the hell did he come from? Why is he here? We're supposed to meet tonight at the park.*

"What's the matter, Donovan? Cat got your tongue?"

"Hi, Jack. I'm just surprised to see you here. That's all. O'Brien said we were meeting tonight at the park."

"Yeah, well, I've learned to be flexible with my plans." Jack motioned toward the dining room. "Let's go have a seat. You look like you could use a drink."

Donovan recalled O'Brien's comments about drunks. "Yeah," he laughed nervously "just drinking cola these days. Hey, let me buy you a drink. Bartender, give my friend here whatever he wants."

Jack smiled. "Your money's no good here, Donovan."

The bartender handed Donovan's five-dollar bill to Jack who put it in Donovan's shirt pocket.

"Bring me a club soda with a twist of lime, Johnny and come join us." Jack put his arm across Donovan's shoulders and walked to the table in the farthest corner of the room.

Jack guided Donovan to a chair that left him with his back to the door. Jack sat in the seat that gave him a clear line of site to the door and his back against the wall.

After locking the front door, Johnny the bartender joined them. He set Jack's drink in front of him and took the seat next to him. His own drink was a clone of Jack's.

Donovan took a swig from the bottle of cola. He tried not to make a face as the sweet liquid assaulted his tongue.

Jack chuckled. "Why don't you add some whiskey?"

Still trying to conceal his original intentions, Donovan looked as if he didn't understand what Jack was talking about.

Sighing, Jack said, "The flask of whiskey in your back pocket will make that soda a lot more to your liking." He leaned forward. "However, it will also make you sick as a dog if you mix more than two shots."

"No, it won't."

Jack's left eyebrow shot up. "Oh yeah, I thought O'Brien explained the current situation to you."

"He did." Donovan pulled the flask out and pointed at it. "That's why this contains whiskey that's over twenty years old. My guess is that any booze pre-Order should be safe."

Rubbing his chin, Jack said, "Good idea, Donovan."

Donovan unscrewed the cap and prepared to pour whiskey into the glass bottle of cola. Jack reached out and stopped him.

"There's a slight problem with your idea."

Setting the flask on the table and keeping his hand on it, Donovan asked, "Yeah, and what's that?"

Jack leaned back and tipped his chair so only the two back legs were on the floor. "It's not the booze that's been treated…"

"O'Brien said, he'd seen it being done."

"Yeah, he probably did say that." Jack leaned forward causing the two front legs of his chair to impact the floor. "Think about it, Donovan. Everything we drink starts as water."

Donovan looked from Jack to his flask and then back. "You're telling me that if I mix this untreated whiskey with this cola, I'm going to get sick."

Jack nodded. "I'm afraid so."

"How about if I just drink the whiskey straight up?"

"I'll give you points for persistence, Donovan." He rested his arms on the table. "Let me spell it out for you, buddy. Unless the only thing you drink from now on is untreated booze, you're running the risk of getting sick. You will experience another episode like the one where you puked on Robison."

Donovan licked his lips and stared at his flask for a moment. Then he screwed the top back on it, put it back in his hip pocket and said, "Damn it, Jack. That's just plain un-American."

Jack shrugged. "It has its advantages."

"Such as?"

"I can tell who the alcoholics are in my group in real short order." He stared into Donovan's eyes. "O'Brien's concerned that you're an alcoholic. Is he right?"

"I put away the flask, didn't I?"

"Yeah, you did but can you leave the booze alone for longer than a day? When the going gets tough, and believe me it will; are you going to be drinking to relieve the tension?"

"Try me."

"Believe me Donovan, I will."

CHAPTER 27

Jack Collins studied the wall map, evaluating targets and planning the best escape routes for his people.

A light tap on the door alerted him to cover the map. "Enter."

A young man stood in the open doorway. "Excuse me, General Collins. A messenger just arrived. She insists her orders are to deliver the message to you, in person."

Christ, I hate all this cloak and dagger stuff. He sighed. "Bring her in."

"Yes sir."

Moments later Corporal Davis ushered a young woman into the General's office.

"Are you General Collins?" Her voice was shy and uncertain. Downcast eyes and slumped shoulders finished the picture of a woman whose spirit is broken.

"What if I say I am? How will you know I'm telling the truth?"

She tilted her head back, causing her long blond hair to trail down to her waist. "I know how to tell the difference between an imposter and the real deal."

"Oh, and how would that be?" *This could be interesting.*

With a burst of unexpected speed and audacity she crossed the few feet separating them. She grabbed Collins left arm and pushed the sleeve up.

Cpl. Davis reached for his weapon. "Stop! Or I'll…"

"At ease, soldier." General Collins raised his right hand, palm out.

She used her body to block the view of the concerned soldier, who kept his hand on his sidearm ready to draw it. She saw the identifying tattoo and then released his arm and the sleeve dropped back down to cover the unique mark.

"My name is Ruth." She looked over her shoulder and then at Collins. "This message is for your ears only." Her submissive demeanor was gone, replaced by that of a strong confident woman.

Collins ordered the guard out as he studied the blond chameleon before him. "All right, Ruth. We're alone. What's so important?"

"We've learned that Erin Foster is with a resistance group somewhere in the swamps."

"That's not news. Certainly not important enough news for all this cloak and dagger nonsense." He motioned at the chair in front of his desk. Ruth sat down as he moved behind the large wooden structure. "What are you really here for?"

She ignored his question. "You have a new recruit named Donald North?"

"Do you always answer a question with a question?"

"We know Donald North found sanctuary and our intelligence says it's with you. If it's not with you, then I'll be on my way."

He sighed in exasperation. "Yes, I have Donald North."

"Good." She leaned forward, arms resting on the desk. "We've located his wife."

"Excellent." Collins jumped up from his chair as if he were spring loaded. "Let me have him brought in and…"

Ruth slapped her palms on his desk and stood up looking into his eyes. "No!"

"I don't understand. We've been hoping for word of her location so we can mount a rescue operation. The man's been inconsolable since..."

"You must tell him our intelligence has confirmed her death."

"What?" Collins slowly sank back into his chair.

Ruth followed his example and returned to her seat. "General, where she is being held, we cannot rescue her. It would be suicide to attempt it."

He drummed his fingers on the desktop, mulling over this development. "You're sure there's no other way?"

She ran her tongue across her lips and shook her head. "He cannot be allowed to know she is alive. He will not understand the futility of trying to rescue her. I'm sure you will agree that he's much more likely to cooperate with your goals if he feels The Order has killed his wife." Ruth stood up. "If you would like, I'll break the news to Mr. North."

The general stood up. "That won't be necessary. I'll tell him." He cleared his throat and called out, "Davis."

The door opened and Ruth's escort entered. "Corporal Davis, our guest is no doubt tired and probably hungry. See to her needs and have Donald North sent to me."

"Yes sir."

After his guest was gone Collins considered how he would tell this lie to a man he'd come to respect. He sighed. *This is one of the reasons I never wanted to be more than a street cop. All the politics and decisions. It's crap. Nothing but crap.*

Donald knocked but didn't wait for permission to enter. "I

heard there was a messenger. Did they bring word of Yvonne? Tell me, Jack. Where is she?"

Collins walked to Donald and placed a hand on his shoulder. "Donald…"

"Whoa! This can't be good news." Donald turned away, wringing his hands and pacing. Collins' hand dropped down to hang by his side. "I mean, you used my full name." He laughed nervously. "You know I think that's the first time you've called me Donald."

General Collins never moved from the center of the room. His voice was as bland as if he were reporting on a golf game. "She's dead, Don. The messenger…"

Donald cleared his throat and swallowed hard. "I guess I kind of knew that. I mean, well, there was no way Yvonne would co-operate and…" He intertwined the fingers of both hands and cracked his knuckles.

"I'm sorry, Don. I…"

"Please, don't…" Donald put up his hands palms out and backed toward the door. "I should go. There's a lot of work to do yet. If Operation Chaos is going to work, I need to…" He turned and opened the door. Just before he pulled it open to leave, he said, "Thanks for being the one to tell me, Jack."

CHAPTER 28

Donovan didn't like being left in the dark. He felt that as Jack Collins' right-hand man, he should be included in all meetings and should be briefed on those he was unable to attend.

Collins had a different opinion, only including Donovan in meetings he deemed necessary for Donovan to attend.

This led Donovan to take matters into his own hands. One day when he knew Collins was out of his office he slipped in and placed a listening device on the underside of Collins' desk.

The device transmitted to a small digital recorder; Donovan had hidden in the corner of a room few people ever entered. The device had the capacity to hold several hours of recordings.

News had traveled throughout the ATO about the messenger from outside. The news she brought had devastated Donald North.

Donovan wondered if there had been any other news, news that Collins' was keeping to himself.

Donovan walked into the tool room of the abandoned factory ATO used as its headquarters without a glance in either direction.

He slipped the earpiece on and fast forwarded through the meetings he had attended

When he came to the messenger from two days ago, he played with rewind and fast forward until he found the beginning.

When he finished listening, he downloaded the recording of the meeting to a storage device.

You never know when information like this might come in handy.

Not wanting anyone to ask him why he was smiling, Donovan replaced his grin with his usual dour expression as he headed to his quarters.

He needed to think, to make a plan. As Collins' right-hand man, he had private quarters. Sitting at his desk leaning back in his chair, he stared at the ceiling,

Who else wants Erin Foster dead as much as I do? Of course, Bishop Snead, father of the late Peter Snead.

Donovan still had connections in the police department, and he decided that was the best way to get a message to the Bishop.

Yeah, I'll meet with him and together we'll work out a plan to capture Ms. Erin Foster. Well, capture or kill, it's all the same to me.

CHAPTER 29

Bishop Andrew Snead studied the man before him through narrowed eyes. "Why should I listen to you? You have forsaken The Reverend Master and God, abandoned your country and the badge you once wore."

"So, you know who I am?"

"Yes, I've made it my business to know the faces and names of every person even remotely connected to the killing of my son. You are Michael Shamus Donovan, formerly a police sergeant. You have a drinking problem that grew worse after..." He paused. "Ah yes, your lifelong friend Norris Parks was killed that day too."

Donovan's face was expressionless. "So now we both know why we want Erin Foster dead."

The bishop raised an eyebrow. "I never said I wanted her dead. I have often stated that she needs to be brought to justice."

Shaking his head in disbelief Donovan said, "You can drop the act. There's nobody here but the two of us." He waited but Snead said nothing. "Anyway, the plan is simple. I know you have Yvonne North in custody. Make her location known to Erin Foster and I'm betting Foster will try to rescue her."

After a moment's consideration, Bishop Snead asked, "Wouldn't it be more likely that her husband would try to rescue her?"

135

Donovan smiled. "Don't worry about him. I've already taken care of that. He's under the impression that she's dead."

"Just make a video of her and make sure it falls into the right hands so that it makes its way to the Swamp Rats. Foster will see it and the rest as they say will be history."

"And just what shall Mrs. North be doing in this video?"

"Damn, you want me to do all the work?" He shrugged and sighed. "I don't know have her plead with her friend to surrender herself, rather than be killed fighting a losing battle."

Bishop Snead studied Donovan for a moment, before replying, "While capturing Erin Foster is desirable, capturing Donald North would be more beneficial to the cause."

Donovan looked at the man before him in disbelief. "You mean to tell me, that you'd rather catch Donald North than Erin Foster. What kind of father are you?"

"The kind that wants to move up in the ranks. Donald North is more of a threat to our cause than Erin Foster. His knowledge of the power grid is helping the resistance be more effective in their raids, not to mention that random blackouts are a public relations nightmare."

Shaking his head, Donovan said, "Tell you what Bishop, you help me get Erin Foster and I'll see what I can do about Donald North. Deal?"

"Hmmm. What guarantee do I have that you'll do your part after Erin Foster is out of the picture?"

Donovan puffed his chest out and said, "I'm a man of my word, Bishop. If I tell you I'll do something, then I'll do it. You just make sure Erin Foster is captured or killed. I really don't care which." He smiled. "A woman like her, maybe a lifetime in one of your reorientation facilities would be a better punishment than death."

An evil grin slowly spread across Donovan's face. "Yeah, I like that idea."

"Very well, Mr. Donovan. We have a deal."

CHAPTER 30

The day arrived when Erin swung her legs over the edge of her hammock, planted her feet on the ground and stood up, all in one easy motion. It dawned on her, getting out of the hammock was painless and didn't require the use of her cane. She did a quick set of the exercises Dr. Upton prescribed, testing for any remaining twinge. Nothing.

Six weeks to heal from the gunshot wound. How long will it take me to get over Alice?

Wearing her leave-me-alone expression, she headed to where Camp Liberty's canoes were tied up. A quick glance around showed her she was alone, for the moment. The aroma of breakfast being prepared sailed past her on a breeze. She moved toward the smell and for an instant was torn between the canoe tied just feet away and the smell of bacon and eggs frying in a skillet.

While the idea of food was appealing, Erin felt a more urgent need for quiet and contemplation. She stepped into the first canoe she came to, as if it belonged to her. Two-minutes later she rounded a bend and Camp Liberty disappeared from sight.

She paddled strongly for an hour against the current and then she stopped paddling and allowed the canoe to drift with the current. Sweat reflected the sunlight, giving her arms a glimmering look. The tree canopy was sparse here allowing a light breeze access. It carried the scent of oranges.

There must be a grove nearby. Must be a late blooming variety.

A smile began at the corners of her mouth as she remembered how Alice loved the smell of orange trees in bloom. The smile faded when in her mind's eye the movie of Alice's death played in fast forward.

Erin closed her eyes, drew in a long deep breath, and released it slowly. She clenched and released her hands several times. Her eyes closed in a meditative state, and she allowed the water's gentle current to carry her back to Camp Liberty.

It was early afternoon when she stepped from the canoe onto the dock at Camp Liberty and found herself face-to-face with Paul. His muscular arms hung at his sides; his face was expressionless.

"Where have you been?" Without waiting for a reply, he continued, "Colonel Mason wants to see you."

She shrugged, as if to say big deal.

It's been days since she came to see me. Maybe she finally got the idea that I'm not going to be her friend. Wonder what she wants to see me about?

Erin found her heart rate was up and her breathing became rapid at the thought of seeing Colonel Linda Mason.

The duo walked in silence to Colonel Mason's office. Paul stopped in the open doorway, knocked on the frame and announced, "Colonel Mason, sorry it took so long to find her. Seems she went for a joyride in one of the canoes."

Sitting behind her desk Colonel Mason looked up and smiled. "Thanks Paul. Won't you have a seat, Erin?"

Erin's heart skipped a beat. She felt a surge of desire when she looked into the colonel's green eyes.

Colonel Mason cleared her throat and said, "I received notice from Dr. Upton that he's releasing you. He says as long as you don't stop anymore bullets you should live a nice long life."

"Great." Erin's deadpan monotone was in total contrast to her choice of words.

Why is it so hard for me to be around you? What is it about you, Linda Mason that makes me want to wrap myself around you and make love to you?

"What are your plans, Erin?" Mason leaned forward resting her arms on the desk.

"Plans?"

"Yes. What do you intend to do with yourself?"

Erin's eyes flashed as she redirected the passion, she was feeling for Linda into the hatred she felt for The Order.

"I plan on killing as many of the Reverend Master's followers as I can."

A faint smile brushed the colonel's mouth and then was gone so quickly, Erin couldn't be sure it had ever been there at all. "With what goal in mind?"

"Goal?"

"Yes. What do you plan to accomplish by killing the Reverend Master's followers?"

"I don't know." She shrugged. "Guess I didn't think that far ahead."

The colonel leaned further forward drilling Erin with a stare. "Come on, Erin, you're an intelligent woman. I think you know exactly what your plan will result in, your own death."

Erin fought the urge to look down the open neck of the colonel's shirt. Still, she felt her nipples getting hard. To hide the physical evidence of her desire, Erin crossed her arms on her chest.

"If you knew the answer to the question, why did you bother to ask it?"

Sitting back in her chair, Mason fanned herself with a manila envelope. "I suppose I wanted to see if you were aware of the end result of your so-called plan. If you want to commit suicide, there are quicker ways."

"Will any one of those ways also result in the deaths of Moralists? If not, then I'm not interested."

"What would you say if I told you that I knew of a way you could kill a large number of Moralists, maybe even the Reverend Master himself?"

A smile as warm and friendly as a glacier spread itself across Erin's face. "What do I have to do?"

"Join us." Her voice was full of the fervor of a true believer. "We need people like you. You know how to handle a gun. From what Hank has told me you know how to fight. Join us, help us train those who need training and lead them on missions to fight The Order."

"Why should I?"

"Because you stand a better chance of actually accomplishing something with us, than without us." Mason stood up. "We may not look like much, but we have weapons and more importantly we have a network of contacts."

Erin watched her pace behind the desk, as she imagined those long legs wrapped around her. "So, what do you need with little ole me? You've got weapons, and a network, where

141

do I fit in?"

"Come on, Erin. Stop playing stupid!" She paused. "You know exactly how you fit into the big picture. You're probably the only person in Camp Liberty who has actually fired a weapon against the enemy, and you have prior military training."

Erin straightened up in her chair. "How do you know that?"

Smiling Mason said, "We have our sources. Not everyone out there is in favor of the new government. Are you with us or not?"

Erin studied the floor for several seconds before looking up and meeting the other woman's eyes. "What if I say no?"

"You'll be blindfolded and escorted out of the swamp, back to where Hank found you. Everything that was in Hank's truck is there. At least, it was the last time we sent someone to check." She paused. "Hank has generously agreed to let you keep everything."

"And if I say I'll join you?"

"You'll begin hand-to-hand combat training. You'll be tested on other aspects of fighting. As soon as you've proven yourself ready, you'll be given the rank of Lieutenant and assigned a troop."

Erin rose. "How long do I have?"

"I need an answer before noon tomorrow."

"You'll have one."

CHAPTER 31

Erin sat on the dock watching the sunset, mulling over her options. She became aware of a presence behind her.

"Mind if I join you?"

Without glancing back, she said, "No, deputy. Have a seat." She watched him fold himself into a position facing her with his back against a piling. "Colonel send you to sway my decision?"

"Hardly. I doubt anyone would think I could make an effective argument for you joining us. After all it was my fault, you got shot."

"So it was."

She looked away and watched the setting sun turn the sky from pink to lavender to a deep purple in a matter of seconds as it sank in the western sky. "Pity your aim wasn't better."

Hank raised his eyebrows. "You know if you're so all fired determined to die, why don't you just kill yourself?"

"Because that's the coward's way out and I may be a lot of things but I'm not a coward."

"I suppose that's a matter of opinion."

Erin snapped her head around to face him.

He raised his hands in defense. "No, no, not that you're a coward. What I meant was that not everyone would consider suicide the coward's way out."

"Oh." She returned to watching the sky transition from light

143

to dark.

"So, if you don't want to commit suicide but you'd prefer to be dead, why not join us?" a mischievous smile split his face. "Trust me I'm sure some of the upcoming battles could easily get your wish granted."

"I have considered that, but you see my problem with that is this, if I take on the position of lieutenant then I'm responsible for those under my command."

She looked away and in a quiet voice added, "I don't want to be responsible for anyone's life but my own."

He sighed. "Yeah, I can see where that could be a problem."

They sat in silence as the sun sank lower and soon left them in darkness. The sounds of the swamp floated across the still water accompanied by an occasional burst of laughter from the quarters.

Hank got to his feet and said, "Think about this, if you don't join, those same people will still go out on dangerous missions, without the benefit of your leadership. That lack of leadership could be the cause of some or all of them being killed. So, by not joining and providing the best leadership available wouldn't you still be responsible for their deaths? Directly or indirectly, to some degree we're all responsible for one another. Think about it, Erin."

CHAPTER 32

Sgt. Paul Skinner stood on the soft sand of the training area, bouncing on his toes to keep his leg muscles loose. The group of women before him wore expressions ranging from defiance to terror, highlighted by the light sheen of sweat from the stretching exercises they'd just completed.

"Remember ladies, you have an advantage over a big guy like me. You can move quicker and slip away easier," he smiled "unless you let me get a good grip on you. Then all bets are off." He paused. "Who wants to take me on? Come on girls, you're never going to learn how to defend yourselves without participating."

Andrea stepped forward. "All right, big guy. Let's see what you've got."

Paul dropped his arms by his side and smiled. "How did I know you'd be the one?" Palms up, arms outstretched he continued, "Well, what are you waiting for? What's the matter afraid I might hurt you? I promise I'll take it easy on you, little girl." He spoke in a singsong mocking manner.

Without warning Andrea flung her five-foot four, hundred twenty-five-pound body forward. Paul stepped aside. She landed face down in the sand with a thud.

"Oops, was I supposed to stand still and let you land on me? Sorry. I promise I'll do better next time."

She didn't move. Paul stopped dancing around like a junkie

in need of a fix. "Andrea, are you alright?"

"Maybe one of us should go for the doctor," was a suggestion from the sidelines.

"Hold on. Don't bother the doc just yet. She's probably just knocked the wind out of herself." He grabbed Andrea's left shoulder and rolled her onto her back. His reward was a face full of sand and a swift kick to the groin that sent him sprawling.

Colonel Mason and Erin emerged from the trailhead in time to see Andrea's attack. "Well, sergeant I see you've gotten farther in the first lesson than I anticipated."

"'Ten hut," said Andrea, as she sprang from the ground.

"Colonel," Paul slowly rose from the ground blinking sand from his eyes and trying to stand at attention, "we were just..."

"At ease, everyone." Suppressed laughter could be heard in the Colonel's voice. "Especially you, Sergeant."

"The sergeant was encouraging us to use unorthodox methods, street fighting tactics ma'am."

"I see." She turned her attention from Andrea back to Skinner. "I've brought you a new recruit. Erin Foster, this is our hand-to-hand combat instructor, Sergeant Skinner. She's all yours." Linda turned and headed back toward camp calling over her shoulder, "Come see me after lunch, sergeant. I'll want a full report on this morning's training."

"Yes ma'am."

Andrea moved back with the other women, leaving Erin alone in the center of the sandy arena.

Paul flushed his eyes with water from his canteen.

"That was an interesting maneuver, Andrea." He spoke as he dried his face with his t-shirt.

146

"She sucker punched you and you think it was interesting. She used the fact that she's the 'weaker sex' to lure you into dropping your guard." Erin shook her head in disbelief.

"Yes, she did, and the reality is that tactic will work very well against the enemy you're going to be fighting." He paused. "How about if we see what you've got besides a smart mouth?"

"Fine."

Paul assumed a fighter's stance and began circling her. Erin never moved. After making two full orbits, Paul straightened up and asked, "Are you going to fight or not?"

"I was about to ask you the same thing. Now that you've gotten a good look are you ready to get started?"

Without a word he moved forward to deliver a roundhouse punch to Erin's jaw. She grabbed his extended right arm and used a hip throw to put him on the ground.

"Sorry Sarge. Hope I didn't hurt you. It's been a while and I'm probably a bit rusty, but I was in the military once. Besides that, I grew up in a neighborhood of boys."

CHAPTER 33

That evening Erin was sitting on the dock meditating when a young woman's voice interrupted her. "Ms. Foster?"

A sigh of exasperation escaped her. "I suppose I could say no but then the colonel would just send someone else, wouldn't she?"

"Yes ma'am. I imagine she would."

Erin got to her feet. "Her office I presume?"

"Yes ma'am."

"Stop calling me ma'am. I'm not an officer, at least not yet, and I'm not that much older than you are." *Though I feel old enough to be your grandmother.*

As they walked past a group of women, Erin heard a voice say, "Too bad the deputy didn't kill her when he had the chance."

Erin stopped and turned around. "I couldn't agree more. Who said that?"

No one stepped forward. "I see, a cowardly back-stabber." She started to turn when Andrea moved out of the group.

"I said it."

"Good for you. Now would you mind telling me exactly what I've done to offend you, so that you want me dead? I know why I wish the deputy had been a better shot. I want to know why it matters to you."

"You shot your lover in the back rather than let her leave

148

you. Everybody knows it."

Erin inhaled sharply and clenched her fists. *I tried to tell the Colonel this would happen.*

Still controlling her response Erin asked, "And this matters to you why?"

"It matters to me because I don't like sharing space with a murdering coward, especially one that masquerades as a hero."

"Exactly what do propose to do about it, Andrea?" The surprised look on the woman's face amused Erin. "Yes, I know your name."

"I plan on..."

"What's going on here, Andrea?" Colonel Mason had approached the group unnoticed.

"Ten hut." Andrea snapped to attention. "Nothing colonel."

"Ms. Foster, General Wayne isn't used to being kept waiting."

Erin looked Andrea in the eyes and said, "We'll finish our discussion another time." Then she turned and walked away.

Walking beside her Linda asked, "Exactly what was that all about?" She waited but received no answer.

When they reached her office Linda performed the introductions. "General Anthony Wayne, this is Erin Foster. Erin, General Wayne."

Erin wasn't interested in socializing. "Nice to meet you General Wayne. Now will someone tell me why I'm here?"

General Wayne and Colonel Mason exchanged glances. Then the general pushed a button on a small battery-operated DVD player. All eyes moved to watch the screen.

"In the government's latest attempt to convince Erin Foster

to surrender authorities have released this tape," stated the talking head news anchor.

A video of a woman, wearing the standard black, high-necked, long-sleeved dress of The Order filled the screen. It resembled a Granny dress minus the frills.

"Yvonne!" Erin moved toward the screen like a woman dying of thirst moves toward a glass of water.

"My name is Yvonne North. I saw the error of my ways and placed myself in a local Reorientation Facility so that I might be able to return to society in my proper capacity. My husband and I were friends of Erin Foster and Alice Davis for many years. Erin, please surrender. You know you've sinned against God and man. Ask forgiveness for your crimes. The Reverend Master in his benevolence has intervened with the government on your behalf. It's obvious you're mentally ill and an agreement has been reached to take you into a special rehabilitation facility The Order has created for people such as yourself. Please, before you kill again, surrender yourself. I ask you as your friend."

Click. The screen went dark.

"I take it you know that woman," said General Wayne.

"Play it again." Erin fell to her knees in front of the machine frantically scanning the various buttons, trying to figure out which one would replay the video. "Damn it! Somebody play it again." Tears streamed down Erin's face as she looked from General Wayne to Colonel Mason and back again.

"Since you insist," said General Wayne. He pressed the play button.

"Without the sound."

"Gladly." He held down the volume button until the audio

was silent.

Erin stared intently at the tiny screen as the general and the colonel watched her, just as intently. When the recording ended, she jumped to her feet. "I have to get out of here."

"Where are you going? Surely, you don't intend to surrender to them."

"Hell no! I have to get Yvonne out of there."

"Out of where?" demanded Colonel Mason.

Erin took a deep breath. "Let me explain something to the two of you. Yvonne and I grew up together. She was the first person I came out to. When we were kids we developed a special sign language, so we could communicate without others knowing it."

Colonel Mason asked, "What exactly did she tell you?"

"She's being held at the old municipal football stadium. It's called a Reorientation Facility for Women." She paused. "A fancy way of saying it's where The Order brainwashes women into obedience."

"Be that as it may," General Wayne said, "what makes you think it's not a trap? You just said it's where The Order does its brainwashing. Maybe your friend told them about the sign language."

Erin leaned forward, palms flat on the desk, her face inches from General Wayne's. "Haven't you realized it doesn't matter to me? If it's a trap and I get killed, that's my problem."

"But if you get captured, it's our problem."

"Are you planning on keeping me under lock and key, with an armed guard, twenty-four-seven?" She straightened up and looked from the general to the colonel and back. "Cause that's the only way you're going to be able to stop me from

151

going after Yvonne."

"Give us a moment Erin." Colonel Mason moved in closer to General Wayne for a private conversation. Erin stepped away from the desk toward the door.

Hank came through the office door, blocking Erin's escape. "I apologize for being late General Wayne." He acknowledged the two ladies. "Colonel Mason, Erin."

"That's all right, Lt. Bartholomew. You're here now and we have much to discuss." General Wayne looked from face-to-face as he spoke. "Colonel Mason has an idea we need to refine into a plan." His eyes locked with Erin's. "You may get your death wish granted yet, Ms. Foster."

CHAPTER 34

Erin didn't know what Colonel Mason said to General Wayne and she really didn't care. Whatever it was it worked. General Wayne gave Erin until 0800 hours to present a viable plan to him.

The first part of the plan was the major selling point. Erin would be taken from Camp Liberty blindfolded. If she was captured there was no way she could lead anyone back.

The plan was simple; get Erin committed to the reorientation facility where Yvonne was incarcerated. Once inside she would locate Yvonne and in the middle of the night they would escape.

Colonel Linda Mason wasn't pleased with the plan. It lacked any details on how Erin and Yvonne would escape. To her this was a suicide mission, one she knew she wasn't going to be able to prevent.

Arnold Norton was driving the car and Erin was sitting in the passenger seat questioning her own sanity.

I just met this man yesterday and here I am allowing him to turn me over to The Order. Will he turn me over as his rebellious wife or will he tell them who I really am?

He stopped at the vehicle barrier and turned off the engine. "Are you sure you want to do this?"

Looking straight ahead at the guard shack manned by two black-uniformed Peacekeepers a voice inside Erin screamed at her to say, no, she did not want to go through with the plan. Not trusting her voice, Erin nodded her commitment.

"All right then. It's show time." Arnold got out, walked around to the passenger side, and opened her door. "Get out of the car woman!"

Erin looked at him and yelled, "Go to hell, man!" She emphasized the 'man' as if it were an insult.

He reached in and grabbed her arm, dragging her from the vehicle. Pushing her in front of him he continued to berate her as an embarrassment to himself and God.

As she stumbled along in front of Arnold, she kept telling herself, "I'm Barbara Norton. I'm Barbara Norton."

The older Peacekeeper demanded, "Halt. What business do you have here?" Both Peacekeepers advanced toward the pedestrian barrier, though the younger one stayed a few paces back.

"Good afternoon, sir. My name is Arnold Norton." He glanced at Erin standing next to him. "And this, I am ashamed to say, is my wife Barbara."

The guard glanced at Erin and then returned his attention to Arnold. "Your business here Mr. Norton?"

"This past Sunday I heard Deacon Withersby speak of a program for wives, to help them see the error of their ways and ..."

"Did Deacon Withersby tell you he had an opening for your wife?"

"Well, I really don't know about an opening." Arnold scratched the back of his head. "All I know is that she becomes more and more disobedient with each passing day. I'm at my wits end, sir."

The Peacekeeper looked at Erin as if she were a car he was considering buying. The scarf covering her head hid most of her face. "Tell her to remove the scarf."

"I'm not an idiot you know. You can speak to me directly. If you want the scarf off, ask me yourself."

Arnold yanked the scarf from her head and slapped her face, all in one fluid motion. "Have you no consideration for the shame you cause me woman?"

He turned to the Peacekeeper. "You see what I mean?" He pointed at Erin's freshly shaved head. "That's her latest stunt. She shaved it all off. She had such beautiful long hair and now... Look at her!"

Erin stood defiant, refusing to cry even as Arnold's handprint blossomed red on her face.

"Wait here." The older Peacekeeper stepped back a bit and spoke to his younger counterpart. The older man returned to the guard shack leaving his partner to keep an eye on Arnold and his wife.

Arnold and Erin looked past their guard to the one in the guard shack. They watched the man's face as he spoke with someone on the phone. His conversation was short. He hung up the phone and rejoined them at the pedestrian barrier.

"I've been instructed to have you taken to Deacon Miller. He will be the one to decide if your wife is a candidate for the program and if there's room for her."

"Bless you, sir. Bless you for asking him to give me a hearing. What is your name so I can include you in my prayers?"

"Peacekeeper Joseph Bromley." He called to the young Peacekeeper. "Peterson, take these two to Deacon Miller and then return here."

"Yes sir."

As they started away, Arnold Norton asked the young man, "What is your name sir? I'd like to include you in my prayers as well."

"Peacekeeper Adam Peterson at your service, Mr. Norton. If you will follow me, sir."

They walked past the guard shack toward the old ticket seller's window, moving past that they entered a tunnel that led to the stands. About twenty feet in they came to an intersection, the guard turned left, and they went through an open doorway that was the entrance to a long, narrow hallway.

Erin made a point of surveying her surroundings.

Not the ideal escape route. Too confined but you never know what will happen.

The corridor widened and she could see that to her right was another tunnel that opened onto the field. Approximately eight feet beyond the tunnel intersection they stopped at a door and the Peacekeeper knocked.

"Enter," said a deep male voice.

Peacekeeper Peterson opened the door and motioned for Arnold to go in. "I'll wait out here with your wife, Mr. Norton."

Erin started to object but acquiesced when Arnold raised his arm for another bruising blow.

Ten minutes later a heavy jowled man, whose belly threatened to pop the buttons off his vest came into the corridor where Erin waited with the Peacekeeper.

"So, you're Barbara Norton." Erin looked into the eyes of her worst nightmare, a man firm in his belief that he has been

156

chosen to do God's work and that his religion is the only true religion.

"I am Deacon Miller. Your husband has left you with us for a few days." He tilted his head and studied Erin's face. "You look familiar. Have we met before?"

Erin held his gaze. "No, I'm sure we haven't. Where's my husband?"

"Ah well, I'm sure it will come to me." His hands were clasped together across his ample mid-section. "As I said, he has left you with us for a few days, in hope that we can help you see the error of your ways." He paused; studying Erin's face and then turned to her guard. "Peacekeeper Peterson, you may return to your duties. I have sent for an escort to take Mrs. Norton to her assignment."

"Yes sir." Peterson performed a smart about face and headed back the way he had come.

Erin watched him go, dreading the thought of being alone with Deacon Miller.

Peterson wasn't out of sight yet when another young man popped out of the tunnel, they had passed coming in. "Deacon Miller, Peacekeeper Kittredge reporting as ordered, sir."

"Yes, Peacekeeper Kittredge" Deacon Miller was still studying Erin's face. "Huh, yes, take Mrs. Norton to the kitchen tent. I'm certain Mrs. Rivers will find plenty to keep you busy, Mrs. Norton."

As they started away Deacon Miller stopped them. "Mrs. Norton, please, be so kind as to keep your head covered, until your hair grows back." Not waiting for a reply, he turned and entered his office.

Erin followed Kittredge through the tunnel and onto the field.

For a brief moment she was overwhelmed by the memory of the last time she was in the stadium. Matthew Anderson, the son of a friend was the quarterback on a high school team competing for the regional championship. Erin and Alice had screamed themselves hoarse, cheering him and his team on to victory.

"Mrs. Norton, are you alright? Why have you stopped?"

"Huh?" Erin looked at the young man and said, "I'm sorry. I was thinking of the last time I was in this stadium."

"Please, keep up with me, Mrs. Norton."

Erin drew in a deep breath, reminding herself why she was here. "Of course." She followed the young man onto the field, down well-worn paths between the many tents assembled on the once well-tended grass.

The stadium's public address system was broadcasting a sermon. Outside Deacon Miller's office it had been a distant drone, standing on the field the words were clear.

"Is that always on?"

Her attendant stopped and looked at her in surprise. "Of course, the sermons are constant. How else are you to learn?"

"There are an awful lot of tents here. How many women have already been sentenced to this facility?"

"We are not allowed to engage in conversation with the students here."

"Students?"

"Please, follow the rules Mrs. Norton."

"But I haven't been given any rules to follow. The only thing I was told was to follow you to the kitchen tent."

"True, still I have told you that I'm not allowed to engage in conversation with you."

"Yes, and yet here we are having a very pleasant conversation, Mr. Kittredge."

"Kittredge," a strong male voice called. "Is that the new student Deacon Miller called me about?"

The young man spun away from Erin. "Yes sir. I was just explaining to her that I'm not allowed to answer her questions."

"Leave her with me. I'll see that she gets to the kitchen tent."

"Yes sir." Kittredge saluted, performed a smart about face and headed off.

"This way, Mrs. Norton."

Erin was certain that trying to get information out of her new escort would be a futile effort and only arouse his suspicions.

From outside, the large green tent with its canvas sides rolled up, reminded Erin of the old television series her mother used to love, MASH. A different era. A different war.

Just inside the kitchen tent various smells battled for supremacy, with none winning. Instead, they all joined together to create a nauseating combination of hot soapy bleach water, grease, meat and various other foods cooking, and trashcans in desperate need of being emptied.

"Mrs. Rivers, here's another pair of hands to help. Make sure you instruct her in the proper etiquette for reorientation students. She's your responsibility until her mentor is assigned."

Erin watched Mrs. Rivers' expressionless face as she hesitated for a fraction of a second before responding. "As you say, Peacekeeper Braxton."

With a self-satisfied smirk Peacekeeper Braxton spun on his heel and left the tent.

"So, what's your name?"

"Barbara Norton."

"Do you have any experience working in a kitchen?"

"No."

"Of course not." The heavy-set woman sighed. "It would be too much to hope for that they send me someone with restaurant experience." She pointed toward a large sink full of dishes. "It doesn't take experience to be able to wash dishes. Have at it."

Erin's nose wrinkled at the odor of bleach rising from the hot soapy water. She looked around. On the shelf at the back of the sink stood a bottle of liquid detergent next to it was a gallon of bleach. "Are there gloves? My mother always…"

Mrs. Rivers snorted. "Your mother doesn't work here, little girl. The purpose of the hot water is to cleanse, not only the dishes but you. Now get busy."

Women came and went; each one stopped to get instructions from Mrs. Rivers, none of them gave Erin more than a cursory glance until a petite blonde with ice blue eyes entered the kitchen.

"Hello Mrs. Rivers. How goes the feeding of the sheep?" Her tone was light and breezy.

Watching out of the corner of her eye Erin noticed the older woman's body stiffen. "What can I do for you Mrs. Hardtack?"

The blonde looked past Mrs. Rivers at Erin and said, "Rumor has it that we've got a real rebel in our midst." As she spoke, she walked past Mrs. Rivers, heading for Erin. "I came to see for myself."

Erin continued washing dishes as she tried to place the name 'Hardtack'.

I know I've heard that name. But in what context? In relation to who?

Standing just behind Erin, Mrs. Hardtack said, "You seem rather docile for a rebel." With those words she snatched the scarf from Erin's head.

Erin picked up a dishtowel and dried her hands before turning around. Looking into the other woman's eyes Erin softly said, "I'm learning to choose my battles." Erin extended her hand. "You would be wise to do the same. My scarf, please."

Emily Hardtack smiled. "Sure." She tossed the scarf in Erin's direction.

Erin caught the scarf, never taking her eyes off her antagonist.

"You look familiar. What's your name?"

"Barbara Norton."

Emily repeated the name. "Hmmm. No, I don't know anyone by that name. But your face looks familiar. What was your maiden name?"

Erin stepped closer to her and whispered in her ear. "None of your business." Then she stepped back.

Emily Hardtack held her gaze for a few seconds and then moved toward the exit. Just before leaving she turned and said, "I'll think of where I know you from eventually, Mrs. Norton."

Erin barely got the breakfast dishes done in time for lunch. Lunch dishes were minimal since that meal consisted solely of fruit and cheese. After cleaning up from lunch, it was time to serve the evening meal. Each woman received a bowl of thin soup and a chunk of bread.

When they finished serving, Mrs. Rivers and Erin ate their own meal. As soon as the dishes were stacked and ready for washing Mrs. Rivers said, "Our shift is over. Come with me. I'll show you to your tent."

As the two women stepped from the tent the stadium lights came on replacing the fading sunlight. Erin blinked several times until her eyes adjusted to the change in light.

Mrs. Rivers led the way down a path between two rows of tents. After passing a couple of tents Erin asked, "I noticed that the tents to our left are flying pennants with letters on them but not the ones to the right. Why is that?"

"The lettered tents designate the first letter of the last name of the tents occupants."

"So, the ones with no flags are vacant?"

Mrs. Rivers sighed. "Some of them are used for storage but for the most part they're unoccupied."

They stopped outside a tent flying a pennant bearing the letter N.

"Here you go, Mrs. Norton, this is your tent. May God bless you and keep you." Mrs. Rivers turned around to head back to her own tent.

Looking east between the rows of tents Erin noticed two large wooden posts coming out of the ground. She called out. "Mrs. Rivers." The other woman turned around.

"Yes."

Erin pointed and asked, "What are those? They weren't there when I was brought in this morning."

Mrs. Rivers stepped to where she could see what Erin was

162

pointing at. Shaking her head in dismay, she looked at Erin and said, "Pray that this is as close as you ever come to those. They're the pillars of repentance. Some call them the Sinner's Posts." Without another word she spun around and moved quickly to her own tent.

Erin moved her gaze upward to the stadium seats. Empty, not even guards to keep the women from climbing up and going over the wall. She smiled, pushed aside the flap and entered her assigned tent.

The dank smell of wet canvas was joined by the odor of too many bodies in too small a space. She wiggled her nose to stifle a sneeze. She had no desire to draw attention to herself.

Erin counted twenty cots. Ten to a row, separated by a five-foot wide aisle. Light was provided by a series of bare bulbs strung on wire. Eleven bulbs per side, one over each cot with an extra one for the empty space near the flap.

Halfway down the right-hand row of cots a small woman of undetermined age rose and moved to greet Erin. "Good evening, sister. How may I be of service to you?"

Erin refrained from telling this subservient creature that they weren't sisters. "Mrs. Rivers said this was the tent I'm assigned to. My name is Barbara Norton."

"My name is Miss Nabors. If you'll follow me, I'll show you to your cot." Without waiting for a reply, the woman turned and walked back the way she had come.

Erin followed Miss Nabors, who paused at every cot long enough to recite the name of the woman kneeling next to it. Erin strained to hear the soft voice of her guide.

"Why," Erin's own voice sounded so loud and booming in this place it startled her and she paused. Consciously

163

speaking in a quieter tone, she began again. "Why is everyone praying?"

Miss Nabors stopped and turned to face Erin. "This is the time of evening prayer. We thank God for sending us Reverend Master Calton. We also pray for the salvation of those lost souls who continue to resist the word of God."

She moved toward Erin and lowered her voice to a barely audible whisper. "Do you know there are people who have tried to kill Reverend Master Calton? Can you believe that anyone would want to harm that saintly man?"

Erin painted what she hoped was the appropriate expression on her face and said, "Imagine that."

Miss Nabors resumed her glide-like walk. The second to last cot was vacant. Erin's guide paused and said, "Mrs. North." She moved on and then stopped at the foot of the last cot. "Here is your cot. There are five minutes left for evening prayer, so you'll have to hurry. Afterward we are scheduled to assemble at the Pillars of Repentance."

Before Erin could form a question, Miss Nabors walked away, returning to her prayers. Erin hesitated for only a second before getting on her knees and assuming the expected position. Instead of praying her mind raced through possible scenarios that would explain why Yvonne wasn't at her cot.

The only two scenarios that seemed logical were, one, Yvonne worked a different shift than the other women in this tent, or two, she was the reason they were scheduled to assemble at the Pillars of Repentance.

CHAPTER 35

Yvonne's arms and shoulders ached unmercifully and the rough rope bit into the soft skin of her wrists. She longed to lower her arms and be able to place her weight on her feet. However, her toes just barely touched the ground, and the leg cramps were returning.

Peacekeeper Doyle opened the door to her cell and pushed her. Unable to prevent herself from swinging Yvonne tried to ignore the searing pain running from her wrists to her shoulders and back again. She flexed her feet upward in an effort to at least relieve the leg cramps.

"Still think your little joke was funny?"

Before Yvonne could find the breath to reply, Deacon Miller entered the room. "Mrs. North, are you prepared to repent?"

Knowing that nothing she was willing to say was going to do anything to improve her situation Yvonne remained mute.

"Very well. Lower her and escort her to the Pillars." Deacon Miller turned to leave the room. In the doorway, he stopped and looked over his shoulder. "I expect her to arrive unharmed, Peacekeeper Doyle."

"Of course, Deacon."

Doyle released the rope that kept Yvonne dancing on her toes, and she collapsed to the floor in a heap. He unclipped the five feet of hemp that was attached to the length of cable running through the pulley set in the ceiling. He used the rope as a leash to pull Yvonne to her feet. The involuntary cry of pain she emitted brought a smile to his face.

"If you think that hurt, you're in for a real surprise *woman*." He spit out the last word as if it were something nasty he had found in his mouth.

Yvonne's attention was focused on keeping up with Peacekeeper Doyle. She had little doubt that if she lost her footing, he would simply drag her to the Pillars.

Erin tried to be as inconspicuous as possible among the crowd of women gathered before the Pillars. She and her tent mates stood in the two front rows.

The setting sun was behind them. In front of them was another tunnel leading into the bowels of the stadium.

Sweat trickled down Erin's back as she stared down the tunnel anticipating the worst, knowing there was nothing she could do to stop whatever was about to happen.

The murmuring of hundreds of women ceased, and a silence born of fear hung over the crowd like a stagnant cloud.

A Peacekeeper emerged from the tunnel. His black uniform looked hard as coal; the dark lenses of his sunglasses protected his eyes against the brightness of the flood lights aimed at the pillars.

Yvonne blinked against the bright lights and raised her hands to shield her eyes. A tug on the leash brought her hands down, she stumbled but managed to catch herself and keep up with her tormentor.

Her escort stopped when Yvonne was standing between the two ten-foot-high round wooden columns that looked like the pilings used to build piers.

Doyle turned toward her, removed the rope from her wrists;

166

grabbed each of Yvonne's arms in rapid succession and placed the metal shackles hanging from the columns around her already raw wrists.

Erin's jaw tightened. It took every ounce of her self-control not to grab a gun from the nearest peacekeeper and start shooting.

Next, he secured Yvonne's legs in the same fashion as her arms. When she was spread-eagled, he stepped aside.

Deacon Miller stepped in front of the crowd. "Tonight, is a sad night. Tonight, we must discipline one of our children. How she sinned is not important. It is only important that you know she sinned." He glanced over his shoulder at Yvonne and then back at the women before him. "Her tears of regret are a beginning. But this woman has refused to ask forgiveness and until she does so her punishment will continue."

He nodded his head and a Peacekeeper moved forward, carrying what looked like a long pole.

"Yvonne North, do you ask the forgiveness of the Reverend Master and of God for your transgressions?"

Deacon Miller waited for a full ten seconds. Yvonne remained silent. The deacon nodded and the staff was pressed against Yvonne's abdomen.

Electricity coursed through her body, which shook like a rag doll in the mouth of a dog.

A universal gasp of disbelief came from the audience of women. Erin clenched her hands into fists. Her fingernails dug into her palms. Tears of helpless rage ran down her cheeks as she vowed to kill all those responsible for this atrocity.

Twice more the deacon asked Yvonne to repent. Twice

167

more she was shocked with the prod.

Deacon Miller faced the audience. "Our intent is educational, not lethal. Therefore, this sinner will remain where she is and in the morning with the rising sun, we will again ask her to repent. I ask that you bow your heads and say a prayer for this sinner. Pray that she sees the error of her ways."

Erin counted each of the immeasurable thirty seconds before Deacon Miller spoke again. "Go to your cots and your duty assignments with the image of this sinner in your minds. Ask God's forgiveness for your transgressions and pray for the soul of your sister."

Returning to her tent Erin examined her surroundings carefully. She didn't want to trip over anything later, in the dark. She also noted the faces of the women around her. Many of them were closed and unreadable. There were some she could tell took pleasure in Yvonne's torment. Others wore expressions of horrified disbelief.

When Erin's group split off for the entrance to their tent, she made note that one of those pleased at Yvonne's predicament entered with them.

As she moved toward her cot Erin saw that each of her tent mates dropped to her knees as soon as they were at their cot, supposedly praying. Upon arriving at her cot Erin imitated their posture. However, her form of prayer was to work on altering her original escape plan.

No way is Yvonne going to be able to climb to the top of the stadium seats.

"Sisters, we have among us a new sister."

The short plump woman Erin remembered as looking

168

delighted over Yvonne's torture walked toward her. Her soft southern accent was tainted by the superior tone of her voice and her body language. "For those who haven't met her, her name is Barbara Norton. I would like for each of you to rise and say your name." She stopped next to Erin who had already gotten to her feet. "My name is Sally Mae Nilbert. I have been assigned to be your mentor during your reorientation period."

Erin nodded her head in acceptance.

Sally Mae smiled. "If you'd been that meek and accepting of your husband's rules perhaps you wouldn't be here, Mrs. Norton."

Erin felt her face grow hot and she knew it was red as a boiled lobster. Another insult to be stored for later action. She locked eyes with Sally Mae and held her gaze throughout the recital of names.

After the last woman stated her name, Sally Mae nervously licked her lips, cleared her throat, and let her eyes move over each of the others as she said, "You will now all bear witness that I am informing Mrs. Norton of the rules she must obey."

She tossed her head back and looked at Erin with a self-important expression. "First, every God-fearing man is your better. We are the weaker gender and as such must learn that the men in our lives will always take care of us. You will follow all orders without question."

Erin knew instantly that Sally Mae was a bully and a coward. She also knew the easiest way to make her kind nervous was to continue to look her in the eye.

As she spoke Sally Mae ran her hands down the front of her dress as if ironing out wrinkles. "You have been assigned to the kitchen and you will report there every other morning no later than 6 a.m. You will work there until 6 p.m. You are required to attend all prayer sessions. Prayers are held at 5:00 a.m., noon and 6:05 p.m. The prayer session at 6:05 p.m. is generally held in each tent, supervised by the tent matriarch."

Sally Mae curtsied. "I am this tent's matriarch."

She acts like this is the senior prom and she's been crowned Prom Queen.

"You will only work in the kitchen every other day because those days you are not working you will be in class. Classes are to instruct you in your proper place in society. The woman's purpose for existence has been so distorted by the godless that these reorientation classes are a necessity." She paused and locked her gaze on Erin.

A hint of a smile played across her face as she continued, "Humor is a very dangerous thing. Ask Yvonne North if you don't believe me."

Erin longed to wipe that smile off Sally Mae's face.

"Deacon Miller may not wish to remind you of Mrs. North's sin, but I will. She made a joke that caused one of her betters, Peacekeeper Doyle, to look foolish and you all see where it got her." She paused before continuing in a matter-of-fact tone.

"Curfew is at 7:15 p.m. You are not allowed to leave the tent after that without a guard as escort until the 4:45 a.m. bell rings calling us all to morning prayers. There is a small port-a-potty in the corner of the tent," she pointed to the corner closest to the tent flap "however, keep in mind that whoever uses it, cleans it."

170

Sally Mae paused and looking directly into Erin's eyes said, "I think I'll sleep in Mrs. North's cot tonight, so I'll be close at hand if you should think of any questions during the night."

Suddenly every other light bulb on the power line inside the tent went dark. All the women removed their shoes and got into their cots, fully clothed.

"Goodnight, ladies. May the lord keep you through the night and wake you with the new day."

CHAPTER 36

Erin lay on her cot, listening, when she was sure her tent mates were asleep, she sat up and swung around planting her feet firmly on the ground between her cot and the one holding Sally Mae.

The steady rise and fall of Sally Mae's breathing indicated sleep; however, her eye movement told Erin she was only pretending to be asleep.

Erin leaned toward her and softly said, "I know you're awake."

The other woman opened her eyes and sat up to face Erin. "Why do you continue to resist the inevitable? You seem relatively intelligent. Why not beat them at their own game?"

Erin looked around the quiet room and then brought her attention back to Sally Mae. "There's a very old saying. I may not have it verbatim, but I have the intent down pat. Basically it's this, 'anyone willing to surrender their freedom for security, deserves neither'."

A cynical smile tugged at the corner of the other woman's mouth. "Hmmm. Pretty words but they're not practical." She leaned forward to ensure none, but Erin heard her. "I'm a realist. A survivor."

Erin held her gaze. "No, you're a coward and a traitor."

Before Sally Mae could do more than look insulted, a single blow from the edge of Erin's hand crushed her windpipe. In the same movement Erin grabbed a pillow, put it over the other woman's face, pushed her down onto the cot, and waited for her feeble resistance to cease.

A quick glance around the tent assured Erin her activities had not disturbed the sleep of any of the other women.

She shed the full-length Granny dress of The Order to reveal black pants and a black long-sleeved t-shirt. From the hem of the dress Erin removed a length of wire. This garrote was the only weapon she brought with her.

Using the dress, her pillow and Sally Mae's pillow, Erin made it look like she was under the covers of her cot. Like a mouse sneaking out of a granary, she slid under the tent edge and out into the night. She paused, letting her eyes adjust to the darkness.

The stadium lights were out now. However, there were spotlights at opposite ends of the field. Erin watched the timing of the light sweeps and the pattern they followed.

The Reverend Master's sermons were more audible out here than they'd been in the tent. She focused on tuning out his self-righteous voice and cocked her head, first one direction then another, listening for sounds of anyone approaching.

She heard two distinct male voices that were not part of the sermon. Unable to make out their words, she concentrated on determining where they were. Staying in the shadows of the tents Erin moved toward the pillars and Yvonne. Every two steps she stopped and listened. She was getting closer to the voices.

"I'll be around later to check on you, Mr. Snyder. Right now, I have an appointment with Deacon Miller."

173

One of the spotlights swept across the face of the man speaking, as he moved away from the other fellow. Erin recognized the one with the appointment as the peacekeeper who brought Yvonne to the pillars. She waited until he disappeared from sight.

Less than six feet from her target Erin stopped. If memory served her, they were between two empty tents.

Erin stayed low until the last possible moment. Then she rose to her full height, looped the wire around the guard's neck and pulled him backward as she turned placing her hips low against his. She continued the turn and draped the off-balance guard over her shoulder. He clawed at his throat trying to get his fingers under the wire. When he stopped struggling Erin lowered him to the ground.

She removed his boots, gun belt, shirt and cap and then lifted the edge of the nearest tent and rolled him into the tent. Dressed in Peacekeeper attire Erin continued toward the Pillars of Repentance, dodging the spotlights as she went.

Despite giving the outward appearance of a Peacekeeper, Erin knew that if questioned her voice would give her away.

Any fear she felt dissolved when she saw Yvonne sagging from her shackles between the pillars. The raging fire of hatred she had been stoking since Alice's death was building to an inferno.

Calm down girl. You've got to keep a cool head and remember why you're here. Once you and Yvonne are out of this hellhole, then you can blow your top.

Without hesitating Erin bent down and pressed the trigger release for the shackles around Yvonne's ankles. Gently shaking her friend, she whispered, "Von, you've got to wake

174

up. Come on girl."

Yvonne opened her eyes and squinting asked, "Erin, is it really…"

"Quiet, you'll get us both killed." Erin whispered in Yvonne's ear.

"Peacekeeper, what are you doing with this sinner?" The voice startled Erin and she snapped to attention, cleared her throat, and deepened the tenor of her voice as much as she could. "Deacon Miller demands the presence of the woman in his office."

The man hesitated and Erin was just beginning to reach for the knife on her belt, when he said, "Carry on, Peacekeeper. I'm not one to question the doings of my betters."

He turned his back to leave but before he could walk two steps Erin pulled her Billy club and hit him in the back of the neck.

As he dropped to the ground Erin saw someone emerge from a tent. A quick glance showed her the large red H on the white pennant.

Shit! Just what I need is one more complication. H. It has to be that Hardtack woman. What the hell is she doing sneaking around?

Before Erin could form another thought Emily was standing in front of her.

"Take me with you, Erin Foster." Not waiting for a response Emily moved to Yvonne and released the remaining shackles that held her.

Together they gently lowered Yvonne to the ground and using the ropes available hoisted the peacekeeper into Yvonne's former position. Uncertain about whether the man

175

was alive or not, Erin removed the bandana from around his neck and used it to gag him.

They half-carried, half-dragged a nearly unconscious Yvonne into the tunnel. Sitting Yvonne down and propping her against the tunnel wall, Erin ignored Emily.

"Damn it, Von. There's no time for this right now. You've got to get on your feet and walk. It's our only hope of escaping." She paused and looked around. "Come on, girl. I know you can do it."

Yvonne licked her cracked lips and tried to speak. Erin spotted a bucket of water. She carried it over, made a cup of her hands and offered Yvonne a sip. The water dribbled down her front.

Erin placed her left hand over Yvonne's mouth and with her right hand poured the bucket of water over her friend's head. Yvonne was more alert, but she remained on the ground. Erin removed her hand from Yvonne's mouth.

She set the empty bucket down and said, "Damn it, Von, I need you to function." Erin wasn't sure how loudly she'd spoken. She looked around to see if she had attracted unwanted attention.

Careful to speak quietly, she continued, "I got your message girl but if you want out of here, you're going to have to get on your feet." Yvonne nodded.

Erin stood up. "Get up. We're headed for Deacon Miller's office."

Yvonne tried to get to her feet, but her legs refused to support her.

"Go. Leave me. Save yourself. Just give me a gun." Her voice was soft, but Erin could see the resolve in her eyes, to never be taken alive again.

Emily was growing impatient. "You heard her. Let's get out of here while we still have a chance."

Erin got in Emily's face as she said, "I came to get my friend out of here. If I'm leaving anyone behind, it's you. Do we understand each other?"

"Fine. Then let me help you carry her."

Yvonne again mumbled, "Just give me a gun and go."

"I didn't come all this way to help you commit suicide, so shut up and cooperate." Erin pulled the 9mm from its holster and placed it in Yvonne's hand. "Watch my back." She smiled remembering what a lousy shot Yvonne was.

"If you see someone coming up on our rear, shoot at them. Don't worry about accuracy. Just get a shot off fast. His aim won't be much better than yours when he realizes we're not unarmed and helpless."

Without another word Erin scooped Yvonne into a fireman's carry and moved through the tunnel at a steady pace. Following close behind, Emily saw the heavy gun slipping from Yvonne's grasp. Emily reached out to take the weapon and Yvonne was too weak to voice an objection, much less put up a fight.

As they moved deeper into the tunnel the Reverend Master's sermon on a woman's proper place in society became less and less audible.

Light spilled into the tunnel from the intersection with the hallway containing the entrance to the Deacon's office. Erin lowered Yvonne to the ground while they were still in the half-lighted corridor.

She whispered in Yvonne's ear, "Stay here. I'm going to

scout ahead. I'll be right back."

When Erin straightened up, she noticed the gun she'd given to Yvonne was in Emily's hand.

They stared at each other for a moment and then Emily said, "I thought you were going to check ahead."

Erin straightened her shirt and moved toward the light. Before stepping into the intersection, she pulled the ball cap down to hide as much of her face as possible.

To her right she saw the door to Deacon Miller's office.

She looked to the left, knowing that the corridor eventually intersected with another tunnel and that a right turn into that tunnel would lead her out. Of course, it would place them near the guard shack.

The sound of a doorknob clicking open drew her attention back toward the Deacon's office.

As she stepped back into the shadows Erin looked and saw the Peacekeeper who had delivered Yvonne to the pillars standing in the doorway of the Deacon's office, his hand was still on the doorknob.

"Yes sir," he said to someone on the other side of the door. He started to close the door, paused. "Yes sir."

He pulled the door closed quickly, as if trying to cut off any more words from whomever he was 'yes sirring'.

Standing in the shadows Erin's eyes had readjusted to the lack of light; she looked at Emily and signaled silence, drew her knife and waited.

As the Peacekeeper stepped past her, she struck. A quick thrust to his kidneys brought his six-foot two frame to his knees with barely a gasp. Without hesitation Erin grabbed his chin, pulled his head back, and as she drew her blade across his throat she said, "Tell your God, Erin Foster sent you to him." She let his body fall forward to the tunnel floor.

Using the man's shirt Erin wiped her hands and cleaned the blood from her knife before pushing it into its sheath.

"There's no turning back now."

Once again, Erin scooped Yvonne into a fireman's carry and the three women walked past the corpse of Peacekeeper Doyle.

CHAPTER 37

Hank Bartholomew looked at his watch, again.

Where is she? Why hasn't she signaled? His thoughts followed this path, wondering what could have gone wrong.

Did she get caught? Has she just been unable to locate Yvonne? Lots of questions but no answers.

"Lieutenant." A voice whispered in his ear.

Hank jumped and started to admonish Andrea for sneaking up on him. Instead, he clenched his jaw and gave her a look he hoped imparted his displeasure. He watched the self-satisfied smile fade from her face.

"How much longer are we gonna wait? She was supposed to be over the wall by now," she demanded.

"We'll wait as long as it takes." The words were barely out of his mouth when the sound of a car drew their attention from the section of wall they were watching, to the main gate of the compound.

It was a limousine. The vehicle stopped at the guard shack. Seconds later shots were fired, and the limo sped away. Just as it turned onto the road its headlights flashed, on and off three times in quick succession.

Lights in the stadium came on and the sound of hundreds of voices filled with confusion and fear spilled over its walls.

No longer concerned with being discovered, Hank said, "Let's go." He cut a diagonal path from the wood's edge on an intercept course with the limo.

As they ran across the open field Andrea said, "This could be a trap."

"It's not." Hank prayed he was right.

Fortunately, the pace he set wasn't conducive to conversation and Andrea and Michael followed him without another word. When they reached the road, the limo was waiting for them.

Guns ready they stopped a few feet from the sleek black vehicle shrouded in a cloud of dust. The front passenger window moved down to reveal a smiling Erin in the driver's seat.

"Get in." She popped the door locks. "Hurry up. Before they figure out what just happened and how to deal with it."

Hank climbed into the front seat next to Emily, while the others got in the back. As the last door was closing Erin hit the gas and said, "Everybody I'd like you to meet Emily Hardtack. Emily meet the Swamp Rats." She paused and then said, "Michael, can you take care of Yvonne?"

Michael Alpine was the medic of the group. In his life before The Order, he'd been an emergency room nurse.

"What happened to the original plan?" Hank asked.

Erin kept her eyes on the road as she answered, "Yvonne wasn't physically able to climb the stadium seats and shimmy down a rope. She could barely walk."

"We heard gun shots at the guard shack."

"Yeah, the Deacon couldn't keep his mouth shut. He decided to tell the guards who we were." She paused. "Can you believe he didn't want to go for a ride with us?"

"Go figure."

181

They had no trouble getting to the location of the stashed flat bottom boat that would take them back to Camp Liberty.

Erin sat on the deck of the flat-bottomed boat amidships, with Yvonne's head resting in her lap. The small vessel's capacity was maxed out with six occupants. Fortunately, Hank chose one of the larger flat-bottomed vessels for this expedition.

Spanish moss hung down from huge oaks casting eerie shadows on the brackish water. The gentle splash of the poles Hank and Michael used to move the craft forward was the dominant sound.

The pitch black of the swamp on this moonless night was impenetrable to the unaided human eye. Hank and Michael had the advantage of wearing night vision goggles, allowing them to find their way home.

Erin kept her eyes closed and paid special attention to the sounds around her. She stretched her leg out and tapped Hank with her foot. He turned and looked at her.

She pointed at her ear, indicating she'd heard something. He stopped poling and signaled Michael to stop.

The air hung like a warm wet blanket covering everything. For several seconds everyone aboard the boat stayed immobile. Hank opened his mouth to speak, and then he heard it.

The gentle splash of a pole entering the water told them they were not alone. Erin moved to draw her weapon and Yvonne moaned. Erin froze.

From a short distance ahead came a whistle. Hank responded in kind.

Twenty feet beyond the next curve in the stream Erin's

party pulled their boat alongside another flat bottom.

Hank and the leader of the men in the other boat spoke in whispers.

"Mission accomplished. Though it didn't go exactly as planned the end result was what we wanted." Hank looked over the three young men in the other boat. "What are you fellows doing out here?"

A baby-faced young man from the other boat said, "Glad to hear the mission was a success. Per General Wayne's orders everyone has to be scanned, before you get any closer to camp."

Hank looked confused. "Scanned? What are you talking about? We have an injured woman with us. We need to get her to Dr. Upton."

"It'll only take a few minutes."

"Didn't you hear him?" Erin indicated Yvonne cradled in her arms. "She needs to see Dr. Upton."

Baby Face's non-emotional blank expression never changed. "Then the sooner I get everyone scanned the sooner she'll get there."

The two boats quickly maneuvered to a nearby piece of dry land jutting out from among the palmetto bushes. One-by-one each member of the rescue party stepped ashore and was scanned. The only two remaining were Erin and Yvonne.

Erin remained in the boat cradling an unconscious Yvonne. "If you want to scan us, you'll have to come out here and do it."

Baby Face stepped into the flat bottom, ran his scan, and then stepped ashore. He immediately drew his weapon and spun around aiming the 9mm at Erin. "One of them is carrying a tracking device. They're too close together to determine which one."

"What the… Are you out of your mind little boy? No one here has any kind of device on them."

"Then you won't mind sliding your weapons to the bow of the boat and stepping out here."

"Michael, come take care of Yvonne while I prove to this pain-in-the-ass I don't have whatever it is he's looking for."

Before Michael could take a step Baby Face said, "No! Harry" baby face indicated one of his team "cover the others."

Another of the young men from Baby Face's group drew his side arm and trained it on the rest of the rescue party. Baby Face kept his eyes on Erin. "Slide out from under her. Then with your left hand undo the buckle on your gun belt, lower it to the deck and push it toward the bow, using your foot."

Erin's jaw muscles tightened, and her eyes narrowed. Gently she lowered Yvonne to the bottom of the boat. She followed Baby Face's instructions and then stepped ashore. She walked toward the young man, looking into his eyes.

"Stop right there!" He swallowed hard and his hands shook.

Erin raised her arms straight out to the sides as she continued to move slowly toward him. "Don't make me shoot you!"

She stopped with her chest pressed against the barrel of the young man's gun. Still staring into his eyes, she said, "Either shoot me, scan me, or get the hell out of my way."

Baby Face holstered his weapon and quickly scanned Erin, twice. After completing the scans his gaze traveled to the boat. "It's her." He pointed at Yvonne still a huddled mass in the bottom of the boat.

While Harry kept the rescue party covered, Baby Face and his other assistant climbed into the boat and thoroughly examined Yvonne, despite Erin's protestations.

"Hasn't she suffered enough humiliation at the hands of The Order?"

Hank stepped into Erin's line of sight and blocked her view of the boat. "Look, Erin, the sooner they find what they're looking for, the sooner we can get underway. They didn't send a female scanning team, so we just have to make the best of the situation."

"Found it!" said Baby Face's reedy voice from the boat. "It's just under the skin. It won't take much to remove it."

Hank continued to block Erin's view. "Just let them do their job, Erin. Then we can get Yvonne to Dr. Upton."

A moan from Yvonne moved Erin to action. She pushed Hank aside and ran to the shore. She reached the boat in time to see Baby Face pull a tiny device from an incision in the back of Yvonne's neck. He placed the device in the palm of his hand.

Indicating the small cut on the back of Yvonne's neck, he instructed the young man assisting him, "Swab that incision with an antiseptic and bandage it, so these folks can get back underway."

Erin looked at the miniscule thing in the palm of Baby Face's hand. "That's what you were looking for?"

He took a small clear baggie from the satchel that was slung over his shoulder and placed the device into the baggie. "Yes, that is a tracking device designed to be placed under a person's skin or for short term use it could easily be swallowed."

185

Erin licked her lips and looked around as if expecting Peacekeepers to start dropping from the trees. "What's its range?"

"Probably about five miles. Any further away than that and the receiver will lose the signal."

"So, you're telling me that there are Peacekeepers no more than five miles away?"

"Probably less." Baby Face turned to his assistant. "Let's go."

Without another word or a backward glance, the scanning team got into their flat bottom boat and headed south into the nastiest most tangled part of the area.

"Come on, folks. We need to get underway too. The people tracking Yvonne will be through here soon and we need to not be here."

"Why not? We could set up an ambush and – "

"No." Hank indicated Yvonne curled up in the fetal position in the bottom of the boat. "She needs medical attention. Dealing with our trackers is the scanning team's job."

Erin looked in the direction the team had gone and then back to Hank.

He smiled at Erin. "Trust me. They know what they're doing."

The rest of the trip to Camp Liberty was conducted in silence.

Questions bounced around in Erin's head like the steel ball in a pinball machine bouncing off one rubber bumper after another.

Did Yvonne know the tracking device had been planted on her? Was that why they managed to escape? Was their

186

escape part of a bigger plan to destroy the Swamp Rats?
What about Emily Hardtack? Who is she? What's her part in
all of this? Is she a plant, in case the tracking device failed?
Too many questions and no answers.

CHAPTER 38

"…After I killed Doyle, we moved to Deacon Miller's office." The memory of the terrified man brought the hint of a smile to her face. "He led us to the garage. While Emily guarded him, I went around and stuck anything I could find into the valve stems of tires. The vehicles I didn't get to were trapped behind those with flats."

Erin sighed. "I was tempted to just kill the fat son-of-a-bitch right there in the garage. He kept yammering about the Reverend Master and God and how we were all going to hell. Finally, I convinced him to be quiet or I'd slit his throat. He shut up until we got to the guard shack."

She paused to take a breath. "I thought we were going to make a quiet get away when he started squawking about how he was being forced to help us escape. I shot the two peacekeepers on duty and told Emily to shoot fatso and kick him out."

Erin looked at Hank and continued, "I was hoping you'd realize I was substituting three short light flashes for the three short whistles that were the original signal. I'd have tried to whistle but I figured you were too far away to hear me."

General Wayne asked, "Did Emily shoot the deacon?"

"I wish I knew. I know she fired her gun and kicked him out."

General Wayne looked at Erin and asked, "What do you know of this woman, Emily Hardtack?"

188

"Nothing beyond the fact that without her, we might not have made it out." She paused and her eyes darted about the room moving quickly from face to face.

"What is it Erin? Something's bothering you. Out with it."

"It's just…" Erin took a deep breath and looking Tony squarely in the face said, "Up until the moment they removed that tracking device from Yvonne's neck I would have trusted her with my life. Now…"

General Wayne looked past Erin to Colonel Mason.

"Please continue, Erin."

"There's not much left to tell, General Wayne. When we reached the swamp's edge Andrea took the car back a way, torched it, and then rejoined us for the trip home."

General Wayne asked, "Lt. Bartholomew, do you have anything to add?"

"Does that mean you don't want to hear about our encounter with your scanning team? Or perhaps you've already received a report on that?" Erin asked.

General Wayne's eyes met Erin's. "Yes, Erin, I've already received Sgt. Harper's report." He refocused his attention on Hank. "Your report Lt. Bartholomew."

"We were waiting for Erin's signal when we heard a car coming out of the compound. It was a limo. It stopped at the guard shack. Shots were fired, the headlights flashed, and we headed across the field to intercept it."

He grinned. "The Deacon had a nice limo, plenty of room for all of us." His grin faded as he remembered Yvonne's wrists.

"Mike took care of Yvonne's wrists as best he could, and we headed home. Has Dr. Upton said anything about Yvonne's recovery?"

189

Erin thought, why didn't I ask about her? She's my friend. I should have been the one to ask how she was doing.

Colonel Mason spoke up. "Yes, he believes she'll make a full recovery. She may have some scars but other than that she'll be fine, at least physically." She moved her attention from Hank to Erin. "I'm interested in why you felt it necessary to kill five, possibly seven people in your escape."

Erin looked directly into Linda's eyes. "They were chess pieces the Reverend Master no longer has. They cannot help him capture, torture, or kill. They're no longer a threat. My only regret is that I didn't get the opportunity to kill more of them."

"You consider the woman… What was her name, Sally Mae? You considered her a threat?"

"Just because she didn't carry a gun doesn't mean she wasn't doing the Reverend Master's bidding."

"Be that as it may…"

General Wayne interrupted. "I appreciate you two reporting in immediately. Congratulations on a successful mission."

He directed himself to Erin. "I know you're eager to talk with Yvonne, but the doctor has sedated her. She won't be up for conversation until tomorrow sometime." He included Hank as he continued, "I think you should both get some well-deserved rest."

Erin wasted no time in leaving. Hank wasn't quite out the door when General Wayne said, "Hank, on your way could you ask Sgt. Skinner to bring Mrs. Hardtack in for her debriefing?"

"Yes sir."

After Hank and Erin were gone General Wayne turned to Mason and said, "I know you object to Erin's cold-blooded

190

killing. However, you must realize that this is not a war that will be won on the battlefield, soldier-to-soldier. The only way we stand a chance of winning this conflict is to sneak up on the enemy and slit his throat."

He sighed as he sank into a chair opposite the desk Colonel Mason sat behind. "I don't like it any better than you do but I accept it as a fact of life. If we expect to win this, we need as many Erin Fosters as we can recruit."

She pushed herself out of her chair, walked to the window and for several seconds stared out at the swamp. The sun glinted off the brackish water, birds called to one another, and the Spanish moss hanging from trees was almost white in the noon sun.

"I know you're right, Tony." She turned and looked into the pale blue eyes of her mentor and continued, "The scary part is that while the killing repulses me, I feel drawn to the killer."

His look of surprise brought a smile to her face. Before he could say anything, she continued, "Yes, yes, I know all about not fraternizing, especially with someone as volatile as Erin. Don't worry I have it under control."

"I certainly hope so and not because of some antiquated rule against fraternization. We're not exactly your standard military organization. I'm more concerned about you." His tone was that of a father to his daughter. "Trust me, Linda. Erin Foster will only break your heart."

The sound of his words still hung in the air when Sgt. Paul Skinner knocked and said, "Excuse me sirs but Lt. Bartholomew said you wanted to see Mrs. Hardtack."

General Wayne stood up and Mason moved toward the new arrival. "Thank you, sergeant. Mrs. Hardtack, I'm Colonel

191

Mason" she indicated Tony "and this is General Anthony Wayne. Welcome to Camp Liberty."

Smiling and looking every inch the gentleman, he was, Tony gestured toward the chair Erin had occupied recently and said, "Please, have a seat, Mrs. Hardtack."

As she sat down, she said, "Please, call me Emily." She looked from Tony to Linda and back again. "The first thing I'm doing when this insanity is over is divorcing that louse I married and returning to my maiden name." She harrumphed. "With a little luck maybe I'll be a widow."

She sat up a little straighter and continued, "Regardless, I think I'll return to my maiden name now." Looking Tony in the eyes she said, "My name is Emily Legrand."

Mason smiled and said, "Now that we know your name, we'd like to know as much as you can tell us about the time you spent in custody of The Order."

"I'd rather forget everything about that time. Though I doubt that's possible." She drew in a long slow breath. "What can I tell you? I'll be happy to answer your questions if it will help return things to the way they used to be." She paused. "It's the least I can do. I don't know how I'll be of much help in any other area. I've never been in the military. For that matter I've never really been much of an outdoors type person either."

The colonel glanced at Tony, and he said, "First of all we'd like to know a little bit more about you in general. What was your profession?"

"I worked in the IT department of the local network affiliate. If I'd been male, I would have been the head of that department a year ago. Instead, I was kept on as the Assistant Director of IT."

"How did you end up at the reorientation facility?"

Emily swallowed hard. Her voice was filled with emotion, and it was easy to see she struggled to keep from crying. "That was compliments of my dear husband, Lt. Joseph Hardtack."

"Lieutenant? Is your husband in the military?"

"No. He's a police lieutenant with the city of Calton Beach."

Tony and Linda exchanged glances.

"Please continue."

"His ambitions required him to have a stay-at-home Mom for a wife. I wasn't ready to start having children yet. He saw to it that I got fired." She laughed.

"There was quite a scene at our house that night when he got home." She paused. "I told him that the only way he would ever get me pregnant was if he raped me. I think we exchanged a few more un-pleasantries and then he left the house. The next thing I know there's a knock at the door. When I opened the door a couple of young men in Peacekeeper uniforms shoved a piece of paper at me and said something about papers committing me to a reorientation facility had been filed." She shook her head as if to erase the image of that night from her mind.

"That must have been a horrible experience. How long were you at the facility?"

"About six weeks."

Colonel Mason looked at General Wayne and then brought her attention back to Emily. "That's a, uh, a long time to resist the kind of 24-hour brainwashing that we've heard about."

Emily smiled and looking at her said, "Revenge is a great motivator. The longer I was able to resist the less favorably my husband was viewed. These fanatics have some kind of a warped idea that the" Emily used air quotes "man of the family is responsible for the behavior of all family members, especially the women." She snorted. "As if he could have any influence over me where I was."

"He didn't come to visit you?"

"No. No visitors are allowed at all. If you're a good little girl, you might get a weekend pass to visit your family and see how you'll behave back in the world."

Colonel Mason held Emily's gaze and asked, "How did you recognize Erin when no one else in the facility seemed to know who she was?"

Emily smiled. "When I heard what she had done and how she had escaped capture. She became a role model for me. I studied her face carefully because I wanted to make sure I would recognize her if I ever saw her."

Keeping her expression blank, Mason said, "That would be the same thing someone after the reward for her capture would do. How do we know that you're not really here to help The Order bring down the resistance?"

Emily shrugged. "You don't." She paused and looked around the room. Her eyes stopped at Tony for a moment and then she brought her attention back to the colonel. "I don't have any idea how to prove to you that I want to help defeat The Order."

Smiling at General Wayne she said, "But if you think of a way, let me know. Unless you have more questions, I'd really love something to eat and some sleep."

CHAPTER 39

Yvonne opened her eyes and looked around her. The woman sitting next to her cot came into focus. Camouflage shorts, t-shirt, bare feet. She was a petite blonde with an attractive face that broke into a smile when she saw Yvonne looking at her.

"Hello Yvonne. How're you feeling?" While Yvonne considered her answer, the woman stuck her head out the nearby door and called, "Billy, tell Dr. Upton she's awake and then notify the others in order of rank."

A quick inventory of her aches and pains provided her with an answer. "My wrists hurt, and my mid-section feels like somebody hit me with a baseball bat. If I have other injuries, I'm not aware of them at the moment." She paused. "Who are you?"

"Chris Barton." Yvonne flinched as Chris placed her fingers on Yvonne's neck.

"It's all right. I just need to take your pulse." She paused briefly and then continued. "I'm the nurse here at Camp Liberty."

"Camp Liberty?" *Doesn't sound like a name The Order would use.*

Chris placed a thermometer under Yvonne's tongue. "Yes. Don't you remember Erin rescuing you from the reorientation facility?"

195

Erin. Reorientation. Disjointed images and sounds flashed through her mind. Faces. Doyle. Voices. Screams of pain. The Reverend Master's sermons. Blood.

She shook her head and felt a twinge of pain on the back of her neck. Slowly, she reached for the source of this new pain. She felt a bandage and looked questioningly at Chris.

Chris smiled reassuringly. "Just a small cut. Nothing to worry about. Would you like something to eat? Or are you just thirsty?"

"Both actually, now that you mention it."

Chris slid a stethoscope under Yvonne's thin gown against her chest. "Take a deep breath for me."

Yvonne took a deep breath and groaned.

"What hurts? Your ribs?"

"Yeth." She replied around the thermometer.

A tall thin man entered the room and stood behind Chris. "And how is our patient?"

Chris removed the thin plastic strip from Yvonne's mouth and glanced at it. "Temperature and pulse are normal. Heart sounds good. Lungs appear to be clear. She experienced pain in her mid-section when she took a deep breath." Chris gave Yvonne a smile and then continued her report. "She's thirsty and has an appetite."

Without even a nod to acknowledge his nurses' report he stepped between Chris and the cot. "I'm Dr. Upton. Can you sit up for me?"

Yvonne winced and groaned her way to an upright position. Upton removed the clipboard hanging on the wall over the cot and lowered his lanky frame to a canvas stool next to the cot.

He examined Yvonne's abdomen, then positioned his

stethoscope and repeated Chris's request for a deep breath. He removed the listening device and scribbled on the clipboard in his lap.

"Hold out your hands." Yvonne complied and he removed the bandages around her wrists and inspected her wounds. He stood up, made another note on the clipboard and returned it to its hook. "Wash both wrists; apply the cream I prescribed and fresh bandages. And wrap her ribs." He started to leave.

"What can she have to eat and drink?"

He harrumphed and without turning around replied, "It's on the chart."

Yvonne watched both nurse and doctor disappear in opposite directions.

Hmmm. That was interesting. He's about as friendly as a rattlesnake. Wonder what his problem is?

Before she could decide to lie back down, Chris returned with a tray bearing a pan of water and a variety of other items needed to follow the doctor's orders. She set the tray on a nearby table.

"All right, how about if we get that gown off of you?"

Yvonne hesitated. There was only a curtain hanging on a line that was suspended from other lines in the rough ceiling.

"A little shy? Don't worry about it." Chris pulled the cotton gown over Yvonne's head. "Hardly anybody comes in here unless they need medical attention and it'll be a few minutes before your visitors arrive." As she moved the garment down Yvonne's arms, she was careful to not let it touch the raw wounds on her wrists.

"Let me help you up. It'll be much easier to wrap your ribs

with you standing."

Ribs wrapped, Chris grabbed a small stack of fabric from the tray. "Let's get this on you." In seconds Yvonne was wearing an oversized t-shirt. "I've got a pair of shorts for you too. But first let me take care of those wrists." She paused. "Do you want to sit for this part?"

"No, getting up again is too difficult."

Chris' ministrations complete she handed Yvonne a pair of shorts and helped her into them.

"Doctor's orders followed to the letter. Patient dressed. Now let's see what Dr. Uppity, I mean Dr. Upton wrote on your chart."

Yvonne started to laugh and stopped because of the pain it caused. "He is a bit uppity, isn't he?"

Chris smiled.

Yvonne leaned forward and whispered. "Are you sure he's on our side?"

Chris laughed. Yvonne placed her hand against her wrapped ribs. "Even with the wrapping, I think it'll be a while before I'm willing to laugh."

"That's a sound I like to hear. There's not anywhere near enough laughter around here."

Chris introduced the two women. "Yvonne this is Colonel Linda Mason, the camp commander. Colonel, this is Yvonne North."

"I'm pleased to meet you… May I call you Yvonne?"

"My friends call me Von."

"Yes, I believe I've heard Erin refer to you that way."

Yvonne looked around the room, and then locked eyes with the colonel. "Where is Erin? You're the second person to mention her but I've yet to see her."

The colonel looked uncomfortable. "Well, I imagine she might still be asleep. The last time I saw her she was exhausted." She paused. "What was so funny when I came in?"

Chris and Yvonne exchanged looks.

"I see. It was a joke about me, was it?"

"No," was the instant response from both women.

"I just don't think it would be appropriate to repeat the exchange to the colonel is all, ma'am."

"Chris, I thought I broke you of calling me ma'am, except when General Wayne is present, and I don't see him in the room."

"Erin!" Yvonne cried out.

The colonel and Chris both turned and saw Erin standing in the doorway. Chris stepped aside. "Good morning, Erin."

Chris smiled at Yvonne and said, "Don't let her wear you out."

"You sure look a lot better than the last time I saw you." Erin moved her eyes to the colonel. "Good morning, colonel. Nurse Barton."

Yvonne sensed something between the colonel and Erin. She couldn't place her finger on it but there was some kind of tension between them.

"Good morning, lieutenant." She paused. "Please, bring Ms. North to my office after breakfast."

Colonel Mason turned back to Yvonne. "We need to talk. Nothing to worry about. I'd just like to ask you some questions about your time in the custody of The Order."

Chris said, "Come on, colonel. I'll buy you breakfast."

Erin watched as the two women left before she turned to her friend.

Yvonne reached out and gingerly hugged Erin. "I'm so sorry about Alice."

"Yeah. Thanks." Erin disengaged herself from the hug.

Yvonne's hands slid down Erin's arms to hold her hands. Then she tilted her head one way and then the other examining Erin.

Erin asked, "Have I grown a second head or what?"

"Not a second head. It's just the one you have is…bald."

"Oh that." Erin extracted her hands from Yvonne's and ran them across her scalp.

"Yes, that. What happened?" She smiled. "I mean, I know you've always liked it short but that's a bit extreme even for you."

Erin explained the ruse they had used to get her inside the reorientation facility and the original rescue plan.

"Thank you, Erin. I, I don't know what else to say, but thank you." Yvonne took a deep breath and winced, slightly. "You're very brave and I can't thank you enough for saving my life."

Erin was uncomfortable with receiving praise and changed the subject. "So, how's the incision on your neck healing?"

"Incision? Chris said it was just a small cut." She reached up and fingered the bandage in question. "Why would there be an incision on my neck?"

"When was the last time you had a 'cut' there?"

Yvonne thought a moment and then said, "It wasn't a cut, but I had a spider bite that a medic for The Order treated. It was in the same area." She looked at Erin. "What's this all about anyway?"

"Nothing. It's not important."

"You're a lousy liar, Erin Foster. What's the deal with my neck? Did I have some sort of tumor or something?"

"No, nothing like that." She moved toward the door.

Yvonne started to follow her and gasped in pain. Erin spun around and her voice full of concern asked, "Are you alright?"

"Yes, I just can't move too fast until my ribs heal." She took a slow deep breath as she stepped toward Erin and said, "Erin, tell me."

Erin looked into Yvonne's soft gray eyes. "There was a tracking device planted just under the skin on the back of your neck. On the way back to camp a scanning team stopped us and everyone was scanned. That's how it was found before we got here."

Yvonne reached back and touched the bandage on her neck. "Well, but how did they know to scan us?"

"We lost a camp a couple of weeks ago." Erin shrugged "I don't know how they figured it out, but somebody decided the only way The Order could have located that camp was with GPS type technology. Some smart guy checked all the bodies and found one with a tracking device under the skin." She paused. "Since the person with the tracking device was killed in the attack we don't know if he volunteered for a suicide mission or if he was unaware, he was leading the enemy to us. I guess, we'll never know."

"So, I suppose you're wondering if I knew I was betraying you or not."

"Truth is. I don't know what to think." She smiled. "I do know that using our old sign language was almost too clever. The video was almost over before I realized what you were doing.

201

So, I had to sit through it twice."

Tears streamed down Yvonne's face. "I'm sorry about the video. It was just…" She wiped her face and continued, "They promised me I could see Donald if I made the video. I kept trying to think of some way to use it to send you a message."

Erin reached out and took Yvonne in her arms. Yvonne groaned and Erin released her. Yvonne's hands moved to her ribs as if to protect them.

"Sorry, I forgot. You must be pretty sore there."

"Actually, I have a pretty good idea of how a piñata must feel."

Erin smiled. "I'll just bet you do." She brushed Yvonne's hair back out of her eyes. "Don't worry about the video. It worked out for the best. How is Donald?"

Yvonne choked back a sob, took several shallow breaths, and said, "I don't know I never got to see him."

"I'm sorry." Erin paused. "I'll ask Lin… uh, Colonel Mason to check with some of the other resistance groups. He might have made it to sanctuary."

"Yes, and the other possibility is that he's dead." Though she said nothing, Yvonne made a mental note that Erin was used to referring to the colonel by her first name.

"Let's not get our exercise jumping to conclusions. How about a walk to the mess hall instead?"

"Great. But first you should check the chart." She nodded toward the clipboard on the wall. "Dr. Upton wrote my dietary restrictions on it."

"Of course he did. Heaven forbid he lower himself to just tell you what you can and can't have. Arrogant bastard."

"Damn, Erin. Don't hold back. Tell me how you really feel

about the doctor." Yvonne was delighted that her comment brought a smile to Erin's face.

Erin cleared her throat and read from the chart. "Food and liquids."

"You're kidding me. He wrote that on there?"

Erin returned the clipboard to its hook and sighed. "Come on. Let's get some food. I'm starving."

CHAPTER 40

It was almost sunrise when Jack Collins entered the safe house through the screened back porch. He was looking forward to spending most of the day with Helen and their daughter, Donna.

If I'm lucky Donna will sleep late and we'll get to have some alone time.

He moved through the kitchen and stepped into the living room. A bright light hit him in the face, and he brought his hand up to shield his eyes.

"Helen told us you would be here this morning." Collins reached for his gun. "I wouldn't advise any form of resistance, if you ever want to see your family again."

Jack didn't recognize the voice, but he was very familiar with the tone. He'd heard that tone of superiority from every thug he'd ever seen walk on a technicality. He slowly removed his hand from the butt of the gun.

"Have a seat Mr. Collins."

Jack's mind was racing. *Are Helen and Donna here? Have they taken them somewhere else? How do I know they really have them? Helen wouldn't go quietly; she'd have put up a fight. They could both be dead for all I know.*

The Voice became more insistent. "Mr. Collins, please sit down in the chair in front of you."

He did as he was told.

Sitting across the room behind a very bright light was The Voice. Collins put his hands up and squinted, trying to get a look at his captor.

Why don't they just arrest me? There's only one reason to capture my family. "What do you want?"

He could hear the oily smile in the man's voice. "Very astute of you, Mr. Collins." He paused. "We want Erin Foster and the rest of the Swamp Rats."

Despite the situation, Collins chuckled, "I bet you do. That's one gutsy lady, braving the lion's den."

The smile was gone as The Voice said, "Is she worth the lives of your family?"

"No, she's not."

"Then we understand each other." He snapped his fingers and a young man stepped from behind The Voice. "This is David Smith. He will be going with you. If anyone questions you, he's a new recruit you picked up and he will serve as the medical officer for your group."

"I already have a doc…"

The oily smile returned to The Voice. "No, Mr. Collins. Your doctor met an untimely demise." Collins could see the outline of The Voice. He watched him check his watch. "Actually, I should say, he will meet an untimely demise in about thirty minutes."

"How do I know my family's alive and safe?"

David Smith stepped closer to Jack and presented to him an electronic tablet with a web camera.

On the screen Collins could see Helen. She was dressed in the plain black, Granny dress that The Order preferred women wear. She didn't look happy.

"Jack, I'm sorry." She moved closer. He could see the tear tracks on her face. "They snuck in, in the middle of the night. I never had a chance to fight."

"It's okay, babe. Is Donna alright?"

"Yes, at least she was the last time I saw her."

"What do you mean?"

"They took her away and put her in school somewhere. At least that's what they told me."

Smith pushed a button, and the screen went dark. Jack started to object but quickly changed his mind.

"What do you want me to do?"

"You have a man in your organization by the name of Donald North. David will plant a tracking device on Mr. North." He sighed. "We're not going to work out the details for you, Mr. Collins. Figure out some way to get the Swamp Rats to leave their precious swamp. Make sure that Mr. North is part of whatever plan you come up with."

"Why North?"

"His wife, Yvonne, is with Erin Foster... how did you put it? Ah, yes, she's the woman Erin Foster braved the lion's den to rescue. Succeed in helping us capture Erin Foster, alive and you'll be allowed to go on your way with your whore and your daughter." He paused. "Fail us, in any way, and you won't live to know what happened to them."

Collins stood up to leave.

"One other thing, Mr. Collins. Emily Hardtack, the wife of your former lieutenant escaped with Erin Foster. Bring her in safe and unharmed and there will be a bonus for you."

CHAPTER 41

Governor Martin Chandler looked at the video phone on his desk as if it were a snake about to strike. The special ring told him the phone call was from the White House.

He swallowed hard, pasted a smile on his face, sat up straight and pressed the receive button. He spoke as the image of the President of the United States filled the screen on his desk. "Good morning, Mr. President."

"Good morning, Governor Chandler." The expression on President Littrol's face told Chandler it wasn't really a good morning. Ignoring the usual pleasantries Littrol got right to the issue at hand. "Tell me what's going on down there, Marty."

Maintaining a smile Governor Chandler started, "Well, Mr. President, the media is blowing this incident all out of proportion. The truth is..."

"Cut the nonsense, Marty. You know I don't get my information from the media. The Reverend Master called me." He stared at Martin Chandler from the video screen like a disappointed father.

"Let me tell you how I see it. Erin Foster killed a cop and Bishop Snead's son, Peter. Some fool decided to use a friend of this Erin Foster as bait to lure her into a rescue attempt. The problem came when whoever instigated this little plan underestimated Miss Foster. Now, not only has she rescued her friend and made the authorities look like incompetent fools

207

she's taken a police lieutenant's wife, Emily Hardtack along with her. In addition, her body count is now at nine. Is that a fairly accurate picture of recent events, Governor?"

"Yes, yes, Mr. President". Chandler swallowed hard and licked his lips. "That summarizes things quite accurately."

"I thought so. Now what I want to know is what you're going to do about it all, so the next time the Reverend Master calls me I can tell him what's being done to protect the faithful of Florida."

"I've asked local law enforcement to incorporate more Peacekeepers into their ranks and I have a meeting set up for later this morning with the local military commanders to see if they have any ideas on how to go into the swamps and get at these rebels. I also have a call out to anyone with knowledge of the swamps to come forward and assist us in tracking down the group that call themselves the Swamp Rats."

There was silence on the line for a moment, Chandler watched his political ally digest the information. "Swamp Rats, huh?"

"Yes sir, that's what they call themselves."

His face expressionless President Littrol said, "Just remember that the Reverend Master looks upon natural areas like those swamps as God's creation and therefore they're sacred."

"Yes sir. I'm well aware of The Order's stand on that issue." He paused. "However, it may come down to..." Littrol cut him off before he could complete his sentence.

"Marty, find a way to get those rebels, without damaging the ecosystem." He paused and leaned in closer to the camera. "I'm sure I don't need to remind you how much the Reverend

Master dislikes failure."

Sweat began to bead on Martin Chandler's forehead. He paused, weighing whether or not to confess to another massacre of Peacekeepers. *Either I tell him, or the Reverend Master will, if he hasn't already.*

"Yes sir, I don't know whose idea it was to use this Yvonne North person to draw Erin Foster out; however, not only did she actually manage to escape but somehow they ambushed the Peacekeepers tracking them. The Peacekeeper unit received heavy casualties; four dead and ten wounded."

Littrol sighed and leaned back in his chair. "Yes, I'd already heard about that. Believe me, the person who instigated this fiasco is, well, let's just say he won't have any future opportunities to screw up. What kind of response have you gotten to your call for swamp trackers?"

"That call went out just this morning, Mr. President. If you would like I can check with the office receiving those calls…"

And if I don't get them with the trackers, well, I'll just have to wait for a good old Florida thunderstorm to set the swamp on fire for me. It won't be my fault if a lightning strike starts a wildfire.

A moment of silence and then, "No, but I will expect a progress report from you tomorrow, before noon."

The screen went dark, and Chandler pushed himself to his feet with such force his chair rolled back and off its mat onto the carpet. He strode out of the office, headed for his personal gym.

Chandler marched down the corridors of the governor's mansion, moving like a man on a mission. Staff scurried out of his way without so much as a good morning.

In the changing room he quickly stripped down and donned his workout shorts and t-shirt. He caught a glimpse of himself in the mirror on his way to the weights.

Not bad for an old man, if I do say so myself.

He slapped his firm abdomen and grabbed a towel off a shelf on his way into the gym. He sat down at the weight trainer, adjusted the weights for a strenuous workout and started with leg lifts.

An hour later he dove into the lap pool housed next to the gym and swam a quick fifty laps. As he swam, a name from the past popped into his mind.

Chandler climbed out of the pool and pressed the communication device connected directly to his personal assistant. "Cal, find Anthony Wayne."

"Sir?"

He enunciated the name slowly. "Anthony Wayne."

A smile spread across his face. "Better known to the Wild Boys as Mad Anthony." Chandler paused. "Tony and I grew up together. Last I knew he was living somewhere in central Florida. Find him."

"Yes sir."

Chandler disconnected and started toweling off. His step was much lighter as he headed back to the changing room.

If anyone can track that bunch of crazies in the swamp, it'll be Tony.

Later that afternoon Calvin Santiago tapped lightly on the governor's door. Without waiting for a reply, he opened the door. "Governor Chandler?"

The governor waved him into the room. "Come in, Cal. Have you found Mad Anthony?"

The confused look on Calvin's face prompted Chandler to amend his question. "Have you found Anthony Wayne?"

Calvin nervously licked his lips as he fidgeted with the papers in his hands. "I think so, sir. There were several Anthony Wayne's in Central Florida. However, by cross-checking them with your past I think we've located the right Anthony Wayne."

Chandler harrumphed and said, "I really don't care how you found him, just that you've found him." He paused. "Where is he?"

"Not sure where he is at this precise moment, sir." Calvin shifted his weight from foot to foot.

Chandler rose from behind his desk, and squinting at the slight figure of the young man before him asked, "What the devil are you so nervous about?"

Calvin swallowed hard and his tongue darted out to lick his lips again. "Well, governor, it would seem..."

"Spit it out, man!"

He inhaled a quick deep breath and then rattled off the words as quickly as he could say them. "Anthony Wayne is on the watch list, sir."

"On the watch..." Chandler burst out laughing. He moved toward Calvin and placed a comforting hand on the younger man's shoulder. "Don't worry about it, Cal. I hadn't thought about it before, but it's not surprising." He paused. "What got him on the list?"

Referring to the papers in his hands Calvin replied, "He operates a company called, Your Wish Is My Command. From his website the best I can figure out is he provides fantasy vacations for the extremely rich. There was a client whose fantasy was to be a sultan with a harem of fifty women. Anthony Wayne provided him with his harem in a desert setting for a full week."

Chandler laughed. "Sounds like something he would do. He always was one to buck the system, at least as long as there was a dollar to be made from it." He turned from Calvin and stood in front of the window.

After several seconds of staring at the sunlit green expanse before him he said, "I want to talk to him in person."

"Yes, sir."

CHAPTER 42

The verandah surrounding the new governor's mansion was Governor Chandler's favorite location for breakfast. He found the view of the lush green lawn with Crepe Myrtles lining the edges and the fountain surrounded by brightly colored pansies in the central flower bed relaxing.

Sitting just outside the French doors enjoying the coolness of the air conditioning as it spilled onto the verandah Governor Martin Chandler was enjoying a second cup of coffee, along with a second helping of sausage patties when out of the corner of his eye he saw Calvin enter the office. He watched as Calvin decided whether or not to interrupt his boss's breakfast.

God, but that boy is such a nervous wimp. He really needs to grow a spine.

"This had better be good news, Calvin."

"It is sir. Uhh, at least I think it is."

"Well, what is it?"

"It's good news Governor."

Chandler rolled his eyes and sighed. "What is the good news, Calvin?"

"Oh. Of course. The state troopers just came through the gate with Anthony Wayne."

"State troopers? I said I wanted to talk to the man, not have him arrested."

"Oh no, sir." Words spilled out tripping over each other in their rush to be heard. "They haven't arrested him. They pulled him over for a traffic stop and…"

"Never mind." Before either man could speak again, there was a firm knock on the office door. The governor called out, "Come in."

The door opened and a mountain of a man in a state trooper's uniform stepped into the room. Chandler stood up and waved the officer in.

The trooper stopped in the open doorway, a few feet from the table. Now the governor could see there were two other men behind the man mountain.

"Is this the man you wanted to see, Governor?" The man mountain stepped aside and pulled Tony forward.

Chandler was surprised by the soft voice of the big man. The consummate politician he glanced at the name plate on the trooper's chest. Then he met the steady gaze of the man and said, "Yes, Trooper Wells." He offered his hand, and it was swallowed by the trooper's ham of a hand for a quick shake and then released.

"Thank you for finding him."

"Just following orders, sir."

"You and your partner should stop into the kitchen. I'm sure my cook can prepare whatever you would like for breakfast." He paused and then said, "Calvin, take these fine civil servants to the kitchen and tell Marsha to fix them whatever they want."

He directed his attention back to Trooper Wells. "I won't keep you gentlemen waiting long. Then you can resume custody of Mr. Wayne."

Anthony Wayne stood silently during the exchange. Martin Chandler felt the fixed stare from his childhood friend; still he did nothing to acknowledge his presence until after the door closed behind the three departing men.

A smile spread across Chandler's face, and he said, "You're a hard man to track down, Tony."

"All you had to do was contact my office and tell Selena you wanted to see me. Having me picked up off the street by your personal Gestapo was a bit of overkill, Marty."

Chandler's jaw tightened at the accusation of abuse of his office, but he let it pass. "I suppose my instructions need to be more detailed in the future."

He shrugged, motioned for Tony to sit, and sat back down to his breakfast. "I told my assistant I wanted to see you." A smile tugged at the corners of his mouth. "It really is difficult to find good help these days. Can I get you something to eat or drink?"

"Dinner was a long time ago." Tony sat down. "A couple of eggs, bacon and a short stack of pancakes would be nice." He gestured toward the coffee cup on the table. "A half-gallon of that would be even better."

"Same old Tony." Chandler relayed the food order to the kitchen.

Chandler watched Anthony Wayne's eyes take in the surroundings. Finally, his eyes came back to Chandler. "You've got it pretty nice here, Marty."

"It has its perks."

"I've noticed."

Chandler sighed. "All for one and one for all, Aramis." He paused but received no response and decided to try a

215

different tack. "Your country needs your help."

Tony laughed.

"You think that's funny?"

"I think you're trying to make yourself look good for the next presidential election. Assuming there is a next presidential election."

A knock on the office door interrupted any further conversation.

"Come in."

A kitchen staffer wheeled in a cart and pushed it through the office, onto the verandah. It was loaded with the breakfast order, including a full thermal carafe of coffee.

As the staffer laid the meal before Tony, his host said, "We'll talk after your meal."

The two men chatted about childhood events and mutual friends while Tony consumed his breakfast. When he took the last swallow of coffee and placed the linen napkin on the table next to his plate, Chandler cut to the heart of the issue.

"As I stated earlier, I need your help, your expertise."

"So you said."

"You're not the least bit curious about what the matter pertains to?"

Tony shrugged. "I figure you'll tell me when you're ready."

"Even when we were kids your arrogance was annoying. I see you haven't changed a bit."

Tony smiled.

"Very well. I need you to guide a team of National Guardsmen and Peacekeepers into the Central Florida swamps and help them find and destroy the group that call themselves the Swamp Rats."

216

"Why?"

"Because they're harboring a fugitive deviant, Erin Foster. This woman has killed, at last count, nine people, one of them a police officer."

"No, that's not what I was asking. I listen to the news. I know why you want the Swamp Rats destroyed. I want to know why I should help you do it."

A conspiratorial smile spread across Chandler's face. "In other words, what's in it for you?" He sighed. "I could simply tell you it's your duty as a citizen to help the authorities capture this fugitive and those assisting her in her crimes."

"You could."

The governor leaned back in his chair and steepled his fingers. "Yes, I could. Or I could offer you a monetary reward. But I think I have, shall we say, a better motivator."

The two men stared at each other, reminiscent of two tomcats having a territorial squabble.

Chandler grew tired of waiting for Tony to ask what the motivator was and finally he said, "Let me put it to you this way; you'll do as I say because otherwise, I will shut down this perverted little fantasy business of yours. You'll find yourself being sued by more of your clients than you were aware existed."

"What exactly will they be suing me for?"

Chandler tilted his head back for a moment and then brought his eyes back to Tony. "It will depend, everything from breach of contract to corruption of morals. The reality is it won't matter what they're suing you for. The legal fees will bankrupt you and once word spreads about what your business is all about, you'll have more trouble finding a job than a hooker wearing a placard stating she's HIV positive." He paused, irritated because Tony showed no sign of fear or concern. "On top of all that I'll have you sent to a Re-Orientation Facility. Perhaps The Reverend Master's people can make you a worthwhile citizen."

The governor stood up, signaling their meeting was over. "I'll have the troopers who brought you in take you back to your office so you can collect whatever equipment you need. A squad of Peacekeepers and state National Guardsmen will meet you and the troopers at Swamp Grass Park tomorrow morning."

Chandler stared down at Tony. He'd expected to feel a sense of victory by coercing Tony into doing his bidding. Instead, he felt inadequate, but he still refused to look away.

"Do we understand each other, Mr. Wayne?"

"Perfectly, Marty."

CHAPTER 43

Anthony Wayne pushed open the door to Your Wish Is My Command. "Gentlemen, this is Selena, personal assistant extraordinaire. Selena, this is Trooper Wells and his partner, Trooper Garrick."

He continued through the front room to his private office, giving orders along the way. "I need swamp gear for three, including water and trail food. Tell Paul I'll need thirteen flat bottoms at Swamp Grass Park by sunrise and I'll need him to come along on this little adventure. Oh, and make sure that the personal gear for the three of us is delivered to my place before sunrise."

Standing behind his desk he looked at the two troopers. "You boys will need to give Selena your sizes so she can get you outfitted." He paused and looked Trooper Wells up and down. "You may be a bit difficult to find the right sizes for, but we'll do what we can."

Wells looked from Tony to Selena to his partner and back to Tony. "What exactly is all this gear you're talking about, Mr. Wayne?"

"Have you ever spent time in the swamps, Trooper Wells?"

"I went on a manhunt in a swamp once."

Tony smiled. "From the tone of your voice I get the impression you aren't exactly a swamp fan."

Wells' expression showed his disgust. "You're right about

me not liking the swamp. I ended up with leaches and ticks."

"My point exactly. Had you gone into the swamp properly attired and equipped you'd have had a much more enjoyable experience." Tony gestured at the upholstered chairs across the room from his desk. "Why don't you boys make yourselves comfortable while Selena and I get things rolling?"

The two troopers exchanged glances, shrugged, and relaxed into the soft leather chairs.

"Selena, get their sizes and call storage for the Swamp Adventure gear. Make sure Paul picks the three of us up at my place no later than 7:15 a.m. tomorrow."

"I'm on it boss. Also, you had three calls from…"

Tony held up a hand to silence her. "It doesn't matter. We're doing our civic duty for the state of Florida. Business will have to wait."

"I'll call them back and let them know it will be a while before you can get back to them." It was her turn to preempt any comments from Tony. "Right after I get your swamp gear moving." She turned to the troopers. "Gentlemen, I need your clothing and shoe sizes." She handed each of them a pad and pen.

Tony opened a large file cabinet behind his desk. Lying in the bottom of the drawer among the maps was a 9mm Beretta. He pushed it to the dark recess at the back of the drawer. He used the maps he discarded to cover the weapon.

When he turned away from the filing cabinet Tony found himself looking at the business end of Trooper Wells .45 automatic.

Putting his hands in the air Tony said, "I'm crushed Trooper Wells. You don't trust me." He brought his hands forward and

220

displayed the collection of topographical maps. "See just a bunch of maps. No matter how experienced you are, you should never go into the swamps without a map and a plan."

Wells grunted, holstered his gun, and sat back down.

Tony spread one of the maps out on the table across the room. "Selena," he called.

"Yeah boss." The thin pale young woman stood in the doorway.

"How long before the gear will be ready?"

"Tomorrow morning and before you start complaining, take a look at Paul Bunyan over there."

Tony smiled and bowed to Selena. "You are a miracle worker. I actually expected it might take a bit longer than that because of our large friend."

"Oh."

Glancing at his watch Tony continued, "Look fellows the reality is that it's going to be morning before we start this expedition." He spread his arms. "It's mid-afternoon now and in three hours it'll be getting on toward dusk." Tony brought his hands together. "We'll have a good dinner and one last night in a soft bed, then first thing in the morning we'll meet the rest of our party and get underway."

Trooper Wells looked at Trooper Garrick, who shrugged as if to say it was no big deal to him. Wells brought his gaze back to Tony. "That's fine Mr. Wayne but we'll be with you the whole time. Orders, you know."

Tony smiled. "I wouldn't have it any other way, Trooper Wells." With barely a pause he continued, "Selena, make sure everything is at the rendezvous point by sunrise."

"You got it, boss. Paul has the location and the times."

"Wonderful. I know it's asking a lot, but I need you to be here in the office at sunrise, just in case I need to call you for anything. If you haven't heard from me by 0730 hours, lock up and take the day off."

"Thanks boss and good luck."

"Who needs luck I've got God on my side. Catch ya later kiddo."

In the corridor Trooper Garrick blocked Tony's way. He looked at the older man and in a dull voice said, "You shouldn't joke about God like that, Mr. Wayne."

Tony maintained a serious expression and replied, "I wasn't joking. Is it not true that the Reverend Master is God's representative here on Earth and are we not doing the Reverend Master's bidding by bringing Erin Foster to justice?"

Garrick seemed confused. "Yeah, but the way you said it..."

Smiling like a big brother, Tony put his hand on Garrick's shoulder and said, "You have to understand this mission we're going on is dangerous and sometimes people cover their concerns with lighthearted banter."

The two men followed Trooper Wells into the parking lot. "Erin Foster has already killed nine people, that we know of. Rumor has it that she even shot her own lover rather than allow her to surrender and be treated for deviancy."

Wells started the patrol vehicle and cranked up the air conditioner. Tony slapped Trooper Garrick on the back and concluded, "So you see I wasn't really joking. It's just my nature to try and keep things light and easy in a dangerous situation." Tony slid into the back seat of the patrol car, Trooper Garrick joined him, and closed the door.

Trooper Garrick still wore an expression of concern, but

Tony was certain it had more to do with Erin Foster's reputation than with his comments about God.

CHAPTER 44

"Erin, wake up." Nurse Chris Barton gently touched Erin's shoulder and nudged her. "Erin."

"I'm awake. I was hoping if I ignored you, you'd go away."

"Colonel Mason wants you in her office. Now."

Erin considered a smart remark about not giving a damn what the colonel wanted but thought better of it. Something about Chris' attitude told her this was serious business.

"What time is it?"

"Zero three hundred."

Erin got up from the hammock and stretched. "This better be good."

Chris made no reply as she headed toward Colonel Mason's office.

Erin followed her. Approaching the building she saw Hank Bartholomew arriving from the other direction. Chris entered ahead of them. Erin and Hank met at the colonel's doorway.

Hank smiled and said, "Here I thought I was special, but I see I'm not the only one whose beauty sleep was interrupted."

"Yes, but in your case it's a real shame because we all know how much you need your beauty sleep."

Hank motioned for Erin to enter ahead of him as he said, "I think I've been insulted."

Colonel Mason ordered, "You two stop your nonsense and get in here."

Hank and Erin exchanged a quick glance, entered the room, snapped to attention and in unison said, "Lt. Bartholomew, reporting as ordered."

"Lt. Foster, reporting as ordered."

"If you two are through clowning around, we have a mission to go over."

Erin dropped her exaggerated stance and elbowed Hank. He too dropped his over-the-top pose.

Erin studied the colonel and saw the tension in her face and the worry in her eyes. "What's going on, Colonel?" Erin asked.

Colonel Mason turned toward the shadows created by the small flame of the kerosene lantern on her desk. A pale, thin, young woman stepped into the small circle of light around the colonel's desk.

"Selena, this is Lt. Hank Bartholomew and Lt. Erin Foster." The young lady nodded at each of them. "Selena is General Wayne's personal assistant. She does everything from ordering his groceries to making sure his payroll taxes are paid on time."

Always the gentleman Hank said, "It's a pleasure to meet you, Selena."

"Likewise, Lt. Bartholomew, Tony speaks highly of you."

Erin looked at Colonel Mason and said, "I know you didn't drag my ass out of bed at three a.m. to meet the general's assistant."

"No. That is not the reason I had the two of you brought here." She sat down in her desk chair and indicated that everyone should take a seat. Erin was sandwiched between Selena and Hank, with Chris on the other side of Hank.

"Sometime over the weekend Florida State Troopers

225

picked General Wayne up and delivered him to the Governor's mansion." The words came out of her as if she was giving a weather report, but Erin could see the strain the situation was creating for her. It was common knowledge around Camp Liberty that she and the general were old friends. "He left in the company of two troopers. They took him to his office at Your Wish Is My Command…"

"Why in the world does General Wayne…" Hank barely took a breath before he continued. "You mean our General Wayne is really Crazy Tony the owner of Your Wish Is My Command?"

Erin shook her head in disbelief. "And here I thought General Wayne was a real gentleman."

Selena spun around in her chair to face Erin. "And what have you heard here to change your opinion?"

"I've heard about some of the fantasies filled by Your Wish Is My Command, Selena. I don't think a gentleman sets another man up as a sheik with a harem of fifty women. Sounds like a pimp's job to me."

Colonel Mason prevented Selena from responding. "Ladies, you two can discuss the finer points of General Wayne's character after we rescue him." Selena turned back around in her chair and she continued. "We know that around dawn, General Wayne, a group of National Guardsmen, some Peacekeepers and two state troopers will be heading into the swamps."

"You mean to tell me that not only is our wonderful general a pimp, he's also a traitor!" Erin stood up so abruptly she knocked over her chair.

Selena was on her feet ready to attack Erin, but Hank

inserted himself between the two women.

Colonel Mason stood up and said, "First of all, you will never again refer to General Anthony Wayne with anything other than respect. Second, you will immediately apologize to the general's daughter for your disparaging remarks about her father."

"His daughter?"

Selena said, "I don't want an apology from her. I just want the opportunity to kick her ass."

Mason looked at Selena. "As long as you're willing to wait until after she helps us save your father."

"Fine. I respect your opinion colonel and since you think she's necessary to the operation, I can wait."

"Great. You two can kill each other later." She sat back down. "Hank and Chris, please sit between the two of them for the remainder of our meeting."

Looking nervous Hank sat between Erin and Chris, while Chris sat down between Hank and Selena.

The colonel unrolled a map on her desk. "We have limited information on the situation. The troopers never left Tony alone with Selena long enough for him to give her any details. We do know that at sunrise," she pointed at Swamp Grass Park on the map "he will be leaving here with a contingent of National Guardsmen and Peacekeepers." Her finger traced a route on the map.

"If I know Tony, he's going to lead them in a roundabout fashion and sometime around mid-afternoon they'll be here." Her finger rested on the location of Camp Betrayal.

"Why there?" Hank asked.

"Because about a quarter of a mile from there is a narrow

canal. They'll have to form a single line with their canoes and flat bottoms." She straightened up. Her eyes moved from person to person as she spoke, "We'll have troops waiting on each side of that canal and at my signal we'll take them. Erin and Hank, pick your people carefully. I want ten armed personnel on each side of that canal. I don't want anyone who has problems taking orders or who is trigger happy. Chris will be coming along but not as combat personnel. She'll be our medic; in case we need one."

"Hank, I'd like to be one of the ten on your team." Selena offered.

Erin smiled at him and said, "Why don't you round out your team with Andrea? That way she and Selena can compare notes."

CHAPTER 45

In the morning an hour before sunrise Tony woke the two troopers with a call to breakfast.

"Gentlemen, breakfast is ready."

Trooper Wells arrived fully dressed in his uniform, right down to his gun belt. He frowned at Garrick who entered barefoot wearing his uniform pants with his shirt untucked and partially buttoned.

On the table were three place settings. Each plate held a large pile of scrambled eggs, a short stack of pancakes, two slices of bacon, and toast. There was coffee and orange juice at each man's place.

"Have a seat, gentlemen." Tony sat down and took a sip of orange juice. He nodded toward two backpacks leaning against the dining room wall. "Your clothes and some of the personal gear you'll need are in there. After breakfast there'll be time for a quick shower before we leave." Tony smiled. "Enjoy the hot water it could be your last experience with it for a while."

After breakfast and showers the three men met in the living room. Tony wore lightweight custom fitted hip waders, a long sleeve shirt made of a breathable material and a safari hat with mosquito netting that could be pulled down to protect one from the nasty little biters. His two companions were similarly dressed except that their waders were made of a heavy rubber and their long-sleeved shirts were a cotton/polyester blend.

The deep rumble of a large engine drew everyone's attention to the driveway.

"Excellent. Our chariot has arrived." Tony grabbed his backpack and followed the two men to the door. "I'll be right back. I'm not sure I turned off the coffee maker."

Wells and Garrick stopped in the doorway and waited.

Tony's voice preceded him as he walked back from the kitchen. "I was right. I'd forgotten to turn the thing off."

The two troopers stepped outside with Tony right behind them.

At the rear of an overgrown SUV was a man almost as big as Trooper Wells, Tony introduced his associate, Paul Skinner.

"Paul, did you personally inspect all the equipment before it was sent to the rendezvous location? I don't want anything to go wrong out there."

"I inspected all of it. Everything is as it should be." Paul smiled. "Finding stuff to fit the big guy here was the challenge" he looked Trooper Wells up and down "but it looks like we did okay. And like I said, everything else is being delivered to the rendezvous point."

"Excellent." Tony examined the tie downs keeping the load in place on the roof of the vehicle. "Looks like everything's secure. Let's get underway. Trooper Wells, why don't you ride shotgun? That way you can give Paul directions, if he needs them."

Paul climbed behind the wheel, while Tony ushered Trooper Garrick into the back seat and followed him in. Wells hesitated

230

and then climbed into the front passenger seat and said, "Head north on County Road 5A. When you reach US 92 turn west."

Paul nodded and shifted into drive.

For several miles a tense silence filled the vehicle. Then Trooper Wells said, "You see that side road up there just past the on ramp to the interstate?"

"Yeah, I see it."

"Turn right there. Stay on it for about three miles. There'll be a bridge and just before you reach the foot of the bridge you'll see a road to the right, follow that to the parking lot."

Paul glanced in the rearview mirror. Tony smiled at him and then turned to Trooper Garrick and asked, "Have you ever been in the swamps before?"

"No sir and I have to admit I'm a bit nervous about it."

"Nothing to be nervous about as long as you keep your eyes open and your wits about you." Tony leaned forward and tapped Paul on the shoulder. "Isn't that right Paul?"

Paul chuckled. "Yeah. You just have to watch out for snakes falling out of trees into the boat and don't dangle any body parts over the edge of the boat. It might attract a gator."

Tony watched the color drain from Garrick's face. "You mean snakes actually fall out of the trees."

Wells turned around to face Tony and said, "Stop trying to scare the kid." He shifted his gaze to Garrick and continued, "Don't let them get to you Jonny. Snakes don't fall out of trees. Besides we're not going to be in the god forsaken swamp any longer than it takes to do our job and we'll have plenty of company." He locked eyes with Tony. "The governor sent a squad of Peacekeepers we'll be traveling with."

231

Tony frowned. "Oh, just a squad of Peacekeepers. I thought Marty; I mean the governor, said he was sending a squad of Peacekeepers and a squad of National Guardsmen. I'm not sure a single squad will be enough."

Wells didn't respond. He faced front and directed Paul to park next to the military vehicles already in the parking lot.

On the far side of the parking lot a National Guard Lieutenant and a man wearing a black Peacekeeper's uniform were having what appeared to be a heated discussion.

Tony jumped down from the vehicle and headed for the two individuals.

"Good morning, gentlemen." Both men turned and glared at Tony. "I'm Anthony Wayne. Call me Tony. My understanding is that I'm to be in charge of this expedition." He held up a hand to cut off the objections about to be voiced by both men.

"Trooper Wells, I believe now would be a good time to open the orders the governor gave you, so we can settle the matter of chain of command before someone gets hurt."

The governor's orders were straight forward. Tony was in charge of the mission until the Swamp Rats were located. Then the highest-ranking Peacekeeper took command.

As Trooper Wells passed the orders to the National Guard Lieutenant, Tony said, "So now that we know the pecking order, how about if we all shake hands and get on with the job at hand?"

The man with the orders looked up from them and introduced himself to Tony. "Lieutenant Garth Holbrook, sir."

Tony shook his hand and turned to the Peacekeeper who said, "I am Lieutenant Timothy Barnes, sir." He paused looking past Tony. "And while you have introduced yourself sir, you haven't told us who these other gentlemen are." He indicated the two state troopers and Paul.

"State Trooper Wells, State Trooper Garrick and my associate Paul." Tony looked around to where the other members of his staff were. "Over there directing the loading of the first flat bottom is Jason, the other side of him is Pierre."

Tony paused and turned to Paul. "I requested all flat bottom boats. Why do we have canoes?"

Paul shrugged. "I got what was available on such short notice."

Tony looked over the collection of men waiting to embark on this adventure. He sighed and said, "Well, it will be a bit cramped but I think we'll all fit."

By full light all the gear was loaded, and personnel were distributed between the four flat bottoms and the nine canoes.

Before stepping into his canoe Tony addressed the group. "Listen up." Conversations stopped and all eyes turned to him. "Whether you've ever been in the swamp before or not is irrelevant. Because you've probably never been on a seek and capture mission in the swamp before and that's what we're on today."

He paused and let his gaze travel over the group. "I'm sure there has been much speculation about the target of this mission. The group we're going after is well armed and dangerous. They're all wanted on death penalty offenses, so they have nothing to lose by resisting arrest." He indicated the thick vegetation behind him. "That is their home. They probably know it like you know your own neighborhood. At best this is a hostile environment. If my people tell you to do or not to do something, it's because they know this environment almost as well as our target. Listen to them." He looked around the group, making eye contact with the men closest to him. "Sound carries a great distance over water, so once we get underway, I don't want anything above a whisper. If you can deliver your message with hand signals, do so."

Tony and Trooper Garrick manned the lead canoe of the thirteen-vessel flotilla. Paul brought up the rear with one of the flat bottoms. In between was a mix of flat bottoms and canoes each carrying gear and men. Alone in a small canoe, Jason served as messenger, moving up and down the ragged line of boats.

Not a breath of air stirred at water level. There was no escape from the stench of rotting wood and decaying leaves. The sun hammered down on the green canopy creating a sauna affect. Those few places where the canopy opened and allowed direct sunlight to enter offered no relief.

Around noon Jason delivered a message from Lt. Barnes to Tony that the men needed a break.

I'm surprised it took him this long to start crying Uncle. Tony's response was, "Tell the lieutenant that we're almost to a hammock where we'll all be able to stretch our legs."

Thirty minutes later Tony steered toward a small piece of land growing out of the water. When his canoe's bow ran aground just shy of the hardwood hammock, Tony tapped Garrick with his paddle. When Garrick turned around Tony signaled him to go ashore.

Garrick whispered back, "You mean you want me to step into the water?"

Tony fought off the urge to smile at his companion's obvious fear and nodded his reply.

In a few minutes each of the thirteen vessels crowded around the only piece of dry real estate they had seen since they began. Tony, Paul, Jason, and Pierre kept a tight lid on conversations, reminding their traveling companions that sound traveled great distances over water.

The men stood around in small groups occasionally whispering to each other and constantly looking around as if expecting some monster to step from behind a tree or rise up out of the water and devour them.

"Did you hear that noise a little way back?"

"Which noise?"

"I don't know how to describe it. Almost like a roar but not quite."

Another guardsman laughed nervously. "Yeah, it was a gator. I heard one at a zoo once."

His companion swallowed hard. "Well, this ain't no zoo. Bad enough we got the queers shooting at us, now we got to worry about gators."

"Don't forget the snakes."

"Snakes?"

Tony stepped up to the small knot of men and placed a finger across his lips to remind them of the need for quiet. *Ah yes, by this afternoon these boys will be so jumpy they're apt to start shooting one another.*

The tension among the group was a palpable, living breathing thing. All too soon they were ordered back into the cramped boats.

Lieutenants Barnes and Holbrook approached Tony. Barnes did the talking. "Mr. Wayne, when can we expect to reach this rebel camp?" He waved in the general direction of

235

the boats. "These men are not accustomed to these primitive conditions." He narrowed his eyes and looked at Tony suspiciously. "I don't understand why you couldn't have come out here located the camp and directed our helicopters and airboats to the target."

Looking past Barnes as if he weren't there, Tony addressed Lt. Holbrook. "Are you in agreement with this idiot?" Holbrook shifted his gaze between Tony and Barnes but said nothing. "So, you're the kind of gutless wonder the world is full of these days. Pity, for a moment I thought you were a man. My mistake." Tony started to walk away from the two men.

Barnes raised his voice. "Mister Wayne, I demand an answer!"

Tony whirled around. Standing nose-to-nose with Lt. Barnes he spoke in a strained whisper. "If you raise your voice again you can explain to The Reverend Master James Calton III how it was that the Swamp Rats knew we were coming. That is assuming you're alive to explain anything."

Invoking the name of the Reverend Master brought fear to the eyes of the young man before him. Tony drew a deep breath and quietly continued. "Helicopters and airboats make enough noise to wake the dead. And believe me that kind of attack would lead to the death of a lot of those young men whose discomfort you're so concerned about. So, what'll it be lieutenant, a little discomfort or a lot of death?"

"Very well, Mr. Wayne. We'll do it your way...for now." Barnes spun on his heel and climbed back into the flat bottom boat with Trooper Wells.

The heat was relentless, and the mosquito repellent was washed away by the sweat pouring off them. Every splash,

236

every rustling among the bushes raised the level of apprehension. The enforced silence only aggravated the situation.

Two hours after leaving the hammock Barnes pulled his craft alongside Tony's and asked, "How much longer, Mr. Wayne?"

Tony looked around as if determining exactly where they were, then he looked at Barnes and said, "A short distance ahead this stream narrows. We'll go through it single file. If the water level has dropped, we may have to carry the boats a short distance. Just beyond that section the stream spills into an open area, a short distance in there's an old, abandoned fish camp. If I'm right the rebels are using that camp for their base."

Ten minutes later Tony rested his paddle across his lap, placed his hands above his head, signaling for a single file formation.

CHAPTER 46

Calvin Santiago hesitated at his boss's office door. He took a long deep breath and then knocked.

"Come in."

Calvin stepped into the Governor's office and closed the door behind him. He remained by the door as if he might need to leave at any moment.

Martin Chandler glanced up from the papers on his desk and asked, "What is it, Cal?"

"There was a news item just now about Anthony Wayne."

Giving his full attention to his aide, Chandler stood up and asked, "What was it about?"

"A few minutes ago, his house blew up. I thought you should know, sir."

Martin Chandler experienced a sinking feeling in the pit of his stomach. As he searched the internet for the news story, he prayed that it had been something as innocent as a gas leak.

"...We're outside what's left of the home of Anthony Wayne the eccentric businessman and owner of Your Wish Is My Command. Moments ago, I spoke with the Fire Marshall and was assured this explosion was no accident."

The camera showed the still smoking remains of what had once been a house. "When I interviewed some of the neighbors, I learned that Mr. Wayne left here this morning in

238

the company of three other men. Eyewitnesses have stated that all the men were dressed as if they were headed out on a safari. At present the police have no suspects however…"

Chandler closed the lid on the laptop and stared off into space. His mind was racing trying to figure out how Anthony Wayne had once again made a fool of him. Only this time it was more than just a teenage prank.

This is my third strike. First Erin Foster kills a cop and the Bishop's son. Second, she pulls off a rescue from a Reorientation Facility, killing seven people in the process. And now, now I've sent a group of soldiers and peacekeepers into the swamps with Mad Anthony Wayne.

Calvin Santiago looked at Chandler and asked, "Is there anything I can do for you sir?"

"No, Calvin. Thank you for letting me know." Chandler stood up, looking around the room as if he wasn't sure where he was. He cleared his throat. "Why don't you take the rest of the day off Cal. If I need you, I'll call." Not waiting for a response, he moved out the French doors onto the verandah.

Somehow Anthony Wayne is involved with the Swamp Rats. Why didn't I think of that before I sent those men into the wilderness with him? How could I not see it?

He took a deep breath of the warm muggy air, loosened his tie, rolled up his sleeves, removed his shoes and socks and started across the wide expanse of lawn.

CHAPTER 47

Sweat ran into Erin's eyes, blurring her vision. She blinked several times and wiped her face on her shirt sleeve. She looked at her watch.

Thirty minutes? Christ, it feels like I've been here for hours.

Moments later she felt the tickling sensation of a drop of sweat running from her forehead to the tip of her nose. She crossed her eyes to try and see it, entertaining herself with the question of how long it would take to fall. She counted down the seconds, at twenty-one the droplet fell from the end of her nose. It landed on a dried palm frond. To her it was a deafening crash, though she doubted anyone else heard it.

She tilted her head and listened. *There. What's that sound?* She held her breath and counted, waiting to hear it again.

One, two, three, four… It was closer this time. What is that noise? Whatever it is, it's getting closer. Again, she counted to four before the sound floated across the water.

I know that sound. It's an oar scraping the side of a canoe. They're here.

Stationed at the mouth of the canal, Erin was the first to see the expedition come around the bend. Tony sat in the back of the lead canoe.

Erin watched him survey the area, as he gave the signal to form a single line. She watched the occupants of each boat as it slid past her hiding spot. Most of the faces belonged to

240

terrified young men but even the older ones looked nervous.

As the last boat passed her position, Erin released the rope holding up a tree trunk. The huge log dropped across the opening of the canal blocking any attempt to escape. The ground shaking thud startled the occupants of the thirteen boats now trapped in the narrow passage.

"Hands in the air gentlemen." Colonel Mason ordered as she and Erin's other comrades stepped into the open. Panic set in among the boatmen. One young man jumped from his flat bottom boat and tried to run up the bank. Erin saw Andrea plant her foot in his chest and push. He bounced off the side of the flat bottom he'd been in and landed with a splash in the knee-deep water.

A shrill whistle blew. Silence fell and Tony took control. "Listen up, men. You are all now prisoners of war. You will be treated fairly. As long as you do not try to escape no harm will come to you."

The ranking peacekeeper opened his mouth to speak but Tony cut him off. "I don't want to hear any indignant proclamations about how we're all going to hell or any of that other nonsense you people keep spouting. Shut up, do as you're told, and you'll come out of this just fine."

Craning his neck, as if looking for someone, General Wayne called, "Paul."

"Yes sir." The big man stood up from his position in the last boat.

"We're going to move these boats out of here one at a time. I want each occupant stripped down to his skivvies and scanned."

It took nearly two hours to strip and scan all twenty-eight

men, including the boats and the gear they contained.

"General Wayne, they're all clean. Not a tracker among them."

"Good job, sergeant." General Wayne turned to the colonel and said, "Gather your officers, we have plans to make. By the way Paul, have all those uniforms delivered to Colonel Mason's office."

"Yes sir."

She turned around. "General, just what are the prisoners going to wear?"

Tony glanced toward the group of men huddled together. Then he looked at Colonel Mason. "They're covered. Besides, in this heat I'm doing them a favor by keeping them down to their skivvies and t-shirts."

A short time later in her office Mason asked, "So what happened? How did the Governor convince you to hunt us down?"

General Wayne smiled at his daughter and looked around the room at the others present. "The alternative was rather unpleasant."

Erin watched his face, trying to determine from his expression what Selena had told him about her reaction to learning that General Anthony Wayne and Crazy Tony of Your Wish Is My Command were one and the same.

"Erin, it seems that your little jail break created a bit of a furor in high places. Governor Martin Chandler got pressure from the federal level to capture you. Marty remembered me from our days in high school and figured that if anyone could ferret you out it would be me."

Yvonne asked, "You call the governor of the state, Marty?"

Wayne smiled. "Actually, in school some people called him Farty Marty." His smiled faded and he sighed. "I tried to convince him that I wasn't the best man for the job. He wasn't buying any of my excuses." He paused. "He gave me a choice, I could hunt down and capture the Swamp Rats or I would find myself in, what he called, a Reorientation Facility. That's the current regime's fancy way of saying prison."

He stood up from the chair he'd taken earlier. Moving about the room pausing occasionally to look out a window, he continued. "I didn't consider the Reorientation Facility an option, so I agreed."

Hank grinned from ear-to-ear as he said, "I bet he'll think twice about using those tactics in the future."

"I doubt that Marty has much of a future. I got the impression that failure would not be tolerated. Certainly not two such public failures as have happened on Marty's watch." He clapped his hands together, as if scaring away unwanted ghosts. "But that is his problem, and we have problems of our own."

"Yes, right now we have twenty-eight problems being held at Camp Betrayal," said Mason.

"Colonel Mason, those men are not problems. They are twenty-eight opportunities to show the people that we're the more humane and civilized opponent in this war."

She shook her head. "Exactly how is that going to work?"

General Wayne shrugged. "I haven't worked out all the details yet. For the moment let's put those individuals out of our minds. There's another, more pressing issue with which we need to deal."

He looked around the room everyone's attention was

focused on him.

"Just before the Governor's storm troopers picked me up, I received a message from General Collins. He's the leader of a group called ATO, Against The Order. He used to be a cop but when The Order began asserting its power he was fired. He disappeared before they could send him to a Reorientation Facility." He paused. "Anyway, I was hoping he was going to ask us to join an operation I've heard he's planning. Instead, he wants to discuss, and I quote 'your latest acquisition'." He paused and looked around at the people in the room. "Does anyone here have any idea what he's talking about? What have we acquired recently?"

For a moment there was silence then they all started talking among themselves about possible things the message could be referring to. Erin didn't join in any of the discussions. She listened and watched. Then her eyes rested on Yvonne, and she knew what Collins' message meant.

Erin's voice cut through all the chatter. "It's not a what. It's a who."

Wayne looked at her and said, "I'm afraid you're going to have to explain that statement, lieutenant."

Erin straightened up in her chair. "It's not a thing Collins wants to discuss. It's a person. The most recent acquisition by the Swamp Rats is – Yvonne."

Wayne smiled and looked from Erin to Yvonne. "Excuse me Yvonne, no insult is intended." Then he turned to Erin. "What makes Yvonne so important that General Collins wants to talk to me about her?"

Erin sat forward in her chair with her elbows resting on her knees. "There's only one reason Yvonne would be that important." Her gaze moved to Yvonne. "Donald is alive and working for the ATO."

Yvonne gasped.

Moving her gaze to Tony, Erin said, "Yvonne, tell everyone what Donald did for a living."

"I don't see what…"

"Humor me. Tell the general what Donald did."

Yvonne looked at General Wayne. "Donald is, was an Electrical Engineer with Florida Power Source." She smiled. "He used to tell me it was his job to keep the lights on."

Erin smiled as she watched the general's expression change. "At last, the lights have come on, so to speak."

Wayne glared at her. Erin shrugged and said, "If you still have doubts, ask Collins."

CHAPTER 48

The next day Hank, Yvonne, and Erin were called to Colonel Mason's office. The colonel and General Wayne were waiting for them. Word had come back from Collins.

"It would seem that Thor's wife is exactly what Collins wants to talk about." He smiled. "As a matter of fact, he's quite eager to meet. So much so, that he's allowing me to choose the location."

"Thor's wife?"

Laughing the general said, "Yes, we didn't dare use her name. Thor was the Norse god known for throwing lightning bolts, so we decided it was an appropriate code name."

He looked at Erin. "Seems Collins has a code name for you too, Erin."

"I can hardly wait. What is it?"

"The Amazon."

Erin snorted.

"In his reply, he requests that we don't bring the Amazon because he's bringing the Irishman."

"Who the hell is the Irishman?"

Hank spoke up. "That would be Sgt. Michael Shamus Donovan."

"Oh yeah, the cop who's out to get me."

After hours of haggling and rejecting one idea after another, a plan was agreed upon.

It was simple and straight forward. Hank, General Wayne, and Yvonne would meet with Collins and his people at an old research laboratory in a remote area near the county line.

Erin had suggested the place. It was a place she was familiar with because the man, Kevin, who used to work in the lab was a friend of Alice's. When Kevin moved from the area the building was abandoned. Erin hadn't been there in a long time.

Pamela, Lacey, and Andrea were to arrive at the meeting site shortly after the meeting was underway. If anything went wrong, they were to attempt an immediate rescue, otherwise they were simply there to observe.

It was a simple plan, but the more Erin thought about it the more it looked like an opportunity.

General Wayne never spent the night at Camp Liberty. He took a canoe to points unknown. Erin waited until she saw him leave Colonel Mason's office and she followed him to the canoes tied up near the mess.

"General."

"Yes, lieutenant."

"I want to talk to you about something."

"Can't this wait until morning?"

Erin shook her head. "No, sir. It's about tomorrow's plan."

"We already hashed out all the details, lieutenant."

"If you give me five minutes, I can show you a way to make this meeting more effective, in a variety of areas."

CHAPTER 49

Pamela, Lacey, and Andrea were an hour out of Camp Liberty when Andrea signaled a halt. The other two women froze in their tracks and listened. Then they heard it, tweeter, tweeter, tweet, a pause and then the call repeated. Moments later Erin emerged from the palmetto bushes that lined the narrow path.

"What are you doing here? I was told you were confined to Camp Liberty."

Erin ignored the snarl in Andrea's voice. "Things change. Word was sent shortly after you left that I was to catch up with you and take command."

Andrea stared at her through narrowed eyes.

"Look I don't have time to go into detail, right now." She glanced at her watch. "We need to get moving if we're going to hijack that meeting."

"What? Are you insane? Those aren't even close to my orders."

Erin smiled. "Yeah, I know. Like I said things change." She looked at Pamela and Lacey. "You ladies ready for an action-packed afternoon?"

The only response Erin got was a brief smile from both women.

Erin started to take point and move on when Andrea said, "How do I know you're telling us the truth?"

248

"You don't." She paused and held Andrea's gaze. "Either follow my lead or return to camp. I don't care which, but if you're staying, you'll follow my orders." She paused then said, "From this point forward, hand signals only." Without another word Erin shouldered past the younger woman.

Another hundred yards brought them to a cached canoe.

Part of Erin's mind continued to review her plan as another part kept track of her team's speed and location.

She drew in a deep breath of the muggy air. The flavor and smell of it brought back memories of happier times, years ago when she paddled these canals with Alice.

Alice had always made her believe she could accomplish anything she set her mind to. It occurred to her that it was probably best Alice couldn't see her now. She would be appalled at the things Erin had done. She closed her mind to the thought of displeasing Alice, before it led to the last time, she'd disappointed her lover.

A sound brought her back to the present. Erin tapped Lacey on the back with the signal to drift, she passed the signal to Pamela, who passed the signal to Andrea. For several seconds the canoe floated silently, the light current pushing them back the way they had come.

In the bow Andrea turned her head aft and demanded, "Why are we sitting here wasting time?"

Erin glared her down, refusing to violate the silence she'd ordered be maintained.

Splash. Erin looked toward the shore, to her right. A raccoon stared back at her for a moment and then returned to washing its fish.

The foursome returned to their paddling. On schedule they

arrived at the portage point. Erin, Pamela, and Lacey remained with the canoe while Andrea scouted the area ahead.

Sweat trickled down Erin's back as the heat and humidity combined to create a giant outdoor sauna. Her thoughts returned to Alice and her love of the outdoors.

She was always up for any adventure that involved being in the Florida wilderness. I'd give anything to be able to go back to those days.

Andrea gave the all clear signal.

Erin took point, her weapon at the ready as the others stowed their guns and picked up the canoe. Twenty feet later Erin stopped at the edge of the road and listened. Hearing only the wind rustling the palm fronds, the birds chirping and the occasional fish jumping she signaled them forward at double time.

Fifteen seconds later they were across the road and moving toward the canal that would take them east.

They set the canoe in the canal and in less than three minutes everyone had donned the waders needed for their next stop and all were back in the canoe.

The smoother things went, the more Erin was convinced that when things went wrong, they would do so in a big way.

This canal's current is a bit stronger than the previous one. Tide must be coming in. We'll have to pick up the pace if we're going to be on time.

As if the other women had heard her thoughts, they all began to dig deeper into the water with their paddles.

Ten minutes later Erin steered them to the left. The road formed an overpass here, and they tied the canoe up under it, out of sight. With their ride home secured the women waded through the shallow water with slow silent movements.

Erin stopped often, to listen and observe the surroundings.

"Why do we keep stopping?" Andrea hissed.

Erin looked into her eyes and whispered, "Because I'm in command. If you don't like it, you can return to camp."

Andrea opened her mouth to speak but before she could say anything Erin cut her off. "Not another word, Andrea. Either you follow my orders or return to camp. But stop questioning me at every turn. You have five seconds to decide." Erin watched the second hand of her old diver's watch tick off the five seconds.

Andrea didn't say a word. Erin turned around and started forward. She could feel Andrea's optic daggers in her back.

One hundred yards later Erin called a halt and motioned everyone down. She gently pushed aside a stand of cattails for a better view of the man leaning against the pine tree two hundred feet ahead.

In a breathy voice barely audible to the women around her Erin said, "Pamela and Lacey, you're going to move beyond his position. Stay low and hug the bank. There's plenty of cover. You'll come to the mouth of a dead-end canal after you pass him. Follow that canal about ten feet in and then come ashore. There'll be a stand of pine and some underbrush between you and him." She paused. "Andrea, you know what Pamela's bird call sounds like, right?"

Andrea nodded.

Erin moved her attention back to Pamela, "After you do the bird call, listen for my whistle, count to ten and then step out of cover and draw his attention." She paused. "Just make sure you don't look like a threat when you step out. I wouldn't want him to get trigger happy."

An impish grin spread across Pamela's face as she said, "I'll think of something."

Erin and Andrea returned the way they'd come. Pamela and Lacey continued forward.

When Erin was certain the lookout wouldn't see them cross the road they scurried to the parallel canal on the north side of the pavement. Once in the water they moved east again.

If I were setting up lookouts, I'd have more than one for each approach. Erin reached back in her memory to dredge up the details of the landscape surrounding the laboratory.

She was still delving into old memories, trying not to get lost in them, when they reached a vantage point with a clear line of sight to the lookout. Erin removed the crossbow strapped to her back and loaded a bolt. She didn't have long to wait before Pamela's bird call sounded. Erin whistled in response and aimed.

Ten seconds later Pamela walked out of the woods, naked.

Erin grinned. *That girl's as crazy as I am.*

The man reached for his rifle leaning against the tree and then changed his mind. He grinned and took a couple of steps toward Pamela. When he was closer to her than he was to his rifle, Erin let the bolt fly. The projectile quivered in the ground between the sentry and Pamela.

The other three women moved into the open. Lacey handed Pamela her clothes. Andrea bound and gagged their prisoner.

Erin questioned the man, with the tip of her knife against his throat. "Do you know who I am?"

His Adams apple bobbed as he swallowed hard. "Yeah," he

answered around the gag in his mouth.

"Then you know I don't have a problem killing." She could see the fear in his eyes. "How many of you are there?"

He looked skyward as if silently counting. "Nine."

"Does that include you?"

"Uh huh."

"Where are they?" Rather than repeat her question she applied pressure to the point of her knife against his carotid artery.

"Collins, Donovan, and North are at the lab. They've got three guys with them and there are two others on lookout, one northwest and one northeast of the building."

Erin put Andrea in charge of the prisoner. Before they got underway Erin whispered in his ear, "If you even think of causing us any trouble, I'll cut your balls off and feed them to you."

He turned and looked at her. The fear in his eyes told her he believed her, which was what she wanted.

They covered two hundred yards before Erin signaled a stop. She left the others and scouted ahead.

Just around the next bend in the trail the path opened up. Twenty-five feet of open ground lay between them and the barn-like building that was Kevin Beckworth's old laboratory. For several moments she watched two men standing guard at the dock that was downhill from the building. She recognized Tony's canoe tied up at the dock.

Where's the third man? Did he escort Tony and the others inside and then stay? Or is he out here somewhere? Or did our friend lie about the number...

Before she could finish the thought a man came around the

building and joined the two at the dock.

From this point forward there's no room for error. One miscalculation and I'm dead.

CHAPTER 50

The four women and their prisoner shifted their position just enough so that the building kept them from being seen by the trio at the dock.

Stepping onto an old milk crate to reach the window, Erin glanced inside. For an instant, everything looked as it had when Alice's childhood friend, Kevin worked his experiments in the virtually sterile, thirty-by-thirty-foot room. Work benches lined the walls, each one holding an array of scientific instruments relevant to the work being done on that particular table. Despite its location in the backwaters of the Intracoastal Waterway, Kevin maintained the building and equipment in a clean and orderly fashion. She blinked and reality came into focus.

Trash littered the floor, windows were missing their glass, the main thing the work benches held was dust and more refuse. The smells of decay flowed through the open window tickling her nose and forcing her to stifle a sneeze.

General Wayne, Hank, Yvonne, and Donald North sat at a round table in the middle of the room with two men Erin didn't recognize, though she knew one of them was Jack Collins and the other was most likely Michael Donovan.

Tony gave no indication he had seen her, as he spoke to one of the men across the table. "General Collins, I understand your hesitancy at bringing in an unknown group of

255

people to your established plan of attack. At the same time, you have to realize that the more people you have assisting in Operation Chaos..."

Collins leaned forward. "The more people involved, the greater the likelihood for betrayal. Obviously, I already have a leak." He squinted at General Wayne. "Exactly how did you hear about Operation Chaos? And what do you know about it?"

Wayne smiled but said nothing.

Erin filled the silence. "Everyone stay perfectly still, and no one will get hurt."

The man seated to the left of General Collins reached for his sidearm.

Erin fired her crossbow, a bolt imbedded itself in the table between him and General Collins. Everyone at the table froze.

"Yes, I've already reloaded for those of you wondering. The next one will find a fleshier target. Everyone stretch your hands toward the center of the table." They did as they were ordered. "Now, cross your hands at the wrists and hold hands with one another." The center of the table became a jumble of hands holding hands.

Seconds later Andrea pushed her prisoner in through the back door. "On the floor, face down." He dropped to his knees and before he could lower himself to the floor Andrea planted a foot in the middle of his back and pushed him down. "Stay there."

She then moved to the far side of the room, placing herself between the table and the front door. Once she was in position Pamela and Lacey entered. Lacey stayed near the back door and Pamela moved to the front of the room, against the wall between that door and the window.

With her people in position Erin left her perch and stepped inside. Setting her crossbow down near the door, she looked around the room. She paused, half-way between the doorway and the table.

The images of how she remembered this place and its former occupant threatened to overtake her. For the briefest of moments, she thought she caught a glimpse of Alice standing next to Kevin at the workbench closest to her. She turned to look and realized a white paper bag left from some fast-food restaurant was what she'd mistaken for a white lab coat. She shook her head to clear it of the ghostly image.

Despite the holes in the roof and the glass being absent from the windows, the dilapidated laboratory was stifling hot. Not a breath of air moved inside the building.

General Wayne said, "What are …"

"Shut up!" She held his gaze for several seconds before moving to the windowless side of the front door, near Andrea. Erin knew if she could keep Andrea on task the other two would not be a problem.

After a whispered exchange, Erin returned to the table. She stole an occasional glance at her team. Their expressions were confused but they were well trained and didn't ask questions.

She brought her attention back to the people around the table; her eyes moved from person to person, as if weighing the value of each.

She pointed to Yvonne. "You. Get up." Yvonne extracted herself from the grips of her table companions. Erin pointed at Hank and Donald. "You two fill the gap and hold hands." She motioned for Yvonne to follow her.

Pamela moved to the far side of the front window. Erin stood with Yvonne between the door and the window.

She kept her voice low as she spoke. "Get them to come up here with you. Tell them the two generals have reached an agreement and their presence has been ordered by General Collins."

"Why are you doing this, Erin? This wasn't the way things were supposed to go."

Erin narrowed her eyes and said, "I changed my mind. I have my own agenda and General Tony and the rest of you can go to hell for all I care." She paused. "Get out there and convince those men to come up here with you."

"What if they don't believe me?"

Erin glanced back at the table directing her attention to Donald. She brought her eyes back to Yvonne. "I suggest you use all your powers of persuasion."

Yvonne reached for the doorknob. Before she opened it Erin said so only Yvonne could hear her, "Betray me and he'll be the first to die."

The two women locked eyes and stared at each other for several seconds before Yvonne stepped out the door.

"Pamela, watch her. Let me know when she heads back." Pamela acknowledged the order, though she seemed hesitant. Erin returned to her remaining hostages.

Wayne asked, "How did you find out where we were?"

She ignored the question. "General Tony, how about if you introduce me to your friends?"

Anthony Wayne visibly bristled at 'General Tony'. "The gentleman to Hank's right is Michael Donovan and the fellow next to him is Jack Collins." He looked around the table. "I believe you know everyone else."

"General Jack, I've heard of you, the cop who disappeared before he could be packed off to a Reorientation Facility." She smiled and shifted her gaze to Donovan. "Sgt. Michael Shamus Donovan, I've heard of you, too."

Donovan muttered, "Somebody give me a gun and let me kill this bitch."

Erin stared directly into Donovan's eyes. "One of your brothers in blue already tried that. It didn't work out so well for him. Did it?"

He growled and started to get up. Erin pressed the muzzle of her 9mm Glock against his head just behind an ear and said, "Sit down, Mikey."

The vein throbbing at his temple evidenced the internal struggle Donovan was experiencing. His weight was resting on his forearms with his ass inches from the chair seat.

Jack Collins looked at him. "Sit down, Donovan. The day will come when you'll get to kill her but only if you're alive to do it."

Donovan locked eyes with Collins and slowly sat down.

Erin walked around the table as she spoke, "He's very well trained. Is he housebroken, too? Or is that too much to ask?"

She stole glances at Andrea, Lacey, and Pamela occasionally. Their expressions showed their confusion. Erin knew she was running out of time.

She stopped behind Jack's chair and grabbed the back of it. As she pulled his chair away from the table, he released the hands he'd been holding, "Get your hands in the air." He did as he was told.

Turning her back on Donovan, Erin spun Collins' chair, so he faced her and placed the barrel of her gun against his forehead. "So, you think your trained dog will get a chance to kill me. You could be right. But now the question is, will you live to see it?"

Donovan moved with the speed of a cat. He pushed himself away from the table and grabbed the .38 tucked in Erin's back waistband as he pushed her to the floor. Her Glock flew from her hand and slid across the room.

Standing between Erin and Jack, Donovan held the revolver leveled at Erin on the floor. He said, "I'm going to take great pleasure in killing you."

Andrea warned, "Donovan! Shoot her and I kill General Collins." Her rifle was aimed at Collins. Her finger rested on the trigger. "At this range I can't miss."

Rolling over on her back, Erin propped herself up on her elbows and said, "Oh Andrea, I didn't know you cared."

"Shut up! All of you." General Wayne stood up and continued. "This was supposed to be a peaceful meeting to foster cooperation against a common enemy, The Order."

"You have my apologies General Collins for the behavior of Ms. Foster."

Donovan never took his eyes off Erin as he spoke, "I'm sorry Jack but I'm not going to let this bitch live another day." He pulled the hammer back on the revolver. "Get ready to meet the devil, bitch."

"Wait!" Wayne pleaded. "Can't we work something out?" He paused. "General Collins..."

Before he could finish his sentence, the door opened, and Yvonne came in followed by the men she'd been sent to get.

The man directly behind Yvonne, quickly shifted his rifle and aimed it at Yvonne's back. The other two men chose their targets, placing Andrea and Lacey in mortal danger.

General Wayne threw his hands in the air. "Please, can we have just a moment to consider what we're doing here?" He was careful not to make any sudden movements as he looked around the room.

"Donovan, if you shoot her, you'll ignite a bloodbath. Andrea will shoot Collins. One of your people will shoot Andrea. Another will shoot Yvonne, assuming he can get his shot off before Lacey takes him out. And I'm certain that Pamela will get at least one of the other men at the door." Tony took a deep breath as the sweat poured down his face. "General Collins, even if you survive, your Operation Chaos will be no more. Do you really think you'll get Donald North to cooperate with you after one of your men kills his wife?"

Her aim never wavered as Andrea asked, "General Wayne, what's going on here? Erin, told us…"

"Andrea, whatever she told you was a lie. She was ordered to stay away from this meeting. Just hold your position."

"Yes sir."

Collins surveyed the room. "Donovan, there will be other opportunities to kill her. We have got to stop fighting among ourselves if we ever hope to beat The Order." He slowly rose from his chair, with his hands in plain sight and faced Andrea. "Let me talk to General Wayne, in private. I'll keep my hands where you can see them."

She nodded her consent, yet never took her aim off him.

Collins stepped between Donovan and the table. As he passed, he said, "Hold your fire for just a bit longer Mike. Let me see what I can work out."

Collins and Wayne stood face-to-face, whispering for several seconds. Then Jack stepped back. Wayne glanced at Andrea and extended his hand to Collins. They shook hands. Collins walked to Donovan and whispered something in his ear.

"You're lying."

"Donovan, there's way too much at stake here to lie. Believe me. Let me have the gun. Trust me on this."

The big man hesitated.

Erin lay on the floor smiling up at him. "Come on, you big dumb Irishman. Even you can't be stupid enough to..."

"Erin, shut up!" The general ordered as he moved closer to the scene.

Collins took the gun from Donovan's sweating hands. Holding the weapon by the barrel he passed it to Tony and then ordered, "All ATO personnel lower your weapons. Now!"

The three men at the door exchanged glances and then slowly pointed their rifles at the floor.

General Wayne said, "All of my people need to lower their weapons as well."

The women around the room obeyed.

"You people are just no fun. I was ..."

Wayne stepped forward and cut off her words. "These are hard times, and we don't have the luxury of time to spend on trials and such. Therefore, I will serve as judge, jury and if need be, executioner." He paused.

"Erin Foster, I hereby charge you with treason. Your attempt to destroy a working relationship between the Swamp Rats and the ATO group has failed. As with most organizations during war time, traitors receive a death sentence."

Erin rose from the floor and holding Wayne's gaze asked, "Do you really think I care?"

General Wayne dropped his head and sighed. He brought his head up and spoke to Donovan.

"I will give you the option, sir." Wayne removed all but one bullet from the revolver he held. He offered it to Donovan. "You may execute her, or I will."

Donovan smiled and took the gun. He raised the .38 and targeted Erin's head. Then he lowered his aim to her chest and squeezed the trigger.

The impact of the bullet shook her as if someone had bumped into her. She grabbed her chest and blood oozed between her fingers as she sank to the floor.

Yvonne started to run toward Erin. Donald stopped her, pulling her into an embrace. She buried her face in his chest, sobbing.

Wayne exchanged a quick look of relief with Hank and then turned to Collins. "We need to get our people out of here. That gunshot may have been heard and reported. If so, we have very little time before the authorities arrive."

Collins looked from Wayne to Donovan and back again. "We need to finish working out a collaboration agreement. If I remember correctly, there's a piece of high ground about two miles northwest of here."

"Yes. I know the place." General Wayne's attention shifted and his tone softened. "Hank, I want you to bury her. I don't want her body found for a very long time."

"Why not?" Donovan demanded. "I killed the bitch and I want the world to know it."

"Sgt. Donovan, you have had your revenge. However, the resistance needs Erin Foster as a rallying cry. She inspired a great many to stand up and fight The Order. We need her spirit to live on." He paused, looking around the room. "Only those of us present in this room know she's dead and that's the way it's going to stay."

"Says you." Donovan sneered.

General Wayne smiled. "You can shout it from the rooftops that you killed Erin Foster. For those who believe you, she'll be a martyr. However, for those who choose not to believe you she'll still be a rallying cry. A legend. And you'll have a very hard time proving she's dead."

He looked around the room glancing at the faces of his people. Their expressions ran the gamut from confusion to disbelief and shock. Putting as much authority into his tone as he could muster, he said, "Hank, get her out of here. The rest of my people, move to the dock. I'm sure that General Collins and his troops will share their canoes, so we can all get out of here."

Pamela asked, "How will Hank get back to base camp?"

Hank asked, "Where did you leave your canoe?"

"Under the overpass to the south" Pamela said.

Wayne turned to Hank. "You know where she's talking about?"

"I'll find it."

"Good man. You know how to find the meeting place we're talking about?" Hank nodded. He headed toward the door. "Everyone else, let's go."

As General Wayne started past Donald and Yvonne North, she pulled away from her husband and blocking his path asked, "How could you let him just shoot her, you sorry bastard? I thought…God, I don't know what I thought but I never thought you'd let him just murder her and then…"

Wayne looked at Donald and spoke through clenched teeth. "Mr. North, please get your wife under control."

Donald pulled a sobbing Yvonne to him. "That is, unless you have a great interest in becoming guests of the Reverend Master."

He brushed past them and headed for the door.

Yvonne straightened up and pushed herself free of her husband's embrace. "General Wayne," he stopped and turned toward her "I'll stay with Hank and help him bury her. It's the least I can do, considering all she did for me."

Wayne looked at Hank, who nodded almost imperceptibly. Moving his focus back to Yvonne, he said, "Very well."

"Damn it, Yvonne, I just found you again. I have no intention of losing you again."

She wiped the tears from her face and kissed him. "Go with them, Donald. I won't be long. Hank knows where you're going. I'll catch up with you." She moved toward Erin's body leaving Donald a solitary figure. Generals Wayne and Collins moved up, one on either side of him and ushered him out of the building.

CHAPTER 51

Through the open doorway Hank and Yvonne watched their comrades board the canoes and push off. In a matter of seconds, they were out of sight and Yvonne turned toward Hank.

Before she could speak, he looked across the room at Erin and said, "They're gone."

Erin reached up and rubbed her chest where the wadding from the blank had torn a hole in her shirt. "Damn, that hurt." She sat up. "I'm going to have one hell of a bruise there."

Hank smiled. "Hey, it could have been worse. You could actually be dead."

Yvonne's mouth dropped open, and her eyes grew large as she stared at a very alive Erin. "But he shot you…the blood and…"

Hank helped Erin up from the floor. "Come on ladies. The general was right you know. Someone probably reported that gunshot."

"True enough. Just one little touch to add before we go." Erin pulled the hunting knife on her waist from its sheath and cut her forearm.

"What are you doing? Why in the world…"

Erin squeezed the cut until several drops of real blood spattered on the floor near where she'd lain after Donovan shot her. She smiled at Hank and Yvonne. "Just a little something to add to the mysterious gunshot. The combination of stage blood and the real thing should keep them guessing for a while." She wiped the blade clean on her jeans and sheathed it.

On her way to the back door Erin picked up her gun. At the back door she scooped up her crossbow and headed for the canoe with Hank and Yvonne close on her heels.

Erin set a fast pace. When they arrived at the canoe Yvonne grabbed Erin, spun her around and slapped her across the face. "Damn you, Erin Foster. You scared me out of three years."

Rubbing her cheek Erin held Yvonne's gaze.

Hank stepped between the two women. "Ladies, we don't have time for this right now. You two can settle your differences later. We still need to make tracks."

Looking at Hank, Erin said, "No problem, lieutenant. Everything's settled. Let's go."

Hank took the stern position. Yvonne sat in the middle and Erin in the bow. Half a mile later Erin signaled a turn. Shortly after that they ran aground on the edge of a hammock. "This is as far as I go with you."

She grabbed her crossbow and her pack and scrambled ashore. She looked back. "Yvonne, you have to continue acting as if you believe I am dead. If Donovan thinks he's been tricked the whole collaboration could fall apart. He and Collins have to believe, at least until after Operation Chaos."

She locked eyes with Yvonne and said, "You, Hank and Tony are the only people who know I'm alive, no one and I mean, no one else, is to know until after Operation Chaos."

"Not even..."

Erin cut her off. "No one." She pushed the canoe away from the shore. "Good luck." She smiled. "I'll be haunting you."

CHAPTER 52

Yvonne was silent during the ride to the rendezvous with General Wayne and the others. When they arrived, Donald ran to the shore and took her in his arms.

"Sweetheart, I'm so sorry about Erin."

She didn't say anything. Tears welled up in her eyes. They were tears of joy at being back together with her husband. Everyone assumed they were for the loss of Erin. Looking over Donald's shoulder she could see General Wayne, Donovan, Hank, and General Collins. She glared at General Wayne, pulled her upper lip into her mouth, and pulled back from Donald a little.

"Is there somewhere we can be alone?"

He glanced back at the meeting, turned back to her and said, "There are perimeter guards all around us. I doubt there's anywhere private right now." He smiled and brushed her hair. "But tonight, back at ATO Headquarters…"

"No! There is no way in hell. I'm going to be anywhere near that murdering bastard."

Donald tried to pull her to him. "I understand that you're upset and…"

"No, you don't understand at all." She held his gaze. "Erin Foster saved my life at the risk of her own. She got herself committed to a reorientation facility so she could rescue me. Do you have any idea what it was like in that place?"

"No, babe, I'm sure it was terrible."

Yvonne hugged herself and ran her hands up and down her arms as if trying to warm up. "Terrible doesn't even begin to describe it." She was getting up a head of steam and her voice was rising.

The foursome at the meeting looked their way to see what all the noise was about.

Donald tried to calm her, but he was ineffective.

Hank came over and said, "Is there a problem?"

"Is there a problem, he asks." Yvonne got in Hank's face. "How can you even ask such a question? Of course, there's a problem. You're sitting over there making plans with that animal."

Hank moved in close to Yvonne and whispered in her ear. He stepped back, studied her face for a moment and then returned to the meeting.

Yvonne spun on her heel and walked into the brush. Donald tried to follow her, but she held up a hand and said, "I really just need to be alone right now. Please."

Standing at the edge of the woods Donald watched his wife disappear into the brush and trees. He turned and stared at the back of Hank's head.

Fifteen minutes later the four men shook hands all around. Collins gathered his people and they got in their canoes and left. As if on cue Yvonne emerged from the brush and stepped over to stand next to her husband.

Tony didn't seem to be in any hurry to go anywhere. With a couple of subtle hand signals, he asked Hank the results of the scanning he'd done on everybody.

Hank walked over to Yvonne and Donald. "Yvonne, I need

to talk to you about a camp issue." He looked at Donald. "I won't keep her long."

Yvonne followed Hank across the sand, "I don't know why you can't talk to me..."

Tony held his sidearm in his hand as he said, "Mr. North, I have a question for you."

Donald turned to face General Wayne. "Yes?"

"Are you aware you're carrying a tracking device of some kind?"

Yvonne started to push past Hank to go to her husband's defense. "What are you..."

Hank grabbed her.

Donald smiled and said, "Yes."

Yvonne stopped struggling against Hank.

"That statement requires an explanation."

Donald never took his eyes off Wayne as he responded, "One for all and all for one, dear Aramis."

The general hesitated, then looked at Hank and said, "Privacy" as he holstered his gun.

Hank looked at Yvonne and said, "Come on, let's go see how our perimeter guards are doing."

Donald continued to look at Wayne as he said, "It's okay sweetheart. The general and I just have some things we need to discuss in private."

"Well alright, I suppose. Men. Ridiculous." She turned and headed into the brush with Hank muttering, "One for all and all for one. Bullshit."

Once they were alone General Wayne said, "Talk to me."

Donald explained how Jack Collins' family was being held hostage. "He wants your help to rescue his family. He kept

The Order's man in the dark about today's meeting. He's out of range for the tracker he put on me." When he gets back to base, he's going to have to deal with Smith, if that's his name. Time is an issue. He'll only be able to keep the guy on ice for just so long before The Order will decide that Collins isn't going to keep up his end of the bargain."

"Why should I believe you?"

"You and Jack have known each other a long time. He's trusting you with his family's lives."

General Wayne called. "Hank."

Hank walked away from Yvonne and moved toward the two men. "Yes, sir."

"Remove Mr. North's tracking device. Give it to Andrea and tell her where to find the scanning team. They'll know what to do with the device."

CHAPTER 53

Erin settled her canoe in amongst the other canoes at Camp Liberty's dock. It was close to midnight and almost everyone in camp was asleep. Food and a few medical supplies were all she was after.

She headed straight for the supply shed with the extra padlock key in her hand. The sight of the padlock hanging loose caused the hairs on the back of her neck to stand up. Squinting into the darkness she tried to figure out who had left the door unlocked and if they were still hanging around.

The sound of cicadas filled the night air. They were so loud Erin wondered if there were any earplugs around. She opened the door to the pantry shed and stepped inside closing the door behind her before turning on her flashlight.

"It's about time you got here."

Erin's hand was on the hilt of her knife unsheathing the weapon before she realized the voice belonged to Yvonne.

"Shit Von! What're you trying to do? Get yourself killed."

"No. I needed to talk to you."

She pushed the knife back into its home and began filling her backpack with apples, a small sack of flour, some canned meats, and powdered eggs.

"So, talk."

"Do you have any idea what your little charade has caused around here?"

"No" she sighed "but I'm sure you're going to tell me."

Yvonne grabbed her arm. "You're damn right I'm going to tell you."

Erin watched her friend's face. "Linda is devastated. She and Tony are now addressing each other as Colonel Mason and General Wayne. Their friendship is being destroyed."

"What the hell do I have to do with that?"

Yvonne threw her head back, shaking it in disbelief before bringing her eyes back to Erin's. "You'll never convince me that you don't know Linda Mason is crazy about you. Keeping her in the dark is just cruel Erin Foster."

"Keep your voice down."

Yvonne fell silent.

Both women listened. Hearing only the normal sounds of the night, Erin moved close to her friend and said, "I know she is and so does everyone else in Camp Liberty."

Erin continued to pick through the pantry like it was a grocery store while she talked. "What I don't know is how good an actress she is. If she didn't really think I was dead, would she be able to convince everyone else around her that she believed I was dead."

"You mean..."

"Yes, I know she has feelings for me. Her feelings and mine are unimportant right now. The important thing is to defeat The Order. If that means letting Donovan and that other clown Collins think I'm dead, then so be it." Erin turned and headed for the door.

"How do we get in touch with you?"

"For right now, I'm thinking it's better if I come to you."

"I don't agree with you, but for the time being at least, I'll

274

play along. Good luck, Erin."

Erin looked over her shoulder and said, "I'm sorry you got involved in all of this. You and Donald should be home living your lives."

"You really think either of us would be home living our lives, even if we didn't know you and Alice." Yvonne smiled. "How do you think Donald managed to avoid being captured? He got an advance warning that they were after him and he managed to find sanctuary."

Erin turned around. "How come you didn't get advance warning?"

"I'm sure that the phone call coming in as I was answering the door was my warning. Problem was that I answered the door instead of the phone." She shrugged.

"It wouldn't have mattered much. All the exits were covered. Donald was out of the office, or they'd have gotten him too." She laughed. "It was one time he was thankful his boss liked to call off site meetings."

"Yeah, well, remind him to thank his boss when this is all over." Erin turned off her flashlight and started to open the door. Something made her hesitate. She looked back at Yvonne. "How about if you make sure it's clear?"

Yvonne stepped up to the door and then stopped. "If there is someone out there, how am I supposed to explain being here?"

Erin smiled. "Tell them Donald's snoring woke you and you were looking for a midnight snack." She reached over and placed an apple in Yvonne's hand. "Now go."

Yvonne opened the door and stepped out onto the walkway. Erin saw her stop and started to follow her when the shed door closed in her face.

Erin heard her say something, but she couldn't make out what it was. After several seconds of searching Erin found a knot hole to look through, at first all she could see was Yvonne's back.

Come on, Von, move. I want to see who's out there with you.

Then Yvonne stepped to her right just enough for Erin to see that there were two women sitting on the edge of the dock near where her canoe was tied up.

I can't tell who they are. Damn it! Where's the moon when you need it?

Suddenly a light shone on the faces of the two women. It was extinguished as abruptly as it had been lit. In that brief instant Erin saw Linda's face. It was covered with grief and distress. That she'd been crying was evident. Erin bit her lip to keep from calling out to her.

She sank to the floor to wait for Yvonne to give her the all clear.

A few minutes later the shed door opened and closed. "Erin? Are you still here?" Yvonne turned on her flashlight.

Erin was sitting in a corner, her back against the wall, knees up to her chest with her head resting on top of them. At the sound of Yvonne's voice, she wiped her eyes on her arms and lifted her head.

"Where did you think I'd be?" She stood up. "I sure as hell couldn't leave here while you were holding court just outside the door, now could I?"

Yvonne just stared at her. Before her friend could think of a comeback Erin continued, "I take it the party's over, and I can

276

get out of here."

Erin realized too late that she should have stopped goading Yvonne. "The party? Oh yeah, it's a real party watching a woman who loves you mourn your death, while you sit in here holding your own little pity party. I just love lying to people, I care about."

She barely stopped long enough to take a breath before continuing, "Exactly how many people are going to have to suffer because you feel guilty over Alice's death? You didn't kill her. You killed the bastard that did, and you're fighting against the whole world to try and kill the asshole who thinks he's God. How long are you going to punish yourself and everyone around you for Alice's death?"

For once in her life Erin was at a loss for a comeback. She stood and stared at Yvonne, knowing there was nothing she could say that would make a difference to Yvonne. Her mind was made up and so was Erin's.

"I need to go before someone else comes along." She was halfway out the door when Yvonne stopped her.

"I almost forgot Hank told me he needs to see you. Sooner is better, were his exact words. And before you ask, no, I have no idea what it's about."

Erin considered her options. She could wait where she was and have Yvonne bring Hank to her or she could set up a meeting somewhere else.

"Tell him to meet me at the training hammock in an hour." Without waiting for a response Erin slipped out of the shed and headed for her canoe.

Forty-five minutes later she was hiding in the brush around the clearing the Swamp Rats used for hand-to-hand combat training. Her position gave her a clear view of the last ten feet of the path and the entire clearing. She settled in to wait.

Going on the belief that she had fifteen minutes, Erin closed her eyes and tried to clear her mind. Meditation was the only thing keeping her sane right now. She concentrated on listening to the sounds around her.

The rustling of the palmettos nearby was probably an opossum, the cicadas still dominated the night's airwaves, the almost inaudible buzz of a mosquito came and went. Then she heard a twig snap. A moment later, she heard Hank's voice, "Cute trick."

Erin stepped into the clearing. "Yeah, well I wanted to know when you arrived, without having to constantly be watching for you." She looked around nervously, wondering if he came alone.

He smiled and as if knowing what she was thinking said, "I'm alone." He stepped to the far side of the clearing.

"We need to talk, and I don't want anyone overhearing this conversation."

Erin followed him into the shadows on the far side of the clearing. Hank looked around and then stepped in close to Erin. "The details of how we know aren't important. What's important is fixing the problem."

Erin looked into his eyes and asked, "Okay, so what's the problem?"

He licked his lips and looked around one more time. "Jack Collins' family is being held hostage by The Order and he has at least one traitor in his group, maybe more. He doesn't know who the turncoat is, however, his main concern is rescuing his family."

"And I am supposed to do what about it?"

"Nothing for the time being. I have some contacts on the outside. They're going to try and locate Collins' family. Once we know where they are, we can figure out a rescue operation. Right now, the main thing I need from you is a way to contact you, quickly."

Erin worked her jaw and then squatted down, picked up a stick and drew a map in the sand. "Camp Liberty is here. Take the main stream about 100 yards, if you look closely, you'll see a very small canal to your left, take it, follow it until it opens up, continue forward about 20 yards and there's another much shorter canal on your right this time. That one will open up to a lake like area and my camp is on the far side.

There's a small beach there, pull your canoe up and start moving inland; you can't see it from the shore. A narrow band of palmettos, slash pine and scrub oak separates me from the beach." She watched him studying the map, when he looked up, she stood up and using her foot destroyed the map.

Hank rose to his full six-foot two height. "I know you think Donovan is the traitor." He shrugged. "You may be right, but we don't have any proof, one way or the other."

CHAPTER 54

"Hello?" Hank called as he moved inland. "Hello?" He hoped his voice was loud enough to be heard close by and yet not loud enough to carry any distance.

Knowing Erin's violent tendencies, he had no desire to sneak up on her. As he rounded a bend in the path it opened into a clearing. He stopped and looked around.

The ground here was soft white sand. There was a fire pit just outside a sapling and palm frond hut, a hammock was strung between a couple of trees and a canvas chair sat between the hammock and the hut. Erin was nowhere to be seen, yet he knew this was her camp.

Before he stepped into the clearing, he called one more time. "Hello, anybody home?"

"Yeah, I'm home." Hank jumped and spun around.

Erin stood behind him. "I saw your canoe."

He took a deep calming breath. "So why didn't you show yourself? Why sneak up behind me?"

She shrugged. "I didn't know it was you. I only knew someone was here." Erin pointed down and said, "Careful of the trip wire."

Hank looked down and for the first time noticed the monofilament line stretched across the trail head. He looked around trying to figure out what would have happened if he'd tripped Erin's booby trap.

Erin brushed past him. "I don't suppose this is a social call."

He stepped over the trip line and followed her into the clearing. "No, it's not a social call. We've located Collins' family, at least we think we have."

Erin indicated the canvas chair and said, "Have a seat."

Hank looked around and asked, "Where will you sit?"

"Ever the gentleman, aren't you?" Smiling and shaking her head, Erin ducked into the hut.

"Do you have a problem with that?"

She emerged and unfolded another canvas chair. "No, I don't have a problem with it." She almost smiled.

"My mother would have said it was 'refreshing'. I'm not sure refreshing is the right word but... you didn't come here to discuss your impeccable manners."

Erin plopped into the canvas chair and again indicated Hank should sit down. "You came to convince me why I should help with a rescue operation for the family of the leader of an organization that would just as soon my kind, and yours too for that matter, became extinct." She sat with her legs stretched out in front of her and her arms resting on the wooden chair arms.

It was Hank's turn to smile. "I don't think ATO wants women to become extinct."

Erin laughed. "No, but they would like to see homosexuals become extinct." She waved away the issue. "But we're not here to discuss ATO's beliefs. Why should I care about Jack Collins' family?"

"Because they've done nothing to harm you. The Order is using them to try and force him into leading the Swamp Rats into a trap. The Order knows all about the original Operation

Chaos."

"The Original Operation Chaos?" Erin sighed and sat up. "I think this is going to be a long story, so how about you start at the beginning."

"It turns out that Jack Collins and General Wayne went to high school together. They were often referred to as the Three Musketeers by teachers and students alike."

"Hold on. I may not be a math whiz but even I know Collins and Wayne only add up to two, so how did they get to be the Three Musketeers?"

"Yeah, I was afraid you'd ask that. Seems the third musketeer was Martin Chandler."

Before Erin could voice an opinion, he hurried on. "However, in college Chandler got political ambitions and distanced himself from the other two." Hank smiled. "Let's face it being associated with the owner of Your Wish Is My Command isn't going to get you a lot of votes."

"I suppose not." Erin looked at Hank waiting for him to continue his story.

Hank took a deep breath. "Anyway, Collins agreed to set the trap. Then he confided the situation to Donald North. He took a big risk doing that. If Donald turned out to be the traitor... Well, anyway when we ended up with North, he told Tony what the situation was, and that Collins wanted help in rescuing his family." He sighed. "The short version is this, we're going to rescue Collins family, trap the traitor at ATO and move Operation Chaos forward one day. Everybody comes out ahead," he smiled "except The Order."

Erin processed Hank's information before asking, "What exactly do you mean by move Operation Chaos forward a day? And who is the 'we' that's going to rescue Collins' family?"

Hank leaned back in his chair. "Originally the plan was for the chaos to happen on July 4th at the start of the fireworks display. That's the plan The Order knows about, instead things are going to start popping the day before on the 3rd as soon as it's full dark." He paused. "As for the rescue of Collins' family, well, the general wants you, me and Yvonne to handle that."

Erin looked him in the eyes and asked, "What makes you think you can trust Collins? Why risk his family's life? Why not just do what The Order wants and then go on his merry way. This whole rescue operation could be nothing more than a trap."

"Collins is smart enough to realize that even if he does exactly what they want him to do, they're never going to give him his family and let him go. The best-case scenario would be separate reorientation facilities for each of them."

Hank sat forward and rested his elbows on his knees. "As for the trust issue, sooner or later you have to trust someone. You can't go through life without placing some level of trust in the people around you." He looked at his watch. "Whoa. I've got to get back to camp before I'm missed. I can explain a short absence as a joy ride for some alone time but with all this talk of turncoats I don't want to be gone too long someone might get suspicious of me." He stood up.

"I'll think about this rescue idea. But why me?"

"General Wayne, figures that you, me and Yvonne should be able to pull it off." He paused. "If you're not interested then I'll see if I can get Andrea to go with us instead."

Erin walked to his canoe with him but refused to take the bait of Andrea's name. "We're still hammering out the exact details of who will do what on the third."

He climbed into his canoe and Erin pushed it into the water. "Maybe by the next time I visit we'll have the plans in place. If so, I'll try to bring Tony with me so we can see where you might be the most beneficial."

She grabbed the rope that was trailing on the sand and reeled Hank back in closer to shore. "Where are they holding Collins' family?"

Hank smiled, reached in his shirt pocket, and pulled out a folded piece of paper. He leaned forward and Erin reached out and took it from him. "The address is on there. So is a map of the layout of the house."

Erin tilted her head to one side. "How do we know so much about this house?"

Hank laughed. "Turns out The Order never took them out of the house Collins had them stashed in. They just stepped in and took over. Our best intel is that they're being kept in the bedroom at the northwest corner. Yvonne and I will come back tonight and we can do a recon."

Erin tossed the rope into the canoe and gave a final push. She watched him disappear around the bend of the canal and then headed back to her camp.

CHAPTER 55

Hank wasn't overly fond of small, enclosed spaces, so he hurried through the narrow canal to the open water. As his canoe glided into the open, he blinked against the bright sunlight. It only took a moment for his eyes to adjust to the new light level. He located the entrance to the much longer canal that would take him back to Camp Liberty glanced at his watch and dug his paddle into the water.

In his eagerness to get back to camp he failed to notice the woman in the canoe waiting behind the oak tree branches that hung out over the water a short distance from the short narrow canal.

As soon as he was out of sight Colonel Mason paddled her canoe to the mouth of the canal Hank had come out of and without hesitation entered. When she emerged into the open, she scanned the area moving her eyes in a clockwise pattern.

Right there. That beach is the only place he could have landed. Of course, there could be another canal he took and moved further on. But I'm betting this was his destination. Who the hell could he be meeting out here? And why?

She paddled her canoe across the open water and drifted up to the white sand beach, looking for signs that Hank had stopped here. Her search was rewarded with the rut Hank's canoe had made in the wet sand.

She pulled her canoe onto the sand in the exact same

location Hank had used. She made sure it was on the sand high enough that she wouldn't have to worry about it floating away but not so far that it would be a chore to get it back into the water in a hurry.

She wiped the sweat from her face with a bandana. The soft sand looked disturbed but there were no real footprints to give her an indication of how many people and which direction they had gone.

Since she hadn't planned on following Hank, her supplies were limited to the emergency kit that was kept in all the canoes at Camp Liberty. She grabbed the liter bottle of water she'd been sipping on while she waited for Hank's return and finished it off. She put the empty bottle back in the canoe.

Damn if I hadn't lost him when he switched canals, I'd already know what this little disappearing routine of his is all about. There have just been too many times he's vanished from camp and then suddenly he's back. This time I'm going to find out what it's all about.

She examined the dense jungle like foliage lining the shore. Not noticing an opening anywhere, she repeated her examination, only slower this time.

There. That tiny branch is broken.

She walked to the broken branch and found the trail head. A quick glance at the sun's position to get her bearings and she started down the narrow path. As she moved along Mason looked for more signs that others had been this way recently and at the same time paid attention to where she placed each step.

After the second bend in the trail the sand became firmer, allowing it to hold footprints. She bent down to get a closer look.

At least two people or one person wearing different shoes as they came and went. Sand's still too soft to get a really good print.

She stood up and moved on. The light level dropped, and Linda checked her watch.

Sun must have gone behind a cloud. Between that and all these trees I'm surprised I have as much light as I do.

She sniffed the air.

Rain. Crap! I hope it's just a light shower and not a downpour.

Determined to discover what Hank was up to she pressed forward despite the threat of bad weather. She picked up her pace and soon rounded yet another turn in the trail.

Tired, hot, and thirsty the colonel missed seeing the trip line. Suddenly she felt a weight drop on her and at the same time she heard a loud clang.

Erin rolled out of her hammock; gun in hand, ready to do battle. Her eyes darted past the person flailing around under the net. She looked beyond them to see if there were others approaching. By all appearances her captive was alone.

"Stop!" Erin ordered her prisoner.

Bent at the waist with her head down the colonel stopped struggling.

"Put your hands on top of your head and lace your fingers together."

She did as she was told. *That voice. No, it can't be. She's dead.*

Erin stepped over to a tree with a cleat attached to the trunk. Never taking her eyes off her captive, she found the rope used to lift the net. She pulled on it and the net began to rise. "Don't get any ideas. Just stand there until I tell you to move." Keeping the gun trained on her prisoner and tying off the rope was a difficult proposition.

As the weight of the net was removed from her, Mason straightened up. "Erin? Is that you?"

"Linda?" The rope slipped from Erin's hand and the net once again fell on the colonel. This time the unexpected weight caught her off balance and she went to the ground.

"Oh, crap." Erin stuck her gun in her waistband, grabbed the rope with both hands, hauled the net up and quickly tied it off.

"Linda, are you alright? What the hell are you doing here? How did you find me? Did Hank tell you where I was?" She asked as she came over to help Linda.

The colonel got to her feet and with both hands held Erin's face. Smiling and with her eyes wet with tears of joy and relief, she ran her hands down Erin's arms to assure herself that this wasn't a ghost. Erin really was alive. Then without warning she slapped Erin across the face with such force it knocked Erin off her feet.

With her hands on her hips, Mason stood over her. "What the hell is going on? Why was I kept in the dark about your 'death' being a fake?"

Rubbing her cheek Erin started to rise.

She pointed a finger at Erin and said, "I'm not so sure that's a good idea. You might want to just stay down there until the urge to knock you down passes."

Erin took her advice and stayed on the ground. She worked her jaw and rubbed her cherry red cheek. "What the hell was that for? I thought you'd be happy to find out I'm alive."

Colonel Mason paced back and forth, three paces in one direction and then the other. "Yeah, well, the jury's still out on that." After a few more laps she stopped. "Who was in on this? I want to know exactly who to be pissed at. I know it had to be at least Hank and Tony." She paused. "And Yvonne. She stayed behind to help Hank bury the body. I remember that part of the story."

She resumed doing her laps. Erin stayed seated on the ground with her legs crossed.

"If you're going to be pissed at someone it should be me. The whole thing was my idea."

"Oh, don't worry I'm plenty pissed at you." She stopped in front of Erin, took a deep breath, and asked, "Why not let me in on it?"

Erin looked up into those mesmerizing green eyes and said, "I wasn't sure you were a good enough actor."

Her confused expression prompted Erin to explain. "I wasn't sure you could fake the appropriate amount of anger and grief."

She swallowed hard, mentally reviewing her reaction when General Wayne told her how he had allowed Donovan to execute Erin.

"Get up."

Erin smiled at her and said, "I don't know. I feel pretty safe down here."

Mason returned the smile and reached out a hand to help her up. "On your feet, woman."

Erin took her hand. Electrical heat spread throughout her body. Her heart rate increased, her nipples hardened, and the wetness grew between her legs. On her feet she found herself almost right up against Linda.

Her voice soft but firm, Linda leaned in and brushing her lips against Erin's ear whispered, "Surrender Erin. You know you want me, as much as I want you."

She leaned back and looked into Erin's eyes as she ran a fingertip down the side of Erin's face to her jaw to the center of her chin and down her neck. She stopped at the neck of Erin's t-shirt. "Just some no strings attached…fun."

One voice inside Erin's head said, "No strings attached fun. Hmmm. Sounds good."

Another side of her conscience spoke up, "The problem is I've never been much for casual sex."

Jesus, girl stop over analyzing things. Life is short. Enjoy it while you can.

Erin silenced the voices in her mind as she pulled Linda into her arms and kissed her. Linda's soft lips parted, and Erin's tongue explored her mouth, while her hands explored Linda's body.

As Erin's hands found the bottom hem of Linda's t-shirt and pulled it over her head a clap of thunder shook the ground as a bolt of lightning flashed.

Both women leaned their heads back as the skies opened and it began to pour. In a matter of seconds, they were both soaked. Erin brought her head back down to find Linda staring at her. The violence of the storm added to the desperate passion they each felt.

Erin dropped Linda's t-shirt to the sand, pulled her own shirt off and let it fall next to Linda's. Wrapping her arms around Linda, she pulled her into an embrace. She felt the steam rising from the rain landing on their hot bodies.

Linda moaned with desire as Erin moved her mouth down Linda's throat, across a shoulder and down her chest to take a breast into her mouth.

Erin's tongue teased the nipple of Linda's breast as her fingers found the button and zipper combination of Linda's shorts. Linda's shorts joined her t-shirt on the sand. Frantic to feel all of Linda against her, Erin released her long enough to remove the remainder of her own clothes.

Skin to skin the two dropped to the sand, paying no attention to the storm around them. Their own internal storms were far more potent and overwhelming.

Eventually, they moved their love making inside the hut.

Later, Erin gently disentangled herself from Linda and quietly slipped out of the hut. The sun had dried the clothes she and Linda left lying on the ground.

She shook the sand from her shorts and shirt and stepped into the shorts. She lifted the t-shirt over her head.

"I take it she found you."

Erin spun around to find Hank standing behind her. "Shit! That's a good way to get yourself killed. Sneaking up on me like that." She returned the knife in her hand to its sheath.

Hank smiled.

"What are you grinning at?"

He shrugged. "Nothing."

Erin picked up Linda's clothes and shook them out. Linda's intoxicating scent filled the air around her. She paused for a moment, silently wishing Hank weren't there, so she could have more time with Linda. Erin shook her head and started toward the hut. "I'll get her."

"Erin," she stopped and turned to face him. "Let yourself

love. Life is short. You, of all people should know that. Live it while you can."

She stepped closer to him and in a fierce voice quietly said, "What happens when I end up dead for real? The more she cares, the longer I allow this to go on, the more it will hurt when it ends." She paused. "I, of all people, know that all too well."

She spun on her heel and headed for the hut. Hank's voice stopped her again. "Are you talking about her being hurt, or you being hurt?"

Erin continued into the hut without responding.

A few minutes later Colonel Mason came out of the hut. She stared at Hank with her arms crossed over her chest. "I should be angry with you."

A smile split her face from ear to ear. "But at this very moment I can't even dredge up anger at The Order."

Hank smiled. "Yeah, well you better get over that before we get back to camp."

Erin stepped up behind her and put a hand on each shoulder. It was her attempt to control the physical contact between them. Linda was having none of that, she stepped sideways and put an arm around Erin's waist as she pulled her to stand next to her.

Erin's initial response was to give in to the moment, to let herself feel, instead she moved away from the colonel toward the trailhead. "You two should get back before I have half of Camp Liberty here."

She headed down the trail toward the shore without waiting to see if they were following her.

Mason and Hank followed Erin down the trail to the beach.

"Colonel," Hank said "we're going to need a story as to why you were out so long. Did you tell anyone what you were doing?"

Never taking her eyes off Erin, she answered, "Yes, I told Chris, Nurse Barton, that I was going to follow you."

The trio stepped onto the sandy beach.

Hank stopped short of the canoes. "Well, I've already been back to Camp and there was talk of starting a search party because no one could find you. I stalled them by insisting they let me go look for you first. I told them we didn't need a whole bunch of people out crashing about in the woods, especially during a storm."

Erin asked, "What made you follow him?"

"I was suspicious." She looked from Erin to Hank sheepishly. "I'd noticed you going off when I knew you weren't on a mission of any kind." She paused and looked at Erin. "At least, no mission I knew about."

Smiling, the colonel reached out and ran her hand over the top of Erin's head. "You know, I'd have never thought it possible that a virtually bald woman could be so damn sexy."

Erin's knees became weak, and her heart raced at Linda's touch. She cleared her throat and moved a few steps away, looking at the canoes.

"How about this for a story?" She looked at the colonel. "Your canoe ran into a submerged metal pole of some kind that gouged a hole big enough to sink it. You swam to the first piece of dry real estate you could find and that's where Hank found you." She paused.

"What about…" Mason started.

"You two need to go. You can work out the details on the

293

way back." Erin looked at Hank with pleading eyes.

"She's right. Come on, Colonel."

"Yeah." Mason stepped toward Hank's canoe where Erin stood at the bow. She reached out and pulled Erin into her arms and kissed her.

Erin returned the embrace and kiss. When they separated Hank was seated in the canoe. Hesitantly, she climbed aboard.

As soon as the colonel was seated Erin tossed the bowline in and pushed the vessel into the water.

Hank quickly steered the canoe into the canal toward Camp Liberty and they were gone.

CHAPTER 56

Erin wrapped the wide ace bandage around her chest flattening her breasts. With her shaved head, a baggy shirt and her breasts bound she could pass for a young man if the lighting was low, and no one looked too closely.

The information Hank had provided her on the house where Jack Collins' family was being held was good. However, it didn't give her any details about how many guards or where they were positioned? For this information she trusted no one. The only way to find out was to go and look for herself.

She'd spent the rest of the day preparing her equipment and deciding what was necessary and what she could do without.

One last circuit around her chest and she fastened the flesh-colored bandage. Putting on her shoulder holster was a bit difficult due to the binding, but she managed. A few minutes later she went through her mental check list.

Gun with extra ammo, knife, infrared scope, gloves, scanner, night vision goggles, compass, GPS device, canteen, and beef jerky. Looks like I'm ready to go.

Even without a mirror she knew that she presented an intimidating sight. Black pants, black long-sleeved t-shirt and black boots topped off with a black ball cap and wraparound sunglasses with reflective lenses. Without actually wearing a Peacekeeper uniform, she gave the appearance of being a

Peacekeeper. She grabbed the black button up shirt and stuffed it in her pack. She would need it later to hide the shoulder holster.

Two hours later she maneuvered her canoe behind an oak tree overhanging the water and tied it to a branch. An hour after that she was looking out of the woods at the backyard across the street from the target house.

The neighborhood was quiet. Too quiet. Erin used the infrared scope to inspect the target house. There was a person sitting in the living room. Probably watching television. On the back porch a figure paced back and forth. From the look of his body form, he was carrying a rifle of some kind. The bedroom at the northwest corner of the house held two people. By all appearances one was a child.

Two guards? That's it? You've got to be kidding me.

Erin checked out the houses on either side of her target house. Both were vacant. From her position she looked up and down the backyards on her side of the street.

This must be one of those subdivisions that never recovered from the economic meltdown.

The tightly woven branches with the skinny dark leaves of the solid and compact Podocarpus made it perfect for use as a barrier between the neighbors judging eyes and the trash cans every house needed. But now instead of hiding trash cans the short hedge concealed Erin.

Since I can't really do anything until after dark, I'll take a little nap.

When the light of the day began to wane, and the warmth of the sun was replaced by the cooler air of night Erin opened her eyes.

No traffic. No sign of life at all. Nothing. Freaky.

Again, she scoped all the nearby houses, including the ones on her side of the street. The only one with any life signs was the target house. The ghost town atmosphere made her skin crawl. Instead of being comforted by the low number of guards and the lack of bystanders, Erin was concerned. The whole thing began to smell more and more like a trap.

At first blush she had considered doing the rescue by herself, immediately, instead of waiting and working with Hank and Yvonne.

Something isn't right. The whole thing smells like four-day old fish.

Erin stretched out and watched the occupants of the house through her infrared scope.

The person in the living room got up from his chair and went to the bedroom where the prisoners were supposedly being held. She watched him tuck the child into bed and kiss the woman. It wasn't the kiss of a captor forcing himself on a prisoner but more the kiss of a husband and wife who have been married a long time.

Either I was right, and this is a trap or Collins' girlfriend is two timing him. I need to get a closer look.

Erin maneuvered her way around to the far side of the house to her right. The sun had set, and the moon was hiding behind clouds. The lack of light was perfect for her purposes. She was just about to move into the open and cross the road when the streetlight in the front yard of the target house came on. She ducked back behind the large green garbage can.

That was close.

The high halogen lamp created a puddle of brightness that

297

lit up the street and most of the front yard. Lying on the ground Erin scoped the house again. There was no evidence anyone there had seen her or noticed anything out of the ordinary.

If I shine a bright light on it and it'll think it's morning and shut off, at least for a little while.

She moved up to a bush at the corner of the house, scoped the house and the surrounding houses before aiming her flashlight at the streetlamp. Almost instantly the lamp went out. She took a quick look to see if anyone inside had noticed anything, they hadn't, and she took off at a dead run. As she approached the corner of the house, she noticed a motion detector light mounted on the eaves and veered right in time to avoid tripping it.

It was full dark now and she needed a plan to figure out if these were really the woman and child she was supposed to rescue or if this was a trap. She searched her bag of tricks and found a couple of firecrackers.

Hopefully, one will be enough.

She moved up to where she hoped there was a dead space between the motion lights on the front corner and the ones on the rear corner. Standing in the neighbor's yard beyond the range of the lights, Erin lit the firecracker and tossed it into the target house's backyard.

While it was still air born, she ran across the side yard. Pressing her back flat up against the wall she moved under the bedroom window.

"What was that? Is someone shooting at us?" asked a woman's voice.

Through the open window Erin heard a man say, "I'm not

sure what it was, Wendy."

Sweat poured off Erin, more from nerves than the temperature.

The man in the bedroom with the child and the woman called out, "Did you see anything, Al?" His voice was close; Erin figured he was looking out the window just above her.

From the direction of the back porch a male voice answered, "No. Probably some kid trying out his fireworks ahead of time. There's a bunch of occupied houses a couple of blocks away."

Erin stayed put and listened.

"How much longer do we have to stay here, Jimmy? This place gives me the creeps. There isn't anybody in any of these houses except us."

"We got paid a nice tidy sum to stay here until July fifth." Jimmy's tone was conciliatory. "It's not that much longer, babe and then we'll move out of this place. Hey, maybe we'll even move back to Georgia. You'd like that wouldn't you?"

Erin stopped listening and began preparing to return to camp.

CHAPTER 57

Four hours later Erin stepped into the clearing at her camp. "You two make enough noise to raise the dead. Don't you realize how far your voices carry out here, especially at night?"

Hank and Yvonne both jumped and started to reach for their weapons. When they realized it was Erin they relaxed. Ignoring her admonishment about sound, Hank demanded, "Where have you been?"

Standing inches from him she quietly said, "Saving your ass."

Unflinching, he held his ground. "What's that supposed to mean?"

"It means the information you gave me about the location of Collins' family is wrong."

"Wrong in what way?"

Erin sighed. "Look it's been a long day and I'm tired. I need to sit down." She turned to Yvonne and indicating one of the camp chairs said, "Have a seat." At the same time she sat down in the other chair. She smiled at Hank. "There's another chair in the hut." Erin set her night vision gear on top of the backpack she'd shed.

He hesitated and then muttering something about a lousy hostess, ducked into the hut and soon came out with another chair.

"All right." He unfolded the chair and sat down. "Please, explain your earlier statement."

"Not a lot to explain." In the sand she drew five squares separated by a line, to represent the target house and those houses in the immediate vicinity. "There are four people in that house." She sank the stick in her hand into the center of the target house. "One of them is named Al; he's the guard on the back porch. I don't know the child's name, but her mother's name is Wendy, not Helen. From what I heard I got the feeling that Wendy and Jimmy are husband and wife." She paused and looked at Hank. "Where did you get the information that Collins' family was being held there?"

Hank looked directly into Erin's eyes and said, "Donovan."

"And you trusted that lunatic?"

Smiling, Hank said, "No, we didn't trust him. That's why we were all going to go there and do some reconnaissance before we actually tried a rescue." He sighed. "But as I expected you couldn't wait for us to go with you and make it a team" he emphasized the word team "effort. How close did you come to getting caught?"

Yvonne spoke up. "What difference does it make? She didn't get caught and now we know that's not where Collins' family is being held."

Hank turned to Yvonne. "It makes a difference because we don't want them to think we're on to them."

Erin waved away his concerns as she leaned back in her chair. "They think it was some kid testing out his Fourth of July firecrackers and in the morning when they go out to look for any evidence the only thing, they'll find is the remains of a firecracker."

Seemingly satisfied Hank took a deep breath. "Good. We want to hit them at the same time the real rescue of Collins' family is taking place." He smiled at Erin. "We have a team out right now verifying the location."

Erin looked at him through narrowed eyes. "Tell me I haven't just been played."

Hank shrugged. "Not really. However, you have saved Yvonne and me a trek through the woods in the middle of the night." He smiled. "Thanks, Erin."

"Glad I could be of service." She stood up and stretched. "Now if you two would go away I could get some sleep."

Yvonne and Hank both got up. Hank started to walk toward the trail, but Yvonne continued to stand next to her chair. "I don't get it. Why do we want to bother with the fake Collins' family?"

Erin laughed. "Because we want to find out what they can tell us about who set them up as a trap."

"Come on, Yvonne. We need to get back to camp."

"By the way, why did you two come to see me?"

Hank smiled. "We were going to set up a time for the three of us to go check out Donovan's information."

Erin walked them to the end of the trail and watched them leave. Despite the nearly full moon the trail was dark. Overhanging trees kept even the sun at bay on this stretch of trail. She used her flashlight aimed at the ground to guide her feet. As she stepped over the trip wire and into the clearing, she turned off the flashlight and looked around.

The moonlight gave the white sand of the clearing a silver hue, and made the primitive hut attractive, the hammock strung between two palm trees, all surrounded by a lush

302

green forest created a picture of tropical romance. All of which was lost on Erin. She was looking to see if anything was out of place. There was something that wasn't quite right. But other than the fact that there were three chairs out instead of two, everything looked normal.

She removed her boots and socks, took the .38 from the shoulder holster, and climbed into the hammock, keeping the gun in her hand.

CHAPTER 58

Captain Landau was crossing the room to his desk when his phone rang. He placed his coffee cup on the desk and looked at the caller ID.

Cooper. Cooper. Ah yes, the fake Collins family.

"Yes, Mr. Cooper."

"Captain Landau, we had an incident last night."

"What kind of incident?"

"Well, it's probably noting but I figured I should tell you about it anyway."

Landau sighed. "Tell me about what? Please, be specific."

Jim Cooper's nervousness showed in his voice. "Well, the streetlight went out shortly after it came on and then there was what sounded like a gunshot. When I went out this morning to see if there was anything to last night. I found the remains of a firecracker."

Landau was silent for several moments as he digested the information.

"Are you still there, sir?"

"Yes, Mr. Cooper." He paused. "Did the streetlight come back on?"

"Yes, sir."

"Thank you for your report, Mr. Cooper. Cameras will be installed today."

Landau ended the call and immediately dialed the surveillance unit.

"Surveillance Unit. Lieutenant Kurtland."

"Lieutenant, have the cameras I ordered for River Shadow Drive been installed."

Lieutenant Kurtland's swallow was audible over the phone. "Hmmm, no sir. It's scheduled for today."

Landau's jaw tightened. "Your delay in getting those cameras in place may have allowed the rebels to escape capture last night. See to it that those cameras are in place before dark and that there is a surveillance team assigned to watch the feed live."

"Yes, sir. I'll have a team install the cameras immediately but the only people I have for surveillance are a couple of young Peacekeepers. They're pretty green sir."

Landau snapped. "Well, it's about time they got some seasoning. All they are to do is watch. If they see anything suspicious, they're to call it in."

"Yes, sir."

CHAPTER 59

"Collins."

Jack stopped and composed his facial expression before turning to face David Smith. "Yes, Mr. Smith?"

"I just heard that you met with the Swamp Rats several days ago. Is that true?"

"Yes." Collins was amazed it had taken this long for the rumor mill to get that information to Smith. *Of course, it helped that I managed to keep everyone at that meeting doing something elsewhere until this morning.*

Smith looked around to make sure they were alone. "Mister Collins, you really need to be a bit more cooperative if you expect to be rewarded."

Collins stepped into Smith's personal space. "First of all, it's General Collins to you. Second, I have been cooperative. I have answered your questions honestly and I've allowed you to place your device on Mr. North."

Smith sighed. "Hmmm. Perhaps cooperative wasn't the best word to use." He paused but didn't move back from Collins. "Informative. Yes, that's the better word. You need to be more informative, so that I know what's going on."

"I wasn't told anything about keeping you informed. I was ordered to allow you to plant your device and to assist in the capture of Erin Foster and the destruction of the Swamp Rats as a resistance force. How I do that is up to me and you can rest assured that it will involve you as little as possible."

"Regardless, I expect to be included in any future meetings and I need to know what occurred at this past meeting so I can get a report to my superiors."

"No."

Smith raised his eyebrows. "In that case I shall have to report to my superiors that I believe you are planning a double cross."

Collins smiled. "Good luck with that." He paused and stepped back as he called out, "Bonner! Sanders!"

Two men stepped into view from a corridor several yards behind Smith. "Yes, sir," they both said.

"Mr. Smith is confined to quarters until I say otherwise. Post a guard to make sure he stays confined. No communication with the outside." Collins smiled.

"Yes, sir."

"It's just a safety precaution, boys. Treat him gently."

CHAPTER 60

Erin, Hank, and Yvonne waited for darkness to fall. The three of them were across the street from the fake Collins' family's house.

Using the thermal imaging scope Erin studied the house across the street. Just like the last time there were four heat signatures. Always cautious she scoped the nearby houses.

Sitting with her back against a wall Erin said, "Something's not right about this whole thing."

Yvonne asked, "What do you mean?"

"I mean, it's too easy. If these hostages are so valuable, why aren't there more guards? Surely, they don't think they can prevent a rescue attempt with just two armed men."

"Maybe the real family has more guards, remember these aren't the real hostages. This is a decoy."

"I understand that Hank. Still, if I were setting up a decoy. I'd want to be able to either kill or capture as many of the enemy as possible. Two guys with guns…That's just, I don't know what it is." She looked around the corner at the house across the street and then settled back against the wall. "But I do know that somehow this is going to end badly."

Hank shrugged. "There's three of us, we're well armed and we have the element of surprise."

Erin looked at Hank. "Do we?"

"Do we what?"

"Do we have the element of surprise?"

Hank tilted his head as he considered the question, and then said, "How would they know we're coming? We didn't know ourselves until five hours ago."

"Besides the three of us, who else knows the timetable?"

Hank shook his head. "Erin, the only people who knew about tonight are you, me, Yvonne, General Wayne, and Colonel Mason. Do you really think General Wayne or Colonel Mason would betray us?"

"No, I suppose not."

Erin closed her eyes and tried to shake the feeling of doom that hung over her like a fog.

Tony and Linda would never betray us. I trust Hank and Yvonne with my life.

One street over and four houses down from the target house, Peacekeeper Crawford Phillips had lost count of how many times he'd cleaned his weapon, shined his boots, and pressed his uniform during this assignment. Patience was a virtue he lacked. Despite all the religious doctrine pounded into him over the years, no matter how many times he heard and even repeated the phrases about the virtues of patience and how everything had its own time, he was an impatient young man.

He was supposed to be watching the monitors. Instead, he was daydreaming about how he would receive a hero's reward for capturing Erin Foster.

In one scenario, he killed her and delivered her head on a pike to The Reverend Master. But then he decided that was a bit too melodramatic and he changed it, so that instead he delivered a bound and humbled Erin Foster to The Reverend

309

Master.

Crawford sighed and dropped the front legs of his chair back onto the floor and briefly scanned the monitors before him. Each one showed a different approach to the house at 1313 River Shadow Drive. He saw the same empty yard and street he'd been looking at for hours.

"Hey Shane, how long before shift change?"

"Five minutes less than the last time you asked me."

Crawford sighed, stood up stretched and yawned. "I wish I knew what I did wrong to get this assignment."

Shane laughed. "What makes you think this is a punishment assignment?"

"Aw come on. All we do is sit here and watch these monitors." He waved at the screens in front of him.

"The most exciting thing I've seen in the last twenty-four hours was the raccoon that likes to climb the bird feeder in the back yard and eat the bird seed." Crawford plopped back down into his chair and again scanned the monitors.

"Whoa! What… Shane sound the alert."

His friend came from across the room where he'd been studying. "What for? Did the coon bring his girlfriend with him?"

At first Shane didn't see anything and then, movement drew his attention to the monitor covering the front of the house. Three figures close to the ground moved through the front yard. One broke from the other two and moved to the south. The others went north and disappeared. After several seconds spent scanning the different monitors, Crawford grabbed the phone that provided him instant contact with the response unit.

310

"This is Station Delilah. We have intruders. Repeat we have intruders."

"How many, Station Delilah?"

"Three known. Cameras have limited range."

"Will deploy a unit to your location immediately Station Delilah. Estimated time of arrival is five minutes."

"Message received." Crawford hung up the phone and stood up. "Their sending a unit but it won't get here for five minutes." He ejected the magazine of his gun, checked the load, reinserted it, slid the barrel back, released it and holstered the weapon. "I'm not waiting for them."

"What are you talking about you're not waiting for them? Our orders are to watch the monitors."

Crawford smiled. "I'm the senior peacekeeper on site and I'm using my judgment. I don't think the unit will arrive in time to catch these intruders. If all I manage to do is slow them down, it may give the unit the time they need." At the door he turned and said, "Stay here and monitor. I'll have my communicator on." He tapped the device curled around his ear and then he was gone.

The house used for monitoring was one street east and four houses south of 1313 River Shadow Drive.

In thirty seconds, Peacekeeper Crawford Phillips paused next to the same house Erin, Hank and Yvonne had used as their staging area. His heart rate was up, and his adrenaline elevated. Crawford Phillips spent his entire youth wanting to be a superhero.

Finally, I get to show everyone what I'm made of. They all think I'm just this goofy guy that reads comic books and the Bible. I'll show them I'm as good as any member of the

Justice League.

He unholstered his gun and ran across the street. In the front yard he turned south, following the single intruder.

Erin's vantage point gave her a view of the back and the north side of the house, all the way to the street. With her night vision goggles on she could see the person on the back porch, and she saw Hank take up his position at the southwest corner of the yard.

Yvonne's owl call drew Erin's eyes back her way. Yvonne signed that someone had crossed the street and was coming up behind Hank.

Erin jerked her head back to look at Hank. The night vision goggles gave the person moving across the next-door neighbor's yard behind Hank a ghostly appearance. Knowing that whoever it was lacked the ability to see her Erin started to signal Hank but rapidly changed her plan when the individual behind him raised his gun and aimed at Hank.

Without hesitation Erin removed the threat with a single shot. Hank didn't have time to react between the instant he saw Erin aim her gun in his direction and the shot she fired. When Erin's bullet hit Crawford, his finger pressed the hair trigger on his gun and it fired, wounding Hank in the left arm.

After that everything seemed to happen at once. The fake Collins' family began to shoot, seemingly at anything that moved. Flood lights came on causing Hank, Erin and Yvonne considerable pain and temporary blindness. They removed their night vision goggles.

When she could see again, Erin saw Hank coming toward her from one direction and Yvonne from another. Both were dodging bullets every step of the way.

The sound of sirens was growing closer by the second.

Hank and Yvonne met Erin in the neighbor's backyard. They were on the back side of the flood lights that had the fake Collins' family backyard lit up like daytime. A low hedge provided them with cover.

Erin noted the blood running down the back of Hank's left hand. "Can you make it back to rendezvous?"

"Yeah, I'll manage."

"All right. You both know what to do." She looked at Yvonne and smiled. "See you at Valhalla."

With that they each went in a different direction and headed back to Erin's camp.

CHAPTER 61

It was dawn and Erin was on the verge of heading for Camp Liberty when she heard Yvonne's owl call. Moments later Yvonne stepped off the trail into the clearing of Erin's camp.

Leaning back in a canvas camp chair Erin presented the image of a relaxed and unconcerned individual.

Hoping her smile hid her worry Erin asked, "So, how's Hank?"

Yvonne studied Erin for a moment but had long ago given up trying to read her friend. She shrugged and sat down in the chair opposite Erin. "His left arm will be out of commission for a while, but he should be all right."

"That's good." She paused. "Any ideas on how they knew we were there?"

"General Wayne thinks it was a combination of motion sensors and cameras."

Erin was doodling in the sand with a stick, not looking at Yvonne. "He does, does he?"

"Yeah, seems similar things have happened on some other missions." Erin looked up and Yvonne continued, "Only some of them weren't so lucky." She paused. "Good thing it was you and not me, I'd have probably hit Hank."

Erin smiled. "I doubt that. You might not have killed the other guy, but you'd have made sure your shot missed Hank." Erin stood up. "I'm sure you're exhausted. I know I could sure use some sleep." She yawned and stretched. "By the way did they rescue Collins' family?"

"Yes."

Erin really looked at Yvonne as she lowered herself back into her chair. Yvonne was an easy read and Erin could tell there was something wrong. She swallowed hard. "Did everyone make it back okay?"

Yvonne looked up from staring at the sand between her feet. "No." She pulled her lower lip into her mouth to hold back the tears. "Pamela was killed."

Erin closed her eyes and tilted her head back. In her mind she saw the image of a lovely, naked Pamela the way she was the day she distracted the guard.

She shook her head, took a deep breath and looking at the fading stars asked, "How's Lacey taking it?"

"She doesn't know yet."

Erin sat up and looked at Yvonne. "Why hasn't she been told?"

Yvonne sighed. "She's unconscious. Doc won't say whether she'll make it or not." She snorted. "Upton said she could go either way."

Neither of them spoke for a few minutes and then Erin asked, "Is she at Camp Liberty?"

"Yes." Yvonne stood up and wiped tears from her face. "And that's probably where I should be."

After Yvonne left, Erin flopped into her hammock and tried to sleep. Thoughts of how she could have done things differently and maybe Alice would still be alive, filled her mind. They were interrupted by images of Pamela and Lacey together. Finally, exhaustion won, and Erin slept.

When she woke it was late afternoon. She cleaned her weapons, checked her equipment and her supplies. She told herself she was going to Camp Liberty because she needed to see Lacey for herself. She needed to talk to her. What she was going to say, she had no idea.

Erin refused to let herself believe that it was really Colonel Mason she desperately needed to see, to talk to and to touch.

Finally, the sun began to set. Erin grabbed her gear, including her night vision goggles and pushed her canoe from its hiding place into the water.

An hour later it was full dark, with a half-moon hidden by the occasional cloud she knew her risk was minimal. There weren't enough night vision goggles to go around, and she knew General Wayne had decided the goggles would be used for priority missions, not sentries.

The first sentry was tricky getting past. She waited several minutes for her attention to be elsewhere before sliding past. The inner sentry was another story. Erin coasted past her without hesitation. Any noise Erin might have made was drowned out by the woman's crying.

I'll have to tell Linda that she needs to reinforce the idea that on guard duty you don't have time to cry. Save your grief for when you're off duty.

Erin pulled her canoe up to the far side of Camp Liberty's infirmary, tied it to a piling and quietly climbed the ladder to the boardwalk. She stopped and listened.

Nothing. She looked in the nearest window and was delighted to see the only person inside was Lacey. She started toward the door when she heard voices. She stopped and waited. The voices faded.

316

They must have been on the crosswalk.

Erin slipped into the dimly lit room and sat down next to Lacey's cot. "Lacey, can you hear me?" Lacey moaned and licked her lips. Her eyelids fluttered. "Come on girl, I know you can hear me. Wake up."

Another moan and finally her eyes opened. "Must be hallucinating. You're dead." She gave a little laugh and asked, "Have you seen Pamela?"

Erin thought about her reply for a moment and then said, "No, I haven't seen Pamela. She probably crossed over and went somewhere I'm not likely to ever be allowed."

"What? I don't understand."

"Don't worry about it. I'm sure Pamela is in a better place." Erin paused to listen for the sounds of anyone approaching. "Listen to me Lacey. Don't do like I did. Don't be bitter and shut yourself off from everyone. There are a lot of people who care about you. Let them."

Lacey licked her dry cracked lips. "They think I don't know." She paused and tried to sit up.

Erin placed a hand on her shoulder. "You need to lie still." She smiled. "You don't want to get me in trouble with Dr. Upton, do you?"

"Don't know what they gave me but I'm not so out of it that I don't know I'm hallucinating." She swallowed hard. "Doesn't matter. You tell Pamela I love her."

Erin knew she needed to go. There was no way Nurse Barton would leave a patient in Lacey's condition alone for very long. "I will Lacey. Lacey, Pamela doesn't want you to stop loving. She wants you to be happy. So, if you find someone, don't be afraid to fall in love again. Okay?"

317

"Sure, whatever Pamela wants. You make sure to tell her I love her."

"I will. You remember to keep on loving and living." Erin stood up and started for the door. She paused and looked back. Sweat stood out on Lacey's forehead.

On a small table next to the cot were a wash bowl and a cloth. Erin stepped back next to the cot, dipped the cloth in the water, wrung it out, and laid it across Lacey's forehead.

"If I hadn't seen it, I wouldn't believe it."

Erin reached for her knife and spun around. The blade was halfway out of its sheath before she realized the voice belonged to Chris Barton.

She pointed at the knife in Erin's hand and said, "Now that I believe." Erin pushed the blade back home. "Why am I not surprised that you're not dead?"

Smiling Erin said, "Maybe because you think I'm too ornery to die."

Chris stepped closer. Her face looked as if she had just figured something out. "Linda knows, doesn't she? That's why her mood changed a few days ago. She found out you're still alive."

Erin finished closing the gap between them. "Chris, a lot of people took a lot of risks to fake my death. It's important that for the time being I stay dead."

"Okay, I'll keep your secret." She paused. "But if it's so important, why did you risk coming here tonight?"

Erin looked over her shoulder at Lacey and then back at Chris, "I needed to tell her some things. Things she needed to hear from someone who's been where she is."

Chris nodded her understanding.

318

"The longer I stay here the greater the risk but" she paused "is Linda here?"

"No, she's with General Wayne getting things ready for Operation Chaos." Chris watched Erin wilt like a deflated balloon. "Next time I see her, I'll let her know you stopped by."

"Thanks." Erin paused. "But I'd rather you didn't."

Chris sighed. "You know Erin; you should take your own advice." She looked past her at Lacey.

Erin studied Chris' face and realized she had heard what she told Lacey. She pulled her lower lip into her mouth and then said, "It's too late for me. It was nice seeing you, Chris. Take care of yourself." She started out the door.

"It's only too late if you're dead."

CHAPTER 62

Project Flatbed

Eddie Ledbetter was pissed off. An accident on the interstate delayed his arrival at Garter's Hardware and Home Repair and now the Lumber Manager refused to unload his flatbed of pressure treated two by fours until morning.

He fired off an email to the home office explaining the situation and then wondered if there was a restaurant within walking distance. He really didn't want to have to move the truck.

At least the stuffed shirt said I could park on the lot overnight. Since I'll be here when they open, maybe I can get unloaded early and still make it home for the family celebration.

There was a knock on the door of the cab.

Hoping the Lumber Manager had had a change of heart Eddie opened the door with a smile. Looking down the barrel of a .45 automatic erased his smile.

"Don't try to be a hero and you'll live to see your family."

"Whatever you say buddy. You're the one with the gun." Eddie swallowed hard as he pulled his eyes away from the gun to scan the parking lot for help.

"Step down from there. Nice and slow." Adam took a few steps back to give Eddie room to get out of the truck.

"Look buddy, I don't have much money and you can see my

320

cargo's nothing but a bunch of two by fours," Eddie said as he climbed down from the truck's cab.

Adam led Eddie to a corner of the lot where he tossed his prisoner a bottle of water and said, "Drink that. All of it."

Licking his lips Eddie twisted the cap off the bottle but hesitated to drink.

Adam looked at him questioningly and then realized why his captive wasn't sure he wanted to drink the water. "Look man, it's not poisoned or anything. I'm sure you noticed when you twisted the cap off, you broke the seal."

Still Eddie hesitated.

Adam sighed. "I ain't got all day mister." He gestured at him with the gun. "Drink the damn water." Eddie got the message and quickly downed the bottle.

"I don't want you getting dehydrated before they find you tomorrow morning." Adam paused. "It's July in Florida and even the nights are hot."

Once Eddie was bound and gagged Adam got behind the wheel of the truck.

Thirty minutes later he was approaching the top of Midway Bridge. Checking his mirrors and the traffic around him, he shifted gears, jammed on the brakes, accelerated, and turned the wheel hard, all at the same time. His seatbelt saved him from more than a few bumps and bruises as the entire rig tipped over on its side, spilling lumber and diesel fuel.

Adam climbed up out of the cab. He pulled four highway flares from his waistband and lit them. One he tossed into the cab and the other three he spread out over the pile of lumber covering the bridge.

People were beginning to crowd around him and confused

angry voices joined the sounds of burning lumber.

"Hey what are you doing?"

"Stop that. Somebody stop him."

"Mister, are you crazy?"

Waving his gun around for emphasis Adam yelled at the crowd, "You all need to get back. Sooner or later the fuel tank will go."

As he continued to warn them to back away, he took his own advice and began to move toward the foot of the bridge.

Under the bridge he hopped onto the Jet Ski that had been left for him and headed for the west bank of the river.

CHAPTER 63

Project Concrete

It was an hour until sunset. Pierre was right on schedule. He looked around as if he'd heard something. It was his way of doing a final check to see if anyone was watching him.

A puff of breeze blew up a mini dust devil the other side of the gate. In a matter of seconds, he picked the padlock and pushed the gate open. Without running he hurried to the truck, he had been told would be waiting for him. He could hear the mixer running.

Pierre climbed into the cab of the in-transit cement mixer truck. He checked all the gauges and dials. Everything looked to be in order. It felt good to be back in the saddle.

Twenty minutes later he pulled the truck across Southern Cross Bridge. He ignored the yelling people and the honking horns as he let the flow trough swing loose and opened the mixer door. Concrete flowed out and spread over the bridge.

The gun in his hand kept people from approaching him as he stuffed a rag into the truck's gas tank and lit it.

Running from the scene Pierre yelled, "It's gonna blow, folks. You need to back up."

CHAPTER 64

Project Gravel

Oscar left the yard five minutes ahead of Andrea. He drove his dump truck over Volunteer Bridge then turned around and headed west. Using the truck's radio, he called Andrea.

"Hey, Tough Girl, what's your twenty?"

"Twenty? What the hell are you talking about?"

"Girl, don't you know how to talk on a radio?"

"What I know is that we have a job to do. Where are you?"

Oscar sighed. *They just had to pair me up with her. Oh well, what's a boy to do?*

"Yeah, I'm approaching the eastern foot of Volunteer. What's your twenty? I mean, what's your location?"

"Meet you at the top in about ten seconds."

"Roger that."

At the top of the bridge Oscar stopped his truck so that he blocked both lanes going west. In the east bound lanes Andrea did the same thing. They climbed down from their truck cabs, walked to the rear of their respective vehicles, released the locks on the tailgates and flipped the switches to activate the hydraulic lifts on each truck's bed.

As the pea gravel began to flow out of the trucks people started getting out of their vehicles and moving toward them.

Oscar reached into the cab and brought out a glass bottle with a rag coming out the top. Inside the bottle was a yellowish looking liquid and the rag extended down into that liquid. In his other hand Oscar flicked open the top of an old-fashioned Zippo lighter. He ran his thumb down the wheel of the lighter and a bright yellow flame came to life.

A voice from the crowd said, "Everybody get back. That guy is crazy. He's playing with a Molotov Cocktail."

Andrea smiled as she pulled her own special cocktail and Zippo from her truck. The two Swamp Rats exchanged glances and shrugged their shoulders. Then they lit their bombs and tossed them into the truck cabs.

In the instant when the crowd turned to run, they both dove under Oscar's truck and out the other side. They ran west with the crowd as the two dump trucks burned amid a mountain of pea gravel.

CHAPTER 65

"Hey folks, this is your radio hostess Selma, sorry to interrupt your evening of music but I've been getting some really wild calls about things that are going on out there in the big bad world. Rumor has it that the three bridges connecting the mainland to beachside have all been blocked. From what I'm being told we're not talking about simple car accidents. If you're out there listening and you can confirm or refute these rumors, give me a call at 253-4633 or 1-888-253-4633." A brief pause and then she said, "Sounds like we've got our first caller. This is Selma, who am I speaking with?"

"My name is Warren Jenkins."

"What can you tell us about the bridges Warren?"

"It's true. I mean, I don't know about the other two bridges, but I can tell you for sure nobody's getting across using Volunteer Bridge for at least a couple of days."

"Whoa! That must be one heck of a car accident if it's going to block the bridge for more than a couple of hours. Warren, you sound a little out of breath. What's going on out there?"

"It's unbelievable but I have to believe it. I mean, I saw it with my own eyes. It's just…"

Selma tried to cajole her caller into being more coherent. "Come on, now Warren. You're scaring me and my audience. Give us some details. What's so unbelievable?"

"They just stopped on the bridge and dumped all that gravel

and then set the trucks on fire."

Before Selma could form a response, she was left in total darkness for about two seconds and then the battery powered emergency exit lights came on.

CHAPTER 66

Operation Chaos was underway.

General Anthony Wayne, General Jack Collins, Michael Donovan, and Hank Bartholomew were at the command post the Swamp Rats had set up in an abandoned factory building outside of town. It was a perfect location. Anyone approaching would be seen long before they could become a threat. The building had very few windows and the ones that did exist were covered with black spray paint.

Occasionally one of the disposable cell phones rang. Units from all over the area were reporting in on their successful missions. As was expected there were a few casualties; however, at this point there were only injuries, no fatalities.

Generals Wayne and Collins were reviewing the graphic that was tracking the progress of their various teams when Colonel Linda Mason entered the room.

"General Wayne, the prisoners are here." Her attitude was formal. There was no sign of the decade's long friendship between herself and Tony.

Wayne looked up from the tabletop monitor. "Thank you, Colonel." He paused. "Your team is waiting for you at your rendezvous point. Before you go, let me introduce you to General Jack Collins."

The colonel stepped forward and extended her hand. "It's good to finally meet you General Collins."

He smiled. "Likewise, Colonel Mason, I've heard a lot of good things about you."

"Don't believe everything you hear" she said, returning his smile.

As she was about to turn and leave another man stepped up next to Collins. It was obvious he wanted to speak to the general alone. However, Collins was a gentleman and signaled the man to wait and he said, "Colonel Mason, let me introduce my right hand man, Michael Donovan."

Wayne held his breath, fearing the colonel's reaction.

Colonel Mason's smile vanished. She turned to face Donovan squarely. "So, this is the waste of oxygen that murdered Erin Foster." She punctuated the end of her statement with a slap across Donovan's face that carried so much force it almost knocked him off his feet.

"A person is known by the company they keep. So do me a favor and keep that" she pointed at Donovan "away from me." Without waiting for any form of response she did a sharp about face and walked away.

Donovan started to go after her, but Collins reined him in. "Let it go Donovan."

"But that bitch…"

"I said, let it go."

"Sorry about that, gentlemen. With everything that's been going on I wasn't thinking about her running into Donovan here." He looked after her and then brought his attention back to Donovan. "She was in love with Erin Foster."

Mason ignored the voices behind her as she walked out of the room wearing a grin.

CHAPTER 67

The ambulance pulled up to the emergency room doors and screeched to a stop. The back doors were flung open by the EMT, and the driver came around and helped pull the gurney out. The blood seeping through the bandage on the patient was sufficient to get the security guard to buzz them through into the heart of the emergency room.

Even before the door closed behind them Billy and Yvonne surveyed the area. Yvonne leaned down and spoke to their patient. "Looks like it's just security at the door and whoever is on duty inside."

Colonel Mason nodded.

"What have you folks got here?" Without waiting for an answer, the doctor directed them to a treatment room.

The time Billy spent at Camp Liberty's infirmary helping Chris Barton paid off. In a tone of authority he replied, "Not sure what caused the wound, but blood pressure is 170 over 110, pulse is 93 and respiration is 20, shallow and rapid."

Once in the room the doctor helped the EMTs lift the patient from the gurney to the examination table. On the table he began to lift the bloody bandage on Linda's arm.

She pulled the oxygen mask from her face, pressed the barrel of her Glock against his stomach, sat up and said, "Thanks, doc, I feel one hundred percent better already. You're a real miracle worker." She peeled the fake bandage off her arm and stood up.

"What... I don't understand." His eyes went from the colonel's gun to the weapons the other two now wielded.

Mason asked, "Are there any other armed guards besides the one at the door?"

"No, not usually." The young doctor swallowed hard. "Sometimes the guard from the main hospital wanders down to visit, when things are slow."

"How many ER staff on duty right now?"

The doctor licked his lips nervously. "Uh, there's myself, two nurses, and another doctor who's on call". His eyes darted from one face to another as if he were trying to figure out who was the leader.

"He's not actually here right now." He paused, closed his eyes, and took a deep breath. "He's in the doctor's lounge catching a nap. He's due to come back and relieve me in about ten minutes. Look what do you people want?"

Linda smiled and said, "What do you think we want, doc?"

"Drugs."

She laughed. "Oh Doctor" she looked at his name tag "Fallon, you underestimate us. We want so much more than just drugs."

Yvonne was at the door keeping watch. She signaled that someone was coming. Seconds later a nurse entered the room. She was still standing in the open doorway when what was happening registered in her mind.

Before she could step back out of the room or utter a sound. Mason said, "Come in and close the door. Don't try to be a hero and you'll be fine. We don't want to hurt anyone. We need some supplies and equipment and then we'll be on

331

our way."

Figuring the nurse would be less likely to risk the doctor's life, the colonel sent her and Billy out for the things they needed.

Though Billy and the nurse were only gone a few minutes it seemed like an eternity to those waiting for their return.

It was a slow night in the ER and the other nurse on duty was too engrossed in catching up on her paperwork to notice that Dr. Fallon and Nurse Fredrick weren't around. "Did you get everything?" Linda asked.

Billy smiled. "Nurse Fredrick was very accommodating. We got everything on the list."

The colonel spotted a yellow and black box attached to what looked like a hand truck in the corner of the examination room. "What is that?"

Dr. Fallon glanced in the direction she indicated. "Oh that, that's nothing."

She pushed the gun into his midsection a little harder. "What specifically is 'nothing'?"

Nurse Fredrick said, "Don't hurt him. It's a portable x-ray machine." Fallon glared at her. "I'm sorry Dr. Fallon but it's easier to replace equipment than doctors."

Yvonne smiled at the colonel saying, "Gotta love a practical woman."

"Yeah. Wouldn't doc just love a portable x-ray machine?"

Using the first aid tape on hand Yvonne gagged and taped up doctor and nurse. While Yvonne was dealing with them, Billy went and got the other nurse. As soon as she entered Treatment Room 2 and saw her colleagues' condition she began to yell. Billy quickly clapped a hand over her mouth.

332

Yvonne stepped over and quickly gagged her and began taping her hands behind her back. Billy opened the door a crack and saw the lobby guard headed his way. He opened the door part way and stood in the opening with his left hand on the door. His right hand, holding a .38 was hidden by the door.

"Sorry about the noise officer. Patient's a little delirious but we've got it under control."

The guard nodded and started to turn to go back to his post. He paused and looked around. He realized there was no nurse or doctor anywhere to be seen. His handed started to move toward his holster.

"Don't even think about, buddy. Put your hands on top of your head with your fingers laced and turn around slowly."

Alan Johnson did as he was told. Billy stood in the fully opened doorway with his gun aimed at him. Using the gun, Billy signaled him to enter the room.

Yvonne took one last look up and down the corridor outside the treatment room before they stepped out. Seeing no one she signaled the others to move out.

The ambulance was parked where they'd left it with the back doors still open and the engine running. Mason and Billy lifted the portable x-ray machine into the vehicle while Yvonne stood guard.

From the darkness at the southwest corner of the building a voice hollered, "Hey, what are you doing there?"

Yvonne spun around and fired at the silhouette of a man.

The colonel yelled, "Get in!" She grabbed the automatic rifle from the back of the ambulance. "Billy, drive. Yvonne get in."

Shots rang out from the bushes at the southwest corner.

Yvonne staggered and grabbed her midsection. From behind her Colonel Mason wrapped her left arm around her waist and pulled her toward the back of the ambulance while she fired at their attacker. At the open ambulance door, she managed to get Yvonne inside. She ended up sitting on the floor with Yvonne in her lap. She yelled, "Billy, get us out of here."

The back doors slammed and opened as the ambulance raced down the driveway. Every time the doors opened Linda fired another burst.

Billy stopped the ambulance a short time later in a deserted parking lot. He left the engine running and ran to the back of the vehicle.

"Help me get her up on the bench." Yvonne moaned as they lifted her. "We've got to stop the bleeding." Mason grabbed a package of gauze and a pair of scissors. She tossed the gauze pack to Billy. "Open that." Then she turned to Yvonne and cut away the shirt to reveal the gunshot wound.

Handing the colonel the gauze Billy asked, "Did it go all the way through?"

"I don't know." She placed a hand on Yvonne's shoulder and on her hip and gently rolled her toward the wall. "Yeah, it looks like it's a through and through. Is that gauze ready?" He tried to hand her the gauze. Both her hands were still propping up Yvonne. "Double that up and place it on the exit wound. Keep it there while I lower her." Once she released Yvonne, she took more gauze from Billy and said, "Look around see if you can find any kind of plastic wrap."

"Plastic wrap? You mean like what you wrap food in?"

The absurdity of it struck her and she fought to suppress her laughter. She knew if she got started hysterics would take over and Yvonne would die. "Yes, I read something somewhere about using gauze on the entrance and exit wound and then wrapping the victim in plastic wrap." She was applying pressure to Yvonne's wound with the gauze. "I don't remember why I just remember it's something you're supposed to do."

Yvonne moaned.

"Okay." He searched storage bins and opened several cabinets before finding a box of plastic wrap. "Here you go. Never would have thought of that for something like this."

"Great. Help me wrap her and then you need to get us moving."

The colonel stayed in the back with Yvonne.

Moments before the ambulance came to a stop at the emergency entrance of the abandoned hotel the Swamp Rats had taken over Yvonne regained consciousness. She licked her lips and opened her eyes. It seemed to take her a couple of seconds to focus on the colonel. "What...what happened?" Her eyes moved slowly, taking in her surroundings.

"Where..." she swallowed, "where am I?" She moved as if she was going to try and sit up. "Ahhhhhhh!" Searing pain ripped through her abdomen.

"Lay still, Yvonne. You've been shot." She put her hands on Yvonne's shoulders.

The colonel's words were less effective than the pain caused by moving.

Gasping from the pain Yvonne licked her lips and tried to speak but Mason told her, "Just lie still. We're at the hospital now."

The back doors opened, and Chris Barton stepped into the ambulance.

The hospital was an old, dilapidated building that had once been a hotel where day laborers rented a room by the week.

"You all right, Linda?" she asked as she looked her friend up and down.

"Yeah. I'm fine. Yvonne's the one…"

He words were cut off by Chris giving orders to Billy and another young man. "Get that gurney in here. We need to get her inside. Linda, go in and tell Lacey to power up room two."

It seemed like eternity waiting for someone to come out and tell her how Yvonne was doing. The inner battle raged about sending Billy for Donald and Erin.

If she's going to recover then I don't need to blow Erin's cover but if she's not going to make it, then I know Erin will want to get here in time to say goodbye.

Colonel Mason spent the next ten minutes making promises to God and deals with the devil while she paced the hallway, occasionally stopping to look through the open door. All she could see was Dr. Upton's back. Finally, Dr. Upton came out.

He looked up and down the hallway to see if the colonel was the only one with whom he needed to speak.

He didn't believe in sugarcoating the truth. He looked at her and said, "At best she has a day, at the worst a couple of hours."

Colonel Mason's knees threatened to buckle and she leaned against the wall. With the wall propping her up, she swallowed hard and asked, "Are you sure? I mean, is it possible…"

She noticed his jaw tighten and his hands clench. "The bullet did a lot of internal damage. If I had an operating room with all the attendant equipment, then maybe she'd survive, even then, there would be no guarantee." He paused. "I'm sorry. Have you sent for her husband?"

She shook her head. "No, I was waiting to hear from you. I'll send someone immediately." She pushed herself off the wall and headed outside where Billy was standing guard.

"How's she doing, colonel?"

"Not so good, Billy. Doc, says she may only have a couple of hours."

"I'm sorry to hear that. She's a real nice lady."

"Billy, I need you to do something for me." She looked around making sure they were alone.

"Whatever you need Colonel?"

She smiled. *He's so much like a little puppy dog.*

"I'm going to tell you something that only a very few people know." He was paying close attention to every word she said, waiting for her orders. She nervously looked around again.

Then she brought her attention back to the young man before her. "There are two people you need to notify of Yvonne's condition. First, Donald, her husband. He should be back at Camp Liberty by now." She paused. "I'll give you directions on how to find the other person."

He waited.

The colonel took a deep breath. "You'll find Erin Foster a short distance from Camp Liberty."

Billy started to say something but hesitated. He studied her closely. "You mean she's still alive."

"Very much so." The colonel suppressed a smile at the memory of how very much alive Erin was. She picked up a twig and, in the sand, drew a map of how to get to Erin's camp from Camp Liberty. She watched him studying the map. After about thirty seconds he brought his eyes back up to meet hers and using his foot erased the map.

"I should get started right away."

"Yes, Dr. Upton, didn't sound hopeful that she'll last more than a few hours. Just remember to watch out for booby traps when you're approaching Valhalla."

"Valhalla?" He looked at her questioningly and then smiled. "I get it."

CHAPTER 68

While the authorities were busy dealing with blocked bridges, a group of Swamp Rats and ATO personnel broke into the National Guard Armory on the mainland. They loaded all the weapons and ammunition they could lay their hands on into two transport trucks.

They drove to the abandoned factory that was being used as the command center for Operation Chaos.

Their cargo was quickly off loaded, leaving them ready and able to accept their human cargo.

General Wayne greeted the truck drivers. "You boys are late."

"Sorry about that General." Paul smiled. "Seems there were some traffic jams caused by power outages between there and here."

"All right, gentlemen. Step aboard your magic carpet to home."

The Swamp Rats herded the blindfolded prisoners into the backs of the two, deuce and a half trucks, fourteen prisoners and six guards per truck.

It was too noisy to carry on a conversation during the ride so Wayne spent the time trying to figure out what he should say to these men when he released them.

He still hadn't worked out exactly what he would say when they arrived at the television station. The facility was automated to the point that there was only one person manning it most of the time. That individual's main duty was to take care of any technical difficulties.

Wearing Lt. Barnes' peacekeeper uniform Tony rapped on the glass door with his ring. Stephen Grimes heard the sound, but it took him a couple of minutes to realize that it was someone at the front door. Standing at the door he saw the two military type trucks and an officer of the peacekeeper corps.

General Wayne yelled through the closed door. "We have an emergency. I need to use your phone."

This was the beginning of Stephen's third year manning this station and he'd never had anyone knock on the door. The rule was that you do not open the door for anyone. However, he was quite certain that rule didn't apply to authority figures like cops and peacekeepers. He unlocked and opened the door. "What's the problem, sir?"

"No problem now, son." He aimed his .45 at the young man. "Hands up and lace your fingers on top of your head." As he was handcuffing the station attendant, he asked, "What's your name son?"

"Stephen, Stephen Grimes."

"Well Mr. Grimes you're going to be part of history tonight." With Stephen secured he turned back and said, "All right Paul, let's get them unloaded."

As the blindfolded and bound men were led through the station's lobby Stephen said, "What is this all about? Who are these men? I don't understand."

General Wayne patted him gently on the cheek. "You don't need to understand. Just do as you're told, and you'll come through this without a scratch."

There was a time when the station did live broadcasts from a studio on the premises. It was still used on occasion, so it was kept clean and operational. Tony had all twenty-eight prisoners placed on the sound stage of that studio.

He passed Stephen off to Paul and said, "Find a nice quiet closet for him. You might want to gag him just to be safe."

"Tammy, the place is yours. I don't want to be any longer than necessary, so do your thing and do it quickly." The red head he was speaking to nodded and headed for the computer system that ran the place.

"Emily, get this studio up and ready. We've got a show to put on."

The prisoners were arranged on the stage in a three-tier formation, as if they were a sports team. While his people went to work getting everything ready for their live broadcast, the blindfolds were removed from the twenty-eight. The only one whose gag was removed was Lt. Timothy Barnes of the Peacekeeper Corps.

Emily signaled the general that they were ready to go. He nodded and Emily began a countdown from five. When she reached one, she pointed at him and the green lights above the cameras came on.

Facing the camera he said, "Ladies and gentlemen, I apologize for interrupting your regularly scheduled programming. However, I have important information to give you. First, let me introduce myself. I am Anthony Wayne." He stepped aside and let the camera pan the prisoners. "Tonight, we return to you your sons, your husbands, and your brothers."

The camera moved to General Wayne's face as he smiled and addressed the twenty-eight. "Gentlemen, your Florida swamp adventure is at an end. When my people and I leave here tonight you will remain, alive and well. Sorry to have kept you from your families and friends for so long." He paused, looking from one face to the next.

"I hope that the time you spent with us has been educational and informative. We are not the devil. We laugh, we cry, we bleed, we love. It just happens that when we fall in love, it's with someone of the same gender as ourselves."

He looked directly at Lt. Timothy Barnes. "Lt. Barnes, how would you feel if you lived in a world where falling in love with your lovely wife, Sharon, was outlawed? What would you do if you were expected to fall in love with a man? Falling in love with a member of the opposite sex was forbidden. Not only was it frowned upon but to do so would make you an outlaw, to be hunted down and sent to a place where the authorities would do everything in their power to change you."

Lt. Timothy Barnes of the Peacekeeper Corps stood up and said, "I would fight until my last breath. Just as I'm sure you will do General Wayne." He paused. "And while you claim that homosexuality is natural for you, my God condemns it as a sin."

General Wayne sighed. "I'm not going to get into a religious debate with you, Lt. Barnes. I have little doubt that your knowledge of scripture is vaster than my own." He paused. "What I will do is ask, why can't you just leave us in peace and mind your own business? Why must you force your religion and your belief system on us?"

Timothy Barnes had been told that General Wayne was

going to ask him some questions during a live television broadcast. He wasn't given any forewarning about what the questions would be.

Looking directly at him Barnes answered, "Because for us to not try to redeem a sinner is in itself a sin. As you claim you have no choice about who you fall in love with, we have no choice on this point. We must try to redeem all sinners or suffer the same fate that God will bring down upon them."

The general turned and spoke directly to the camera. "We did not ask to be saved. We do not want to be saved. If you continue to try and force us to be something we are not, the first civil war this country fought will look like a Sunday church social by comparison. We will fight you." He paused. "This country was founded on freedom. Stop trying to take our freedom away, simply because your religion says we're wrong to love one another.

Tonight, was presented to you, the public, as a demonstration of our ability to fight and our commitment to maintaining our freedom. We have cut the power to most of your city. We've blocked all three bridges between the mainland and beachside. This is only a small sample of what is to come if The Order is allowed to continue running this country.

The government must repeal Amendment 28 and disband the Peacekeeper Corp. All laws enacted since the inception of Amendment 28 must be repealed. We will not stand by and be dragged off to Reorientation Facilities. Equality between the sexes must be returned…"

There was noise outside the studio and then gun fire erupted.

343

"It would seem my broadcast is getting cut short. Here's hoping everyone has a Happy Fourth of July."

Tony stepped past the cameras to find out what the shooting was all about.

Emily said, "We got out and we recorded it." She paused, listening to the voice coming from the earpiece she wore. Then she looked at Tony and smiled, "Tammy says, mission accomplished."

"Excellent." He looked at Paul coming through the door and asked, "What was the shooting all about?"

Paul continued forward without answering until he could whisper in Tony's ear. "A State Trooper happened by and wanted to be a hero. He's dead."

The general lowered his head for a second and then said, "That's the problem with revolutions. People die in them."

He took a deep breath. "Get our people into the trucks."

Emily used a small handheld video camera to continue recording all that was happening.

General Wayne walked back to the stage and looked at each man there. He stopped when he reached Lt. Barnes. "You sir will have some hard decisions to make in the future. You know we're not the evil your leaders have portrayed us to be. How you will reconcile that knowledge with the orders you will receive in the future is something you'll have to live with the rest of your life." He extended his hand, and the two men shook hands.

"General, we need to go, sir." Paul called from the doorway.

"Good luck, to all of us." General Wayne turned and left the room.

Emily backed out of the room filming the twenty-eight men

344

on the stage right up to the moment she stepped out the door. She kept the camera running as she took her seat in the back of the truck, filming their departure.

CHAPTER 69

Lt. Timothy Barnes looked around the studio and found a pair of scissors. He cut the zip ties on the first man he came to and said, "Cut everybody free."

He then turned and looked for a phone.

Before he called anyone else, Timothy Barnes called his wife Sharon. "Sweetheart, it's me. Shhh. Listen, I can't talk. It will probably be twelve hours or more before I'll be home sweetie. I just wanted you to know that I'm back, safe." He paused. "Yes, they released all of us, just moments ago." He paused. "Give Tim Jr. a kiss for me. I have to go now. I've got to call headquarters."

He disconnected the call and dialed the number for headquarters.

"Captain Landau, this is Lt. Timothy Barnes. I don't know if you saw the broadcast... Yes sir." He listened and then said, "Yes sir." He replaced the phone on its cradle and returned to his men.

"I spoke with Captain Landau. He said we're to stay where we are and await his arrival." He paused. "It seems there's a great deal that's happening around the area tonight and it may take some time before he can get here. Until then he doesn't want us to contact anyone, not our families or anyone else."

National Guard Lt. Holbrook said, "I need to call my commanding officer and find out what he wants."

"Captain Landau said he'd call the National Guard and the State Police."

"What's the big deal, lieutenant? Why can't we call our families and let them know we're safe?"

"I don't know corporal. I only know what the captain's orders were."

Barnes rubbed his stomach. "My last meal was a while ago. I don't know about anyone else but I'm getting hungry. Corporal, see if you can find which closet, they put the fellow in that runs this place and let's see if there's anything to eat around here."

Stephen Grimes was released from the closet and untied. He brought out his stash of snacks to share with the others.

Just before sunrise the twenty-nine men in the television station were awakened by the sound of glass breaking. Before any of them could make it to the lobby area to find out what was going on, three men burst onto the sound stage and opened fired at them. In a matter of minutes all twenty-nine were dead.

Before the trio had time to reload, Captain Landau's two most trusted soldiers entered the studio and shot the trio.

The sound of gunfire had barely ceased when Captain Landau entered the television station.

He looked at his two men and said, "Their sacrifice will not be in vain, gentlemen. This will help convince those people still holding on to the notion that these rebels are freedom fighters that they're just your garden variety terrorist." He sighed. "A shame it had to be done this way. But this will send a powerful message to those helping these deviants that they cannot be trusted." He smiled. "They'll find it much harder to get assistance from the general public after this."

Three hours later Captain Landau reported to his colonel. "The terrorists killed the twenty-eight prisoners and the television station attendant just moments before we arrived, sir. My men managed to kill three of the terrorists before they could escape. Surely if we publicize this brutal act, it will help turn the tide of public opinion regarding the rebels."

"Yes, captain." He sighed. "It will help. I just don't understand... I mean, I saw the broadcast. General Wayne seemed quite sincere in his intention of releasing our people unharmed."

Captain Landau bristled. "Sir, please, don't dignify that terrorist by honoring him with a rank such as general."

CHAPTER 70

Donald North was sitting next to Yvonne's bed when Erin came up behind him and asked, "Am I too late?"

The colonel had told him that Erin was coming yet seeing her again was still a bit like seeing a ghost. He stood up and said, "No, she's still..."

"You're damn right I'm still here."

Erin moved to the other side of the bed. "Hey lady, what is this? Payback for scaring you into thinking I was dead?"

Yvonne smiled. "Unfortunately, no. This is the real thing."

"I don't know about that. I always figured you were way too ornery to die." Sweat stood out on Yvonne's forehead.

Donald smiled at his wife and said, "I don't know where she gets these ideas from, I always figured you'd live forever because..." He brushed his fingers through her hair. "...because I wanted you to."

He sniffed, released Yvonne's hand, and turned to the door. "You're hot I'm going to find a cool compress for you. I'll be right back."

Before either Yvonne or Erin could speak, he was out the door.

"Erin, I need you to do something for me."

"I'm listening."

Yvonne smiled. "Not going to say, anything for you?"

Erin's only response was a smile.

349

Yvonne squeezed Erin's hand as a wave of pain coursed through her body.

"Why don't you let Upton give you something for the pain?"

"No!" She took a deep breath and loosened her grip on Erin's hand.

"I want to be present for what's left of my life. Besides I need to talk to you and that husband of mine, together and for that I need to have all my faculties about me."

Torn between wanting to be with Yvonne and not wanting to see her like this Erin said, "Maybe I should go get Donald."

"No, please, stay. If he's not back in a minute or so, but I want to talk to you."

"Okay."

"You need to give Linda a chance. She's crazy about you, you know?"

Erin's last encounter with the colonel flashed across her mind. Just the thought of Linda made her heart rate increase. "Yeah, I know that. I also know that I have unfinished business with The Order before I can think of anything else."

"Yeah, about that…"

Donald came through the door carrying a pan of cold water and a washcloth. "This will help you feel better, sweetheart." He dropped the cloth into the water, set the pan down and then wrung out the cloth before placing it on Yvonne's forehead.

"I'm glad you're back. I don't have much time left and I need to talk you two together."

Erin and Donald exchanged glances and then they both looked back at Yvonne.

"I know both of you feel you have a mission to complete in

this fight against The Order and I'm not going to try and convince either of you to forgive and forget and just live your lives. Because I know it would be a waste of breath."

She paused and took several breaths before continuing. "And obviously, I don't have a lot of breath to waste. So, I'll get to the point, I want you two to work together as a team." Yvonne laughed, which sent a burning pain through her abdomen.

Panting she said, "The looks on your faces. Priceless. I'm serious. Considering the enemy, you two pretending to be a couple will get you a lot farther than working separately."

Erin nodded her head. "True."

Donald agreed and Yvonne continued, "So that's my last request that you two work together to defeat The Order. Do we have a deal?"

Erin and Donald looked at each other across Yvonne and shook hands over her.

"Deal."

"Deal."

Colonel Mason came through the door. "Erin, you have to get out of here. Collins and Donovan are on their way here. They were with General Wayne and Hank when word reached them about Yvonne."

"No, I'm not leaving."

"But..."

"But nothing. Somebody find me a surgical mask."

Without a word Linda left and returned with the requested mask. As Erin covered her face with the mask, Linda asked, "You don't think they'll recognize your voice."

Erin answered with a strong Southern drawl, "Now sugar,

you just let me worry about that. Okay?"

Colonel Mason smiled. "You are a woman of many talents."

In her normal voice Erin responded, "I'm a woman determined to be here for her friend."

The door swung open again and General Wayne and Hank entered the room.

Wayne took in the scene immediately. He narrowed his eyes studying Erin. In a quiet voice he asked, "Are you suicidal? What if Collins or Donovan see you?"

"Are you addressing me sir?" Erin indicated herself by placing her left hand on her chest. The thick Southern drawl was back in Erin's voice. "I'm sure I don't know what y'all are talkin' about."

Hank slapped a hand over his mouth to keep from laughing out loud.

The general shook his head in surrender and turned his attention to Yvonne. "Isn't this a bit extreme to get out of guard duty, Yvonne?"

"I love you too General Anthony Wayne. You're a good man."

Hank and the general didn't stay long. Dr. Upton had told them she didn't have a lot of time left and they both knew she'd want to spend it with her husband.

Alone again with Donald and Erin, Yvonne looked at Erin and, in a voice, barely audible she said, "Remember what I said."

Not trusting her voice, Erin nodded and gave Yvonne's hand a gentle squeeze.

Yvonne turned to Donald. "I love you, Donald North."

"Then don't leave me."

352

"Some things are beyond my control, sweetie." Her eyes closed and gradually the rise and fall of her breathing stopped.

Donald continued to hold her hand while Erin stepped into the hallway. She saw Wayne, Hank, Collins, and Donovan standing with Dr. Upton near the entrance.

In her southern drawl she called, "Dr. Upton, you're needed in here, please sir."

"Excuse me, gentlemen."

Donovan's eyes met Erin's for a brief second before she turned back into the room. Collins looked at him and asked, "Is there a problem, Donovan?"

Rubbing his five o'clock shadow he said, "No, no problem. Just the woman that called the doc seemed familiar. I just can't place her."

Collins smiled. "That's the problem with being a womanizer, Donovan. Every woman you meet reminds you of some bimbo you've been with."

Donovan laughed. "Yeah, I suppose so."

Adam stepped up to the group with a young woman. "General Wayne, a courier just delivered a recording of a recent news broadcast you should see. If you'll follow me."

The four men entered what had once been the doctor's lounge. Adam pressed a play button, and the recording began.

A visibly upset newscaster stood outside the television station where the group of men now referred to as The Twenty Eight had been released. In the background body bags were being loaded into ambulances.

"Ladies and gentlemen, the carnage inside the building

behind me is too gruesome to broadcast. We've been told by the authorities that there are thirty-two dead men inside the building behind me. They aren't releasing the names of any of the deceased until their next of kin have been notified."

A man in a Peacekeeper uniform stepped up next to the newsman. "Captain Landau and his men were first on the scene." He paused. "Captain Landau, what can you tell us about the situation?"

"If only we had arrived a few minutes sooner. We might have been able to save them."

Captain Landau straightened his posture. The grief on his face was replaced with anger as he continued, "They shot and killed every single man in the building. It took us a while to get here because of all the chaos caused by these same terrorists. At least, that particular trio of terrorists won't be shooting anyone else."

Wayne did the math in his head. *Three supposed terrorists killed by The Order, means twenty-nine were killed by those three... I wonder if Tim got to call his wife before... What the hell happened? I know it wasn't any of our people, so who did this?*

A voice off camera called for Captain Landau. "Excuse me sir. I'm needed elsewhere."

The newscaster faced the camera. "There you have it folks. Homegrown terrorists, possibly led by the infamous Erin Foster. Although there have been rumors of her death..."

General Wayne stared at the blank television screen speaking to no one in particular. "What the hell happened after we left? Those men were alive and well."

He sank into a chair and held his head in both hands.

General Collins quietly cleared the room of all personnel, until he and Wayne were alone.

Collins knew that Wayne had come to care for several of the men among The Twenty-Eight. Lt. Timothy Barnes in particular had become like a son. "Tony, we'll find out what happened. I'll get in touch with some of my sources and…"

"No. No, Jack." Slowly the general straightened himself up and got to his feet. Looking his friend in the eye he continued, "That won't be necessary." He paused. "I know exactly what happened. It was something I was afraid of from the beginning."

"So let me in on the secret. What happened?"

"They massacred those men."

"Who?"

"The Order."

"What? Are you crazy?" He paused and studied the general. "You expect me to believe that they went in there and killed twenty-eight of their own men?"

He sighed. "No, I don't expect you to believe it." He paused. "It's the truth but I don't expect you to believe it. Whether it was sanctioned from the top down, or some officer decided it on his own…" He took a deep breath to calm himself. "…either way it doesn't matter. They did it so they could blame us for it."

Shaking his head in disbelief Collins said, "Okay, just for argument's sake, let's say you're right. They went in there and killed all of those men." He paused. "Tell me why."

Tony drew in a long slow breath. "Think about it. What affect will this have on the people that help us? You know the answer as well as I do. They're going to be less inclined to

355

provide us with any kind of help. More of our people will be betrayed and turned in to the authorities after this."

When Collins and his men left to return to their camp General Wayne was left alone in the doctor's lounge for several minutes. He pressed the play button and watched the recorded broadcast again.

Go ahead you bastards! Broadcast your lies about us. See how much good it does you. Thanks to Tammy's programming every time you broadcast anything about us, people will think you're lying.

CHAPTER 71

Erin shoved the last of her possessions into the backpack. She zipped it closed and stood staring at it, as if it could answer all her unasked questions.

"Were you planning on saying goodbye or were you just going to disappear?"

Erin looked up at Linda Mason standing in the doorway. The early morning sunlight was dancing across the red in her hair, making it glitter like rubies, just like the first time Erin saw her. The ruby crown combined with her green eyes took Erin's breath away.

"I considered disappearing." She smiled. "But then I figured Yvonne would haunt me for eternity if I did that."

Linda smiled. "Yvonne haunting you would be the least of your worries, I assure you." She stepped into the room.

They both started to speak at once.

"Linda, I know…"

"I just want…"

Then Linda said, "Go ahead. What I have to say won't take long."

Erin fidgeted with the backpack for a moment and then let her hands hang down at her sides. "I know that either one of us could get killed before we get a chance to get together again, assuming we ever get such a chance."

She swallowed hard, took a deep breath, and continued. "I

want you to know that I love you. However, I don't expect you to wait for me. Believe me, I know the odds are against me. Regardless, it's something I have to do." She looked away and then back at Linda. Looking into Linda's eyes she said, "Find yourself somebody to love."

Linda continued to hold Erin's gaze. "Finished?"

Erin nodded.

"Good." Linda moved in and took Erin in her arms and kissed her. "Know that I love you, Erin Foster. Whether we ever see each other again or not, I want you to know that you're loved."

Erin tightened their embrace and kissed Linda.

"Ahem." Chris Barton stood in the doorway. "I hate to break this up but Donald's ready to go."

Erin released Linda and picked up her backpack. Hand in hand they followed Chris to the dock.

Donald shook General Wayne's hand and stepped into the canoe packed with their supplies. Erin handed him her backpack and turned to the general.

"Good luck with things here sir. It's been an honor to serve under you."

He smiled. "Take care of yourself, Erin."

Erin's eyes roamed over the Swamp Rats that had come to see her and Donald off. Her eyes stopped on Lacey, and she stepped over to her and whispered in her ear. Lacey smiled. Erin gave her a quick hug and without another look back undid the bowline, got in the canoe, and pushed it away from the dock.

Tears ran down her face as she dug her paddle into the brackish water and paddled away.

Colonel Linda Mason watched the receding canoe until it disappeared around a bend in the stream.

About The Author

A native Floridian, Darlene has moved away multiple times, only to be drawn back by the smell of the sea, the sun, and the feel of sand between her toes. She and her spouse live near Darlene's hometown of Daytona Beach.

At the time of this writing, they have one rescue cat named Keke. She's part Russian Blue and quite often Darlene believes the cat is channeling a dog. Keke loves to follow her around and sit on the floor near her chair while she writes.

OTHER BOOKS IN THIS SERIES

A New Beginning in Coventry Beach
A Larissa Carpenter Mystery #1

Larissa Carpenter is the one of the richest women in the country. Eighteen months ago, her spouse, Rachel, died of a brain aneurysm. Looking for a new beginning, she travels to the small town of Coventry Beach and moves into the house she and Rachel bought just before Rachel died.

Using the name Laurel Carpenito to avoid the notoriety that came with winning the largest lottery jackpot in the state's history, she begins to clear her head and think about the future.

Finding the body of a young woman she'd met only 12 hours earlier wasn't part of the future Larissa/Laurel envisioned. As if being a person of interest in one murder wasn't bad enough, she witnesses a woman stab a man on the beach in front of her house.

At the local tea and coffee shop, My Place, Laurel runs into an old high school classmate who, unknown to Larissa/Laurel, is now an FBI agent.

The owner of My Place, Harriet Walsh, has spent two years running from an ex-fiancé turned stalker. Thinking he's lost her trail, she has settled down in Coventry Beach. She and Laurel have become friends, and when Harriet disappears, Det. Murdoch is unhappy with Laurel's hiring of a search and rescue team to help find Harriet.

Will Larissa find a new beginning in Coventry Beach, or will this be just another dip in the roller-coaster ride that her life has become?

Lust & Distrust
A Larissa Carpenter Mystery #2

Since moving to Coventry Beach, Larissa Carpenter hasn't found life in the small beach town to provide the tranquility she expected. Not wanting everyone in town to know that she's the Larissa Carpenter who won one of the state's largest lottery jackpots, she goes by Laurel
Carpenito or LC.

Being a person of interest in two murder cases, one of which still hasn't been solved, is most unsettling and it's not the only unsettling thing in LC's life. Her attraction to Detective Angela Murdoch and the feeling that she's being followed are the other disconcerting issues.

Unsure of who's following her, LC wonders if her former high school classmate, FBI Special Agent Amber Hoffner has something to do with it.

Does the FBI think she's involved in the human trafficking ring? Does Detective Murdoch think she killed Natalie Kramer? Is Detective Murdoch attracted to her or is that a figment of her imagination?

Is LC right about being followed? If so, who is it? The FBI? The local police? Someone else?

Fatal Misunderstanding
A Larissa Carpenter Mystery #3

Follow Larissa Carpenter and four friends on a pre-All Hallows Eve girls' weekend in the mystic town of Cerridwen. The fun comes to an end with the discovery of a dead witch in a cottage in the woods and suspicions about at least one of the women begins. It turns out that the dead woman is the former lover of Larissa Carpenter's current friend with benefits. After spending weeks avoiding Det. Angela
Murdoch, Larissa is forced to call her.

"Ms. Carpenter, you report more dead bodies to me than the 911 dispatcher," said Det. Angela Murdoch.

The Origin of Deanna Dorak
Nedamla Book #1

Is she merely a freak of nature…or is she from another world?

Deanna Dorak suddenly finds herself alone in the world and begins to realize that it may not even be her world. With confusing images forcing their way into her consciousness she struggles to understand who she is and why she's here. She elicits the help of her best friend and former lover, Kate, who believes that all of Deanna's problems stem from her inability to accept her mother's death. That is until she sees the gills that have begun to form on Deanna's sides. Kate brings Deanna to Dr. Jason Alexander, who vows to help her and protect her from government scientists.

Soon after, Kate's body is pulled from the river – someone broke her neck.

A frantic search for answers takes Deanna on the quest of her life. Is she the reason her friend was killed? Is Jason friend or foe? Is he holding her captive for his own scientific research? Is she really from another planet, an underwater world inhabited only by women? Can she trust the detective assigned to solve Kate's murder? Can she trust herself?

Aneesha's Prophecy
Nedamla Book #2

*"The daughter will return and avenge the death of her mother
and those innocents killed here today."*

Dorak Deanna has come home to claim her birthright. Home, to a
planet she remembers only through the implanted memories of her
mother, Miktra. Home to a planet still occupied by the same
Empyrean forces that forced her departure nearly thirty years ago.

The Day of Ascension is fast approaching and the Empyrean
Governor of Nedamla grows more fearful of Aneesha's Prophecy
with each passing day. Especially since each day seems to bring
another unexplained, violent death of at least one of his soldiers.
Yet the Empyror refuses his requests for more troops, assuring
him that since Aneesha's child was killed during the invasion, there
is no heir to ascend to the throne.

By accident Deanna discovers she has the ability to communicate,
with at least one Nedamlan, by using only her thoughts. Is it
possible that there are others among her people with this ability?
Perhaps it will be the secret weapon she needs.

Even with the ability to mind-talk, how can one woman turn a
population of women, known for their pacifism, into warriors? And
if she and her warriors take Nedamla from the troops now
occupying her, how will they maintain their freedom? The Empyror
has more than enough troops to simply send another invasion
force.

As if fighting the Empyre weren't enough to worry about, Deanna
has another problem – she has fallen in love.

Will Deanna fulfill Aneesha's Prophecy? Can she return her people
to a time when they were fierce warriors, asking no quarter and
giving none? Will Jorsta agree to join with her?